PRAISE FOR **A TINY PIECE OF SOMETHI~~NG GREATER~~**

"Tender, touching romance…"

—~~Publishers~~ *…eekly*

"★★★★★… a tender, compassionate look at learning to love another person and oneself at the same time."

—*Foreword Reviews*

PRAISE FOR **IDLEWILD**

NAMED ONE OF KIRKUS REVIEWS' **BEST BOOKS OF 2016**

"A lovely, finely wrought romance that reminds us that to truly love another, we must know our own hearts."

—*Kirkus Reviews*

PRAISE FOR **WHAT IT TAKES**

"[STARRED REVIEW] Sierra (*Hush*) uses rich characterization and lyrical writing to infuse this slow-building romance with depth, humor, and pathos. Readers will savor every dip and peak of Milo and Andrew's relationship as they balance the need for safety with the necessary risk of pursuing happiness."

—*Publishers Weekly*

"This story was so satisfying, and one of the most wonderful depictions of friendship as a cornerstone of romance I've ever read."

—*USA Today's* HEA Blog

PRAISE FOR **HUSH**

"Sierra skillfully captures the frustration of navigating identity and interpersonal relationships for those to whom it doesn't come easy… a worthy read and a valuable addition to the genre."

—*Library Journal*

A Tiny Piece of Something Greater

JUDE SIERRA

interlude 🧩 **press**™ • new york

ISBN 13: 978-1-945053-60-3 (trade)
ISBN 13: 978-1-945053-61-0 (ebook)
LCCN: 2018940092
Published by Interlude Press
http://interludepress.com
BOOK DESIGN AND COVER ILLUSTRATION BY CB Messer
10 9 8 7 6 5 4 3 2 1

interlude press • new york

For Anetia, Rachel and Katie
For being lifesaving pieces in my something greater

This is an #ownvoices book, both in lovely and painful ways. This book does contain sensitive subject matter that may be difficult or triggering for readers.

A Tiny Piece of Something Greater includes the following:

Discussion of mental illness, therapy, and recovery. It includes a portrayal of a cyclothymic character who experiences rapid mood cycles and anxiety. There is non-graphic discussion of past self-harm and off-page relapse. It also contains non-graphic reference to a past suicide attempt.

(www.interludepress.com/content-warnings)

One

REID WATSFORD TAPS HIS FINGERS on the steering wheel. The tap is constant and amplifies in intensity as he pointedly refuses to look in the rearview mirror.

Faced with the thought of her son in a car for more than twenty-four hours, his mother Autumn gave him a gift card he could use to pay for hotels. Knowing it would be months before Reid came home, his father Sean bestowed rare affection; he ruffled Reid's hair and pulled him into a rough, tight hug.

Now, with Wisconsin at his back, Reid's tension gives way to relief. The highway stretches before him, cracked and rough in places, narrowed by construction in others, and disconcertingly smooth and deep black where recently fixed. Reid tries not to deconstruct the loosening of his father's shoulders when Reid had come to them with this plan. This trip is a new start, a *restart*, and he hates to think that his parents need it as much as he does.

Felix told him he'd turn back by Kentucky. He pulled Reid into bed, touched him until Reid's reluctance to sleep with Felix slipped into acceptance, until Reid broke promises he'd made to himself yet again. Felix smirked as he kissed each of Reid's ribs, climbing the ladder of bone with lips that tasted of I-Told-You-So by the time they landed on Reid's.

Reid hits the steering wheel with one final, loud smack and resolves not to linger on any of their worries. Old Reid can't seem to do anything right; not for himself, much less for them.

He rolls down the window. The thick, sharp smell of asphalt is cloying in the hot air. He sits bumper-to-bumper waiting for construction traffic to clear. He turns the radio up as loud as he can stand, and music mixes, cacophonous, with the sound of machinery at work. Reid loses himself in the onslaught on his senses. *There's nothing behind me. Everything is ahead.*

What's waiting for him at The Largos? He has memories of visiting his grandmother when he was a kid. His grandmother tells him he still is a kid at twenty, but it's been years since he felt like one. He remembers that there were lots of old people living in the condo complex. He remembers sitting under a glass-top patio table while his grandmother and her friends, who were always sort of drunk, played various games. He was the only kid around, which was sometimes a bummer but mostly okay. Reid didn't have many friends back home either. Sometimes being alone was what he wanted. Whenever he got angry, when he felt jittery and uncomfortable, holing up in his room with a book and loud music felt safe. Usually when this happened at home, he ignored his parents behind a locked door and yelled into his pillow. Reid has clear memories of himself as a kid, punching his pillow or the wall when he was most overwhelmed.

They all probably should have recognized that wasn't normal behavior. But it's not as if he told his parents. The rational part of Reid's brain now understands that they couldn't have known the warning signs. Reid isn't always rational about this, though, and although he tries his best not to be, and god knows his therapy group has heard about it enough, he's still angry at his parents.

He's angry at everyone, which is why he's running away. Complicit in this is his grandmother, Monica. Even though she wasn't in Wisconsin for any of it—only living here part of the year and spending the rest in the Florida warmth—she was one of the few people Reid wanted to talk to while he was at Sycamore Grove Treatment Center. Despite months of work learning skills and tweaking meds to find out what would work for him, coming home wasn't healthy. After months of struggle and lots of encouragement from his therapy group, Reid finally decided he needed a break: from his parents; from his hometown, Eau Claire; and from Felix, his ex.

Struggling to hold a job and living away from his parents' house were road blocks until his grandmother fell near the pool at her condo in Key Largo. She came back to Eau Claire so Autumn could take care of her but, after only one week with his family, she pulled Reid aside and asked him if he could take care of the condo for her. She worded this to seem as if he were doing her a favor. Wasn't caring for the condo covered by her homeowners' association fees? But he took the offer immediately. One more minute in his home and he might have imploded.

Of course, it took longer than a minute to pull everything together, to convince his parents, to work out how he could still participate in his therapy group, and to gently sever ties with the things and people in his life that were unhealthy. Namely, Felix. Reid is under no illusions about the mess he's made of his life and himself. His boyfriend is a huge part of that. *Ex-boyfriend*, Reid reminds himself firmly.

He's struggling to get to *ex* mentally, and has been. The push and pull, the back and forth, the fundamentally unhealthy codependence between them have had long-term negative effects on Reid. He has ladders of healed cuts on his ribs to prove it.

Reid shifts and fiddles with the radio. Things like this—relapsing a few months ago and the exhaustion of constant practice rebuilding— these are things he can think about later. Right now, he has to get to fucking Florida.

REID SPENDS THE NIGHT AT a Red Roof Inn in Kentucky. He arrives late, painfully exhausted from sitting so long, and barely takes in the beige linoleum floors and spare double beds. He thinks of the countless rest stops he blew past in his rush to get to his destination and regrets not stopping to walk around and unkink his body.

The room is cold, and the bedding is light. At home, Reid's bed was always a sanctuary, with lots of blankets and a heavy comforter, washed often because the smell of the dryer sheets soothes him. Nancy, his therapist, told him once that the weight of blankets and comforters is a therapeutic tool for some people, particularly when going through mixed states or rapidly cycling moods.

Reid is exhausted and anxious about the unfamiliar, sterile, cold room. In the unforgiving lights of the bathroom his skin reflects, pale and drawn. His eyes have borne the same haunted, lost look for months. Under his skin is the beginning of anxiety, or worse, a rapid cycle.

He takes his medications dutifully. As always, he counts out the pills and checks their colors and shapes as he was taught at Sycamore Grove Treatment Center.

Lamictal. Dark blue and round.

Neurotonin. Large oval or, as Mom calls it, my "horse pill."

Ambien. Small and dark yellow.

Klonopin. It looks so much like Ambien. Don't mix them up. Last time I did that, I almost lost my job because I couldn't function.

If I take the Klonopin, will I be able to handle being somewhere new?

The Klonopin helps with anxiety, sure, but it makes him tired too.

He's embarking on a phase in his life that will be nothing but new and potentially uncomfortable. Hell, most of his life has been uncomfortable, to say the least.

Outside the motel room door, he can hear everything: laughter, the sound of a bottle being broken, and cars on the interstate, loud and intrusive. The walls and door and cheap beds offer no buffer against anything or everything that could happen. Reid piles all of the blankets and sheets from both beds on himself. He tucks the extra pillows between blankets in the hope that they will stay in place as he tosses and turns.

After scanning the TV for something to watch, Reid gives up. His tastes run toward fun reality shows rather than conspiracy theory and drama. *Grey's Anatomy* is still on; he takes a moment to marvel at its staying power and yes, perhaps judgmentally, to wonder at the taste of its still-existing audience. Reid tosses the remote onto the nightstand

and huddles under the blankets with his Kindle. He doesn't have WiFi, so he settles down with Paul and Noah, with Tony and Joni and every character and the almost memorized words of his favorite book, *Boy Meets Boy*. Its oddity and loveliness and sharp humor create a little world where Reid got lost over and over as a teenager. He needs this familiarity. Every now and then he lifts the covers for fresh air; the cool relief of clean air is the only cold he can bear. Eventually he falls asleep.

*　　*　　*

MORNING COMES TOO SOON, BUT not soon enough. Noises outside wake him. He considers reading in bed a bit longer, trying to luxuriate on a soft surface before he has to get back into the car, but his Kindle shows a page far past any part of the book he can remember reading last night.

When he showers, he makes the water almost unbearably hot and struggles not to worry the fine lines of just-formed scars on his ribs with his fingertips or to read the story of older, thicker scars he knows all too well. He's untethered enough to worry he'll spiral into something close to relapse if he lets himself linger. He's never grown a beard, but he doesn't have a razor. He considers and decides he can buy one when he's settled at his grandmother's, when he's steadier.

He ignores the mirror and dresses quickly. He grabs his Kindle and charger before stepping out into tepid sunlight and the rushing sound of cars a few yards away. His beat-up white Honda is June-warm, which is nice. His destination is at least another day away. Still, Reid checks the map on his phone. He's not hungry, so he dutifully turns onto the expressway and sends out some positive hope that there will be no more construction. Reid doesn't pray, but sometimes he likes to think that the energy he and others put out into the world might make a small difference.

Two

"TCHAU, MÃE, BEIJOS PRA TODOS," Joaquim Oliveira says, struggling yet again to get off the phone. His mother says goodbye and sends kisses as well. She immediately follows this by reminding him that his cousin is coming to the States and that Joaquim should try to meet up with him. Joaquim doesn't want to remind her yet again that Miami-Dade is at least an hour away and he doesn't have a car.

"Mãe," he says. His mother is awful at letting him off the phone. He misses her and his family terribly, but, after thirty minutes on the phone, Joaquim's finished. He's not a phone person. Perhaps this contributes to his homesickness. He and his sister Sofia keep in touch via email and text, so he gets more constant contact with her, rather than large chunks in weekly phone calls.

On the bed across the tiny room, Bobby, his roommate, laughs at him silently, narrow shoulders shaking. Joaquim throws a balled-up pair of socks at him. He's been folding laundry and talking at the same time, which always gives him a crick in his neck. But he's got to do something. Between the scuba diving classes he's been teaching at the pool at the Key Largo Dive Center, his new responsibilities taking people out on dives, and work at the shop, Joaquim doesn't have time for both a social life and keeping up on chores. Bobby could care less about the clean room, but, if the mess bugs Joaquim, he can usually get Bobby to do something.

"Mamãe, tenho que ir," he tries again. He doesn't have to go, but telling her he wants to might not go over well.

Finally, finally he gets his mother off the phone. He tosses it on the bed and rubs his hot, sweaty ear. "Jesus, Maria e José," he mutters in exasperation.

"You should set a timer for her," Bobby says. His headset is still around his neck, but he's gone back to his computer. He's been gaming since he got out of the shower post-dive, so his tawny brown hair has dried in uneven clumps. Joaquim is never sure what he's playing. Right now, some game with "M-80" in the title. Bobby is happy to unwind in their room playing games, talking to his guild, and Skyping friends he's made online. But Joaquim isn't a big gamer. "Mentally, I have," Joaquim says.

In the two months Joaquim and Bobby have been working as interns at the Dive Center, Joaquim has developed a real friendship with only one of the other interns, Nina, and both of them get along pretty well with Tammy, another intern. They go out together sometimes—nothing too crazy. Joaquim needs to get out of this room and out of the facility sometimes, to sit by the water when he's not working in it, to explore the Keys one by one, to wear his youth. Their jobs leave them so little time. He's used to a more relaxed pace in life and in his approach to work. It's probably good for him, though, to transition into a more American way of handling these things—for whenever he decides what he wants to do with the rest of his life.

Joaquim stacks his clothes haphazardly in his drawers. He checks the time. Almost nine, pretty close to curfew. He didn't have set plans with the girls, but he's hemmed in. Even though Joaquim comes from a much warmer place than Bobby's native North Dakota, Bobby likes it warmer in their room than he does; he loves the Florida warmth and the salt in the air when they open the windows. Sometimes that makes Joaquim more homesick.

The city of São Paulo, where he's from, isn't close to the ocean, so that's not what makes him homesick. Maybe it's the warmth, or the strangeness of a whole new place with a different pace, or the unfamiliar accents. Over his bed is a bulletin board completely covered in pictures of friends and family, of his city, and the jungles and beaches he's visited in the past. His small world map has pins in it, with string connecting them. There's a pin for every place he's visited: a pin in São Paulo, of course, but also in Rio and Bahia and Manaus in Brazil. He's been to Caracas and Maracay in Venezuela to visit friends from grade school. And he went on a trip after high school to Cartagena in Colombia. That's where he first went scuba diving and fell absolutely in love with it. He's been scuba diving ever since. Joaquim has only been to Miami and the Keys in the States thus far. But he and Nina have made loose plans to go on a road trip to Orlando and, if they ever have the time and money after their internship is over, Savannah.

Beyond food and board and a small stipend, Joaquim isn't making money from this internship. He's not saving for future trips now, but as soon as he's certified as a PADI Master Scuba Diver Trainer, he plans to start making and saving money. He wants to visit so many places. He'd love to see snow. Sometimes he makes Bobby describe it to him. Bobby rolls his eyes but humors him.

✴   ✴   ✴

WEDNESDAY'S SHIFT IS BORING, EVEN though he's manning the dive shop alone since Nina is down with a bad chest cold. He understands not diving, obviously, but thinks she was being a bit dramatic when he went to check on her.

The dive shop is slow today, and once he's finished studying, Joaquim straightens shelves. He pulls items from them and cleans and dusts before putting things back. On Thursday, he will start teaching a new beginner's class. He tries to anticipate that.

"Key Largo Dive Center," Joaquim says when the shop phone rings. "This is Joaquim, how may I help you?"

"Um…" Joaquim hears the sound of a throat being cleared. "I was wondering. Well, um. Your website… I'm not sure… Is there a class starting tomorrow?"

Joaquim switches the phone to his other ear. It's an old one, with a spiral cord hooked to the base; the heavy receiver is an unusual shape in his palm.

"We're starting a few classes," Joaquim says, flipping open the schedule book.

"The beginner one? Um, the Open Water SCUBA class?"

"Yes. Usually they're filled up by now—"

"Oh, I'm sorry! I should have thought of that."

"It's okay," Joaquim's fingers fly over the keyboard as he looks up the enrollments. "I was going to say that I could check to see if there were still openings. And, lucky for you, there is one."

"Oh." The boy—Joaquim thinks it's a boy—sounds pleased.

"I'll warn you, sometimes we have kids in these classes. We do this time. Are you comfortable with that?"

"Oh, yeah. Of course. Kids are cool."

Joaquim smiles. "Well, then why don't you give me your information, and we'll get you enrolled. You might have to stop by the shop today to pick up some necessities if you don't already have them."

"I don't even know what they are."

"Well, come in, and we'll go through it all. How's that sound?" Joaquim says.

"I can do that."

TWO HOURS LATER, JOAQUIM HAS cleaned everything he can think of to clean. The boy he spoke to on the phone—Reid Watsford—said he'd come in a few hours. Since Joaquim is teaching the class, he hopes he'll be here when Reid comes in so he can meet him. Maybe he can assuage what seemed, over the phone, to be uncertainty or anxiety.

At exactly two, Reid arrives. Joaquim is behind the shelf with the masks and somewhat hidden from view. This Reid kid is nothing like Joaquim pictured. He's wearing a simple, short-sleeved black shirt, impossibly tight black jeans that are so ripped up they seem to be held together by threads, and a canvas rainbow belt. His hair is dyed blond, dark at the roots, and artfully messy. Joaquim spots several tattoos on his arms; his right arm is a pattern of outlined, layered geometric shapes that stand out in sharp relief against his pale white skin. The design disappears under the hem of his sleeve. His forearm is a riotous splash of ink and color; Joaquim can't tell just yet what they form. Reid wanders to the counter and looks around, presumably for him. Joaquim comes from behind the mask shelf and clears his throat.

"Hi," he says, offering his hand to shake. Reid takes it carefully, as though he wasn't expecting it, or as if this is a foreign gesture. Joaquim swallows. Reid's eyes are beautiful, ice-blue rimmed by darker blue. He's wearing eyeliner, and his eyebrow is pierced twice. His ears sport several piercings, including a barbell and a really cool large triangle that goes through the middle of one ear. Joaquim has never seen that. "I'm Joaquim."

"Reid," the boy says. He seems to be about Joaquim's age. "Joaquim?" He says it slowly, trying out the proper pronunciation. He doesn't come close, but Joaquim appreciates the attempt.

"You can call me J. Most people do. And since I'll be your instructor for the class, you'll be seeing a lot of me." Joaquim eyes the floor as his face heats up. He's lucky his skin is darker so blushes don't show too obviously. He blushes a lot when he's nervous, which is mostly around hot guys he doesn't know. Right now, his hands are sweating.

Quickly, as though he needs the safety of distance from this gorgeous boy, he slips behind the counter and fishes around for a list of things Reid might need.

"J," Reid says, testing it out. "I can do that. But I still want to practice saying it the right way."

Joaquim risks a glance, barely making eye contact, and smiles. He clears his throat and tells himself to chill out. "Okay, so this is a list of equipment you'll need. Some you'll want to buy, and a lot of it you can rent. Have you ever dived or snorkeled?"

"Nope." Reid's unwavering eye contact is both warming and unnerving.

"Well, I'm going to advise that you rent then. Renting some things will help you figure out what you like. Other things are so expensive I'd never advise you to buy them unless you decide you are serious about diving and plan to do a lot of it."

"Great. Okay. So. Um…?"

Joaquim leads him over to the masks, points to several, and describes them one by one. Confidence comes from his competence and, while he's describing what Reid will want or need, he calms down.

"Will these be a problem?" Reid gestures toward his eyebrow piercings. "Any of them?"

"No, your mask will be well above your eyebrows," Joaquim says. He touches Reid's forehead about where it should hit and then snatches his hand back. *Don't be weird. What's wrong with me?*

Reid doesn't say anything, nor does he flinch. Joaquim forces himself not to clear his throat and moves on. He's rather proud that he maintains eye contact and that he doesn't make a ridiculous face when Reid's lips twitch.

By the time Reid has gone, Joaquim is a tongue-tied mess. Holding it together for a student is one thing. As an instructor, Joaquim's quiet, chill nature is a great asset. He's level and personable; his divers appreciate it. He's good at calming the ones who freak out. Cute boys, though? Cute boys are his downfall, and around them, Joaquim often devolves into a shy awkwardness that's totally at odds with his personality. Plus, he's new to teaching, and he's never had to *instruct* someone he's attracted to. Before tomorrow, Joaquim has *got* to get a handle on his idiotic tendency to fall apart around cute boys.

Three

REID ROLLS DOWN THE WINDOWS and blasts the air conditioner. He was in the dive shop long enough for the car to become a sauna. Reid's all for being warm, but the way the car becomes a small greenhouse with a burning steering wheel is too much for him.

He leaves the door propped open and looks back at the shop. *Joaquim.* Reid can't figure out how to think the name with the correct pronunciation. Reid's come here to get himself together, not to get together with anyone, but, *damn.* That kid is hot. He has short black hair that hints at a curl, perfectly smooth, light brown skin, and long, thick lashes framing wide brown eyes. He seemed flustered at first, which was flattering, but then settled into a comfortable groove. Somehow, he reminds Reid of Nancy.

Reid once tried to explain to his mother about people with particular energies. Nancy's office was over an hour from their home, a drive that placed a burden on everyone in the family, be it from shuffling cars or driving Reid themselves. One therapist seemed as good as another to them. Reid didn't know how to articulate the reason, but as soon as he met Nancy he knew he had someone special in his corner, someone who would really benefit his recovery.

"You're kidding, right?" his father said. Dinner steamed on the table, and as he buttered a roll, a familiar story scrolled across his face; his expression said he thought Reid was some sort of alien.

"I'm not saying I read auras or anything." Reid rolled his eyes and ignored the food his mother dished onto his plate. Actively resisting the urge to roll his eyes again, he took the plate from her hands. "I'm just saying I felt calm. She felt calm. I liked being around her energy."

"Reid, she's a therapist," Sean pointed out.

"Dad, you don't have to talk to me like I'm an idiot," Reid said. Familiar frustration rose, tight in his chest and the palms of his hands. He dug his fingernail into the nail bed of his thumb, hard, and exhaled at the small, burning pain. "I've met other people—you know what, forget it and just pass the peas."

There was a long silence while his parents' eyes bored into him. Reid got his pale blue eyes from his mother and his light coloring from them both. When seen together, there was no doubt he was their son; together they seemed like a beautiful family.

Together, truthfully, they were a mess, because Reid was a mess.

"Please," he added. The light played over the tines of the fork he was fiddling with.

They conceded, even if the concession lacked grace. And he never mentioned this kind of energy to anyone again. Nancy's was one of the biggest factors when Reid chose to stay with her and check in via Skype rather than seek out a new therapist in Key Largo. Her energy keeps their therapy group together.

Joaquim didn't seem quite like Nancy. Still, there was something magnetic about him, something that made Reid want to linger.

✳   ✳   ✳

REID'S NOT GENERALLY INSECURE, ALTHOUGH he realizes his anxiety makes him come off that way. And while his initial week in Key Largo goes smoothly enough, that restlessness, tight in his muscles—that anxiety coiling and coiling until he's shaking out his hands and pacing—haunts him. His mood has been good, but he needs to do something more than sit in his grandmother's condo or on the beach contemplating the relatively waveless water. He's even given the book version of *The*

Lord of the Rings a try. He seems to remember liking the movie well enough, but the book is torture, an unadulterated bore.

"Grams, what do you do for fun out here?" he complained the night before his visit to the dive shop. Reid barely spoke to his own parents, but he did call his grandmother every other night.

"Play cribbage and Rummikub with the girls by the pool?" Traces of light laughter made Reid frown. "Go for boat rides with the Kelleys. Have you met them yet, dear?"

"No, Grams." He didn't offer more, because he couldn't think of anything more awkward than a gay twenty-year-old with multiple piercings and made-up eyes knocking on an old couple's door, not that his grandmother's friends would mind. They tried to sucker him into a game of cribbage a few days ago. Since he had no idea how to play, he politely declined.

"Well, I'll try to think of some things. If anything comes up, I'll email you. Have you thought about learning to scuba dive? You did always love the water."

"Oh, huh," Reid said. He was pacing a loop through the small kitchen, through the tiny dining room, and circling the living room, over and over. He'd bitten his thumbnail down until he had nothing left to bite. He shook out his hand. "No, can I? Like, are there special rules?"

"No, Reid, I think pretty much anyone can. Even kids. They have to be a certain age, I think."

"Oh, okay."

"I hear good things about Key Largo Dive Shop. Why don't you give them a call? I'll wire you some money."

"Grams, no one wires money anymore. And you don't have to send me money, either."

"I'll stick it in your PayPal thing and I'll call it wiring, how's that?" she said, with the famous Watsford sass clear in her voice.

Reid knew from that tone that nothing he said or did would deter her.

He hates that he's living off of his parents' and grandmother's goodwill and his own dwindling savings. He's only been here a week, but Reid has never lived on his own. He's never learned to budget for groceries and gas and his own phone. He's never had a job that paid more than minimum wage.

Some people, like Felix, would say that's because he's spoiled. Really, it's because his parents—without meaning to be—are very controlling, as if watching his every move and giving him very few freedoms might manage his mental illness.

WHEN HE GETS HOME FROM the dive shop, he's still agitated, as though tomorrow is miles and miles away. As soon as he's in the condo again, he realizes he needs to get the fuck out. Often, Reid can zone out with mindless television shows; he can't bake for shit and knows nothing about tools, but loves any show featuring large-scale home renovations or cupcakes. *The Great British Baking Show* is his most secret guilty pleasure. Even Felix doesn't know about it. One of the luxuries of living alone is the ability to record anything from the TV without anyone knowing. But now a jittery anxiety curls through him, the kind a television show or even his favorite books won't drown or soothe. It's hot enough outside for him to regret wearing pants, but he doesn't own shorts and is loath to get some, both for aesthetic reasons and because of the cost.

He changes into swim trunks, although the bay water will be too warm. Donning flip-flops, he makes his way out of the screened porch and into the backyard. The foliage, if one could call it that, is different from what he's used to: ferns and a buttonwood tree, tall grasses and a gigantic aloe plant. Almost hidden between the buttonwood and the alien aloe plant he's named Joe is a flight of uneven stairs leading down a steep hill to the water. They're made, as everything here is, from coral. The beach is tiny. The Largos has a larger beach near the big dock and a midsized one near the little dock, which he can see around the curve of land to his right. This tiny beach is meant for the residents of Tamarind, the farthest condo building from the gate, the big dock, and the pool, and few condo residents come here. He guesses that the median age in this building prevents any of them from climbing down the hill, even with those stairs.

This little stretch of beach isn't beautiful. It's scrubby, and there's seaweed on the waterline. The water makes a gentle shush and gurgle as it laps the sand. The thing he's most puzzled by, perhaps disgruntled by, is the sand. Reid's only been to Big Bay Beach on Madeline Island, where his family took an annual summer trip for years when he was a kid, but the sand there was fine. Reid remembers that he loved playing with it. He didn't care to build sandcastles, but would run the sand between his fingers, let it slip through them, bury his fingers in a little pile of it, and enjoy the juxtaposition of softness and graininess.

The sand in the Keys is rougher, with much larger grains. Reid looked it up when he first arrived, only to find out that it's because sand is not natural to the Keys, which are actually coral atolls and not true islands. The beaches here are manmade and the sand scrapes against his bare feet, which he needs to toughen up.

Though it's not the most beautiful of beachy places, Reid likes it. It's solitary. The only noises he hears are the gulls and the water and occasionally a motor as a boat goes by or revs up by the small dock. He's waded into the water a few times, but there's a ton of seaweed and it's incredibly mucky; without water shoes it's definitely gross. And there are jellyfish that look like sea plants. They sit in the shallow water; some sting mildly, some not at all. Reid's picked up a few to examine them. They are diverse and cool and weird. The water on this bay side of Key Largo is different than on the ocean side; over there they get actual waves. It's not far, but he hasn't made the time to go. He hopes that scuba diving will get him in those waters.

Reid loves being in the water. At night, right before they turn out the lights at the pool, he loves to dip in and under, loves the erasure of noise and of his body weight. It's almost worth the crazy motherfucking mosquitos.

Four

ALL DAY, JOAQUIM ANTICIPATES HIS class, partly because a young girl, Erin, is enrolled and Joaquim loves working with kids. Mostly, though, it's because he is intrigued by this Reid guy. He wants to wax poetic about him to *someone,* but Bobby's not that kind of guy and Nina is nowhere to be found.

After his shift at the shop, he flops dramatically onto his bed and stares at the ceiling.

"What's that face about?" Bobby asks. Joaquim is surprised he's looked away from his computer long enough to ask. His color is high, with splashes of pink along his cheekbones.

"Did you have a dive today?" Joaquim asks.

"Mmm." Undiverted, Bobby smiles and turns back to his game. "Must be about a guy."

Joaquim stares at him, but that's all Bobby says.

After Bobby dons his headset and starts talking to someone about whatever mission he's on, Joaquim puts in his earphones, settles into his bed, and texts Sofia.

Joaquim: *Cute boy alert*

It takes a while to get a response.

Sofia: *Where?*

Joaquim: *In the shop today. OMG. Srsly SoSo. Gorgeous*

She responds ten minutes later.

Sofia: *Tell me about the boy.*

Joaquim: *He's in my beginner class tomorrow. I'll know then. Where u at?*

Sofia: *Club w/ Luiz. LOLZ baby. A guy in a mask tells it all.*
Joaquim: *Shut up.*
Joaquim: *You should see him*

Joaquim frowns because he misses his sister so much. But if she's with Luiz, he'll be waiting a while for responses.

He texts Nina to ask where she is.

Nina: *At Salty's*

He groans. Salty John's is a local bar, and Nina is obsessed with a bartender there. If he goes, he'll definitely end up a third wheel.

Instead of pouting, he pulls out his laptop and sends an email to his mom and dad, catching them up on the more mundane aspects of his week. He's working on his specialty certification in wreck diving, which makes for a nicely descriptive paragraph. His Thursday dive had the potential for perfection: the sun was bright and the wildlife on the reef were particularly active. Unfortunately, a diver panicked, and he had to intervene. Joaquim puts a funny spin on the story so as not to worry them.

He doesn't mention meeting Reid. Joaquim isn't out to his whole family. He's not hiding his sexuality, exactly; it's never come up. Maybe they think he is, but no one's ever asked him. Joaquim doesn't tell people unless they ask. It's no one's business unless they're trying to get into his pants, or vice versa. He doesn't walk around asking people if they're straight, after all.

*   *   *

REID IS PACKING UP HIS books at the end of their first class when Nina catches Joaquim's eye from across the room and tilts her head toward Reid. She winks, and Joaquim rolls his eyes. She widens her eyes, the bright green of them flashing in the fluorescent lights, and so he steels himself and sits next to Reid.

"So." He clears his throat. Reid's unwinding earbuds from his phone, which he'd tucked into the pocket of his bag. Joaquim is struck by how tired he seems, and again by how startling his pale blue eyes are with that cobalt ring around his irises.

"So," Reid says back. His lopsided smirk is both lazy and a little playful. His eyes brighten. Although Joaquim deliberately makes eye contact with each student throughout class to get them used to the form of one-on-one connection that will serve them well with buddies and instructors when in the water, the eye contact Reid is making is of a very different sort. It's not-so-subtle flirtation, which is fine, and offers a nice counterpoint to his own, much subtler reciprocation. He's been told his invitation is in his smile, but he's never been able to pinpoint what exactly he's doing or how to replicate it. It just happens. Reid's smile widens, and then his gaze flickers up when Mike, the Dive Center owner, comes up.

"Hi there," he says, holding a hand out to Reid. "I'm Mike Schafer, I run this joint. How'd today go? Joaquim working out for you?"

Reid stand and takes his hand. Joaquim stands as well. Mike likes to check in, make sure that there's a good rapport between instructors and students; what they do is fundamentally tied to the ability to trust the instructor. He's a big guy with a strong grip and a friendly face. Its warmth is meant to combat what is an otherwise intimidating frame.

"Yeah, this is great." Reid kicks at the ground. "I'm excited. Good change of pace for me."

"You're not from around here, are you?" Mike's stance is casual and genuine. He likes to know his divers and students.

"Naw, I'm from a town called Eau Claire, in Wisconsin." Reid tucks his hands into his pockets. Joaquim reads clamming up in the movement, in the tightening shoulders and flickering eye contact. Reid's gone from flirting openly, though quietly, to being slightly agitated and tense. Mike must sense it, too, since he wishes Reid good luck, claps Joaquim on the shoulder, and moves on. On the other side of the classroom, little Erin is lingering with her father.

"I think she's waiting for me," Joaquim says to Reid. Reid's already got one earbud in. "But I'll see you tomorrow?" Unsure of his body language, he refrains from touching Reid or standing too close. Reid nods.

"Yeah, I can't wait."

Joaquim watches him shoulder his bag and walk back through the dive shop.

THAT NIGHT, JOAQUIM, NINA, AND Tammy go to Salty's. Although his beginner class starts at the butt-crack of dawn, he stays out too late, drinks one too many, and word-vomits about how gorgeous Reid is. Nina, clearly amused, shakes her thick mahogany hair over her shoulder when he describes Reid's eyes for the fourth time.

"Why don't you ask him out?"

Joaquim looks around at them, all exaggeration and deliberation. "Where? When? With the fourteen seconds of free time I have?"

Tammy brightens. "Joaquim, it's been so long since you got laid, that's about all you need."

"Oh, my god, woman, shut up!" Joaquim pushes her playfully; she's had more to drink, so she starts to slide off her stool.

"Opa!" he says, catching her one-handed and spilling the Hurricane he was holding in his other hand. She smooths her skirt; her high ponytail is slipping, blonde hairs escaping. They frame her pretty face.

"Everyone okay?" Sam, the bartender who is the object of Nina's admiration, asks.

Nina groans and smacks her forehead. "You guys are a lightweight freak show."

"Oh, my god, woman, shut up!" Tammy says, in a poor imitation of Joaquim's accent.

"I do not sound like that!" he protests. "And besides, who are you making fun of anyway?"

"I honestly have no idea," she replies. Her drink, in her loose grip, balances so precariously that Nina grabs it.

"You're gonna drop it, break a glass, and get us kicked out," Joaquim says. Now that he's more tuned in, Tammy seems drunker than she should be. "You're not taking a group out tomorrow, are you?" he asks.

Tammy shakes her head. "I'm just tired, I think."

Joaquim checks his cell and shakes his head. "Yeah, we need to get back. My eight a.m. won't teach itself."

"Please do not sigh and act like you cannot wait to see that boy again, time of day or not," Nina says.

Joaquim struggles not to smile and shrugs. She's not far wrong.

Five

BETWEEN SITTING BY THE BEACH, walking along Highway 1 listening to music, and wandering in and out of kitschy tourist specialty shops too many times, Reid can officially state that he's going to lose his mind. Not because he's, you know, crazy, but because he's bored.

Reid is itching for fun, though he loves his diving classes. Well, really, he's enjoying his crush. Diving Theory isn't all that thrilling. At least they've moved on to instruction in the pool. He can't wait to go out in the ocean. Yesterday was Reid's first time using a respirator and, of course, he made a total fool of himself. Reid is used to fear; he knows its every flavor and shape. The second he began using the respirator underwater, he was caught off guard by instant, painful panic. Reid could breathe, sure, but it felt different and that compounded the problem. The mask, the respirator, the silence that wasn't silence, all combined to create claustrophobia.

No one else freaked out. First-time panic couldn't be that unusual, however, considering Joaquim's practiced response.

"It's normal," he said. Reid shook his head, knuckled water from his face, and closed his eyes. He tried to regulate his breathing, and, when he opened his eyes, Joaquim's eyes were unerringly on his. He matched his breathing to Reid's. Once Reid calmed, he realized that they were both still crouched in the water with Joaquim's hands on his shoulders and a whole world still spinning around them.

"Ugh, I feel so stupid," Reid said.

"Really, don't." Joaquim squeezed his shoulders once and dropped his hands. "It's very natural. Our instincts run completely counter to breathing underwater. And it feels different. Really different."

"But I'm a strong swimmer." Reid huffed and squared his shoulders. "Shouldn't that—"

"Well then, maybe your brain is too well-trained, and your instincts about what you do and don't do underwater are automatically kicking in," Joaquim said.

Reid let himself look at Joaquim. He let Joaquim meet his gaze and thought about trust: learning to trust himself, learning to trust others. Joaquim helped him with his mask and positioned them both with their chins above water. He counted back from three and, when Reid slid into the water, Joaquim went with him. Reid forced himself to keep his eyes open. Joaquim used one hand, lifting and lowering, to guide Reid's breathing. Even through their masks, he could see Joaquim's eyes clearly. Reid wrapped it all around himself: the motion of Joaquim's hand, his steady eyes, the white noise that could be kind, should Reid let it.

Joaquim is the most interesting thing on this whole island, and not only because Reid wants to fuck him. He's very good at eye contact, which is nice but also a little difficult to receive. Reid's never sure how one is supposed to hold eye contact. He becomes incredibly self-conscious and then isn't sure where to look or how long or how often.

Joaquim is also gorgeous. He has unblemished skin Reid longs to touch, eyes so dark they're almost black, and a slight accent that sounds like the shapes of the words themselves are melting at their edges. He's taller than Reid; if Reid had to guess, he'd say just shy of six feet. What really interests Reid, though, is Joaquim's calm, the antithesis of his own jagged edges and shifting energy. Reid wouldn't mind basking in Joaquim's presence for days.

Unfortunately, Reid cannot sneak into the Dive Center's pool and paddle around after Joaquim to share cosmic energy, or whatever fucking weird thing he's thinking. Reid shakes his head, and an earbud flies out. He's pacing the grounds from one condo building to the next, enjoying the shift of coral pebbles that make up the paths through the wooded areas on the property.

The sunlight dapples the ground as the wind tosses the trees above him. He's trying to talk himself out of his own strangeness, counting his steps one after another, and he's repeated and repeated the same route for over twenty minutes when he bumps into someone.

"Fuck, I'm so sorry!" Reid rips his earbuds out, then winces when he sees it's Roy Wilson, the condo manager. "Oh fuck, language." He cringes when Roy laughs.

"Don't worry about it." Roy waves it off.

Reid isn't sure if he needs to make small talk or if he should move on.

"Spoke to your grandma the other night," Roy says casually. Reid freezes.

"You *spoke* with her?" Fucking great. Another family member checking in on him behind his back. He never thought Grams would pull this kind of crap. His parents do this to Reid all the time. No one trusts him to manage on his own. How the hell is Reid supposed to trust himself if no one else will?

"Yeah, did she not tell you? She and I—"

"Wait, what?" Reid shakes his head.

"Oh, damn, son. She's gonna kill me for this."

Reid squints into the green foliage surrounding them and tries to wrap his mind around this. "So wait, you are like, together?"

"Well, uh." Roy scratches his head. He's almost bald and sweat glistens on his scalp.

"Wow. Um, congrats?" Reid hazards. "Be good to her?"

Roy meets his eyes, and they both laugh. "I am, I promise."

"Knowing Grams, I should be asking her to be sure she's nice to you." Reid loves his grandma, who is amazing, but also a handful.

Roy shrugs sheepishly. "Well, anyway, I spoke to her, and she mentioned that you were getting a little bored."

He's momentarily annoyed that his grandmother is sharing personal information with a man who is, by all standards, a stranger to Reid. He is so busy being unsettled, he misses the next part.

"I'm sorry, come again?"

"My bud Shel over at the Shell World needs a cashier."

"You know a guy named Shel who works at Shell World?" Reid repeats slowly.

"I know, I know," Roy says. "Anyway, you have any interest? It's right across the highway and down a bit. You can walk if you want." When Reid meets his gaze, he sees that Roy's eyes are lined with kindness. It's probably been impossible for people to miss the young man wearing dark clothes and obsessively walking the grounds with his head down, day after day. "You got a lot more commitment to this healthy exercise thing than I do," Roy says, as he pats his belly.

Reid squints and tries to recalibrate. Nancy is forever trying to point out that Reid perceives constant judgment from the world, and that sometimes his reactions—when his perception is off, overreactions—only worsen a situation. With that in mind, he doubts that a seventy-year-old man, who is dating Reid's grandmother and rubbing his own belly with what could only be called affection, is judging Reid as harshly as he thought.

The constant hum of cicadas envelops them. "Yeah, um, that sounds cool," Reid says. He doesn't have a burning desire to work at Shell World, but he is incredibly bored, and Reid and bored is a dangerous combination. And he really, really wants to have some independence from his family.

"Great! I can give him a call. Or, you know, he's there all day today," Roy says. Reid tries not to bristle; he doesn't even like when his family tries to push or guide him, and this guy is definitely not family.

Reid inhales and shakes his hands out once, trying to move the irritation off and out. It's a constant buzz right now; it colors everything he sees and hears and, probably, everything he perceives.

"Yeah, I got time," Reid says. He puts his hands in his pockets. Roy looks at him and he looks at Roy and nothing much happens other than the unceasing soundtrack of the cicada song. Finally, Roy clears his throat, pats Reid on the arm, and wishes him luck.

After he's left, carrying with him the crunching sound of sandaled feet on the path, Reid closes his eyes and tries to settle into the hot, humid air. He tries to transform the rasping cicada song into calm white noise. He tries to relax in his skin, which crawls against the fabric of his clothes and the sweat that dews it at all times because he has no weather-appropriate clothing. Reid's aesthetic has never included shorts or tank tops. In Wisconsin, sweating through the warmest parts of summer was manageable.

But he can't. He can't and can't. His hands out of his pockets, he shakes and shakes them out. Then he takes off toward the gates of the complex; he needs to do something, and he might as well take a positive step. With money, at least he can buy new clothes. And maybe a change of scenery will help.

Outside the complex, the sound of cars rushing past on the Overseas Highway is a welcome balm. There are few sounds and sensations he consistently likes; they shift and cycle the way he does. Since he's been here, he's found that the only thing that consistently calms him is the water.

REID'S BEEN IN SHELL WORLD. It's less than a mile south and so is one of the places Reid's visited on his long walks.

There is tourist kitsch and then there is *tourist kitsch*. Shell World is kitsch on steroids. Reid likes that about it. It wears its genuine self unabashedly. Also, there are a lot of shell wind chimes, the sounds of which are soothing. Reid wonders if they might always be so, if he'll always need soothing, if he'll always be stuck in these cycles of never-fully-okay. He recognizes the chain of thought, but then lets it wash away. His therapist calls this skill "using Teflon mind." He thinks it's a pretty stupid phrase, and so do Rachel and Elise, the most consistent members of their Dialectical Behavioral Therapy group. Even Nancy, his therapist, agrees that it's iffy. But it's part of the program, so they all go with it.

Reid wanders the store; it's overstocked, and the frenetically filled shelves are too close to each other and carry a dizzying array of goods. It's a long store and, to find the register, anyone entering has to walk almost its entire length.

Manning the desk is a curvy, dark-haired girl in a tight black tank and acid-wash shorts who wears a seriously unimpressed face and the body language of the deeply bored. When she spots Reid, she plasters on the fakest smile—Reid's impressed—and chirps, "Welcome to Shell World. Have you found what you're looking for?"

Reid presses his lips together. He doesn't want to seem as though he's laughing at her.

"Well, I'm looking for Shel," he says. "Not *shells*." He tilts his head and stresses the word. Not everyone gets his humor, and often his sarcasm is read as rude. He's learning to try to give body language cues to match his intentions, but he sucks at it.

This girl speaks irony and sarcasm like a pro, because she gets it. Her next smile is real.

She cocks a brow at him. "About a job?"

"Yes. I'm interested in applying for a job."

"Great." She reaches under the counter and roots around, then comes up with a job application. She yawns and hands him a pen. "Have at it, kiddo."

"O-kay," he says. He scoots down the counter, out of the way of any customer who might be on the hunt for a conch shell engraved with their name, and fills out the application. His square, all-capitals printing barely fits in the tiny boxes, but he gets the job done just as the doors chime a customer arrival.

"Done." He holds it out to her, but she doesn't take it.

"Hey, Shel!" she shouts over her shoulder. "There's a guy here for ya."

Reid stifles an intense urge to roll his eyes—he doesn't know how important to this operation Sassy Girl is—and waits patiently.

Six

THE FIRST TIME TAKING DIVERS out on the reef is the most stressful, but rewarding, part of teaching the beginner classes. As an instructor, Joaquim must always be on. In this line of work, that means calm, friendly, confident, and enthusiastic.

On the ride out, he keeps an eye on Keith, who's turned a little green. The waves are high with the wind, but not enough to worry about getting the students in the water at Molasses Reef. He briefed them before they boarded, but will brief them again once they're there. On the way, though, he makes small talk with all of them. They'll talk more on the way back, when everyone is relaxed and enjoying the sunshine and reliving the dive experience—those who liked it, of course.

Joaquim sits next to Reid, who is turned to watch the water as it jolts by and completely silent. He's wearing one of his white swim shirts. Joaquim's embarrassed to admit that he knows that Reid has three that he rotates. They each have distinct colored stripes at the shoulders: red, blue, and green. It's the blue today, with coordinated swim trunks. They always coordinate.

"How's it going?" Joaquim pitches his voice to be heard, but not to shout.

Reid flashes him a smile. "Good."

Should he coax more out of him? He badly wants to know more about this boy. Their class is almost at an end. Often, Reid seems flirty, and his glances are definitely reciprocal, more so than when they began class. That first week, Reid vacillated between happy and anxious, and was often quiet or withdrawn by the end of the session. Joaquim doesn't usually do the asking out when it comes to boys; he's working on that, though. When he's teaching, there's no room for hesitance, and he loves sharing this world with others, teaching them and introducing them to diving. Nina's been coaching him to carry that confidence into the rest of his life.

"Just good?" Joaquim teases, hoping for another smile.

"This is nice," Reid says after a bit. His hair ruffles in the breeze. Joaquim guesses he doesn't bother with product when they're about to go in the water; without it, his hair is still messy and obviously thick, but flatter. The effect is sweeter, and blonder, without his dark roots showing. "I like being on the water like this."

"Yeah, me too." Joaquim's gaze takes in the rest of their group; he needs to help Keith out, because he's a little less steady. Joaquim pats Reid on the shoulder, crosses the boat, and steadies himself with one hand on the roof when they hit a wave.

THE PRE-DIVE SAFETY CHECK GOES about as well as usual for Joaquim. First open water dives are anxiety-producing for divers, especially if they're the sort to second guess themselves and worry. Being in charge of setting up and donning gear strikes them as more daunting with the wide expanse of ocean rocking steadily and unceasingly under the deck of the boat. His class handles the prep and entrance well enough, but when it's Erin's turn to enter the water, she balks.

"You've got this," Joaquim says to her from the water. Claude, the boat driver, is at her back with his hand on her tank, murmuring encouragement. The boat pitches up and down with a wave. Erin is so short. Joaquim can imagine how daunting it must feel, taking a step from a boat into open water, weighed down by unfamiliar gear. She's shaking.

But then Erin squares her shoulders. When she steps off, Joaquim exhales hard around the sharp edge of pride he often feels when he watches others tackle moments of fear. Although she continues to shake all the way down, she takes Joaquim's hand and meets his eyes like a champ. Ten minutes later she's comfortable enough to let go of his hand to point at a barracuda hovering yards away in their periphery.

The actual in-the-water dive runs about thirty minutes. The hours sandwiching those thirty minutes, though, with the details to attend to, the nerves from buoyance checks, the waits for ascent and descent, all slip from his students' minds in their first moments back on the boat. They've taken his group to Winch Hole, named for a large winch believed to be from a ship that ran aground in the 1800s, and it is a great spot for first-time dives.

Joaquim loves touring his divers. With each student, Joaquim has the privilege of sharing this thing he loves or watching others come to love it too. Post-dive, Joaquim's muscles sink into a wrung-out, pleasant thrum. The debriefing is one of his favorite parts, especially after a first dive, when students can't wait to tell each other what they saw and how it felt.

"Did you see that group of grunt fish?" Erin asks; her cheeks are pink, bearing marks from her mask. "They were under that overhang, you know?"

"I definitely spotted some Spanish grunts," Keith says. He looks at Joaquim. "At least, I think we did. They had a yellow stripe at the top and some black stripes. Is that right?"

"Spot on," Joaquim says. "That's what they were."

They saw a school of parrot fish, and once Reid gestured over Joaquim's shoulder toward a nurse shark meandering amongst the coral. It was a great dive; the reef teemed with schools of fish, the sun was bright, and the water clear. After the dive, Reid doesn't speak as the group catalogues what they've seen. Mostly they talk about the fish, although Keith and Roger have many questions about the coral and sponges; Joaquim and Claude are drawn into a conversation with them about the delicacy of the reef. Although they've learned about it in class, it's another thing for divers to see the reef and understand how careful they must be to preserve it. Joaquim's not always so lucky. He has been with divers who have no respect for nature. This group, however: This group is fantastic.

Past Claude's shoulder, he sees Reid settle next to Erin. He offers his hand and they execute a complex high-five and handshake Joaquim's seen them working on in class. Unlike the other divers, Reid never treats Erin like a little kid, never condescends to her. Reid isn't working to include her because she stands apart; left to his own devices, Reid has naturally, quietly connected with her. Their laughter catches on the wind.

Seven

REID'S ENTRANCE INTO THE WATER is less than graceful but, all in all, better than he anticipated.

The minutes leading up to the dive were slightly stressful. All of the things they learned in the pool and all of the equipment to check and wear seemed more overwhelming on the ocean. By the time they finish descent, though, all of that stress is forgotten. All he hears is the sound of his own breathing through the respirator and the constant crackling and popping along the reef. His world narrows to blues and grays, to the work of his body as he learns to keep himself horizontal in the push-pull of currents. Once adjusted, Reid needs a moment to take in the tableau before him, the blue-gray giving way to stunning color. Pictures pale in comparison to the actual vibrancy of the reef. His classmates move along the periphery of his vision; he spends long minutes watching the delicate lace of a sea fan, brown with startling purple veins, undulating in the same currents that envelop him. A brilliant angelfish darts in and out around the crimson and honey-colored coral and sponges. Gorgeous, inspiring reminders of a beautiful world he never thought he would see or experience are right at his hands. They're necessary indicators of the life Reid can have, can work for: full of surprises, of beautiful things, of beautiful places.

After the dive, Reid drowses on a damp towel in the sun and listens to Keith chattering with his wife, Janet, about the fish they saw. The sky is a clear, rich blue, cloudless and open, the water is a constant slosh against the sides of the boat, and Reid can still remember the absolute peace underwater. He smiles. He was a little worried that Keith would puke on the way to the dive, but Keith held it together. He's telling Janet it was nerves. With his eyes closed, it's easier for Reid to eavesdrop. They've got a book, and they're marking the fish and coral they've seen. It's very sweet. Reid has his own notebook for this very purpose, but he's not ready to let go of the wonderful lethargy of muscles well-used and the peace of the moment.

The boat hasn't started yet. They're all snacking and unwinding and writing in their dive logs. A small thump next to him startles Reid. The sunlight assaults his eyes, so he squints and turns to find Joaquim next to him. The can of pop in his hand drips cold condensation onto Reid's arm, and Joaquim wiggles the can.

"Want?"

Reid is so much better than he was on the way out to the dive site, so much more present and alive. He sits up slowly and looks into Joaquim's eyes.

"Yeah," he says, making no move to take the can from Joaquim's hand.

"Did—" Joaquim stops to clear his throat. "Did you enjoy today?"

"Oh my god." Reid says. "That was fucking amazing." He darts a glance at Erin and winces, but she doesn't seem to have heard him. "I've… That was beautiful. And I've never felt like that."

"Right?" Joaquim's eyes brighten and the corners of his mouth lift. Reid likes that.

Without the wind off the water, it's hot on the deck. Joaquim is shirtless, just wearing his trunks. His body is incredible; he's taller than Reid and has somewhat thicker muscles. Either he's naturally more built or he works out. Reid couldn't say when he last exercised, unless walking until his shoes are worn through counts. He's lost weight since coming to the Keys. It's not apparent when wearing a swim shirt, which he is. He's too warm, but there's no way he'd take the shirt off in front of these people—or anyone, really.

Sweating now, he takes the can from Joaquim, making sure their fingers touch, and then drinks half of it in one go. Joaquim smiles. Claude calls for him from the front of the boat; Joaquim's sigh seems annoyed.

"Hey," Reid says, softly. "We'll talk later, right?"

Joaquim lets his eyes linger on Reid's lips and hair and run down his torso. "Definitely."

Oh, man, he is so fucked.

AFTER REID IS DRESSED AND has taken care of his gear, he emerges from the locker room and onto the pool deck. On the boat ride home, he talked himself into taking this chance and, although his heart is beating a little fast, he's interested in Joaquim, he's attracted and intrigued. Joaquim isn't on the pool deck yet. Reid gets drawn into a conversation with Nina, another instructor, and Mike. He's more physically worn out than he anticipated and deliciously present in his own bones.

When Mike is called away by Erin's father, Reid spots Joaquim carrying tanks. Nina watches him watching Joaquim and pats his arm.

"Go get him, tiger," she says, and he blushes bright and hot under his already sun-touched skin. "You guys are killing me. Go get it over with."

"Oh god, shush," he says, ducking his head, but he decides to go with it. That is his purpose here, after all.

"Hey," Reid says as he catches up with Joaquim. He pitches his voice a little lower, even though they're around the corner, at the side of the shop. He doubts anyone can hear them, but they saw him come this way. He isn't sure how out Joaquim is, and Reid doesn't intend to make trouble for him.

"Hey, yourself," Joaquim says. He stands slowly; Reid leans against the green stucco wall and crosses his arms.

"So, I was wondering, I mean, um, do you wanna—"

"Want to?" Joaquim prompts. "*Now?*" His voice rises, and Reid shakes his head and waves a hand.

"No! No, I didn't mean that. I meant, do you want to go out? Not to hook up, but like, a date. Ish?"

"Yeah," Joaquim says. A sweet smile creases his face. "That would be nice."

He never used to be shy about this kind of thing. *Fucking Felix.* Reid concentrates and expels the thought. He starts to speak and then stops. He bites his lip. He's so dumb. "Oh, god," he says, and runs his hand through his messy hair. "So now, I have to admit I didn't think this through and I don't know this town well enough to know where to take you."

"That is adorable," Joaquim says. Reid scrunches his eyes.

"I'm not so much going for that," he admits.

"What are you going for, then?" Joaquim asks, almost whispering. The conversation is intimate, despite the group a few feet away around the corner. Reid shifts his feet. "Don't worry, you don't have to answer that." Joaquim's smile is a little naughty, which is surprising. It doesn't quite match the picture of Joaquim Reid's constructed in his mind.

"Have you been to Anne's Beach?"

"No, I've mostly stuck around bayside where I'm staying."

"We can go there if you want."

"Yes," Reid says, grateful that Joaquim knows what he's doing. "When works for you? My work schedule is probably easier to manage than yours." The dive shop keeps the interns busy. From what Joaquim and Nina have said, Reid can tell that they put a lot of hours into teaching and learning.

"Um, yeah. This week is crazy busy. But I'm free at five-thirty tomorrow. Can you swing that?"

"Definitely!" Reid almost rolls his eyes at himself. That was way too much enthusiasm; he doesn't want to scare Joaquim by coming on too strong.

"Let me text you my number when I have my phone back, and then we'll set things up."

"Don't you need my number?"

Joaquim gives him a *look* and then Reid does laugh at himself. *Duh.* "You have my number in the shop, yeah?"

"Yeah." Joaquim seems as if he wants to say something else, but then Nina calls for him. "I'll text you," he says again, and they share a look.

*   *   *

REID PULLS INTO THE TINY, public parking lot for the beach that Joaquim gave him directions to. Joaquim didn't say much about where they were going, just that Reid should wear swim stuff. He's brought a towel, too, just in case.

Joaquim is standing at the edge of the lot near the entrance to a boardwalk. He's got a small cooler at his feet and is wearing yellow Bermuda shorts. He doesn't see Reid come up to him, as he's fiddling on his phone. His red and white-striped tank top shows off his muscled shoulders and rounded biceps Reid wants to touch.

"I thought you said to wear a suit," Reid says when he approaches.

Joaquim smiles at Reid. "I have it on under my shorts."

Reid wants to make a joke about stripping them off, but, again, doesn't want to come on too strong too soon. This is their first interaction without others around them and in a non-lesson context.

"C'mon," Joaquim says. He picks up the cooler, and Reid is grateful to see that he also has a towel. Joaquim leads him onto a boardwalk that goes through the mangroves.

"Did you put on bug spray?" Joaquim texted about that too.

"Definitely." Slapping at mosquitos isn't Reid's idea of a romantic date. "It's pretty here," he says. Picnic tables and shaded areas on the boardwalk face little sections of beach. Other than the barking of a dog, it's very quiet. The mangroves are verdant; they create the sense of a solitary world. Reid is surprised to discover that mangrove swamps smell, well, like swamps. Despite the smell, Reid could see himself lingering here when he needs quiet time.

"It's very peaceful here during the week. I should warn you, though, sometimes there are nudists. And dogs." Reid catches and reciprocates Joaquim's sidelong smirk. "Hopefully they don't scare you."

"No, I'm not afraid of dogs," Reid says.

"Just nudists?" Joaquim bumps into him. Reid can't tell if it's by design or an accident. Reid bumps him back rather than answer.

"So," Joaquim says after a comfortable silence. "Reid from Wisconsin. Tell me about yourself."

Caught up in taking in the scenery, Reid is a few steps behind him and has to take longer strides to catch up. His own curiosity wins out over manners and, rather than answer, he asks, "Where are you from?"

"Brazil," Joaquim says, eyes meeting his. "São Paulo."

"Where's that?"

"South of Rio," Joaquim says. "Is here okay? The beach isn't as great, but it's more private." It's a sheltered stretch of sand flanked by trees. The sun is low but it's still early enough to be hot and bright.

"This is great," Reid says. He follows Joaquim.

"Tide is low, so there's more beach," Joaquim says. "When it's high there's almost no beach. And there's the seaweed. But it's one of my favorite spots in the Keys."

There is more beach debris here than Reid is used to, but Reid loves that Joaquim wants them to have privacy. The water is shallow quite far out and, past slightly dark patches close to the shoreline, clear and lovely.

"It's beautiful here."

They settle their towels and the cooler in the sand and sit together. Joaquim put his towel right against Reid's, so they are shoulder to shoulder.

"So, São Paulo?" Reid tries for the same pronunciation Joaquim used.

Joaquim squints at him and smiles widely. "São," he says slowly, and Reid tries again. He has to shake off embarrassment at his own attempts.

"I promise, eventually I'll get this."

"It's really sweet that you're trying," Joaquim says, and Reid stills. "Most people don't."

"Yeah?" Testing the waters, Reid puts his shoulder against Joaquim's. He's freaking giggling, and this guy is telling him he's sweet. Reid doesn't know boys like this. He doesn't usually let himself *be* a boy like this. Joaquim leans back and pulls his knees up, crossing his arms when he does. His finger grazes Reid's bicep, then draws a short, teasing line up. Reid bites his lip; the touch sends shivers through his body.

"Tell me about it," Reid says, his voice husky.

"Well, it's a city. The state is called São Paulo too, but I'm from the city. It's a huge city, one of the biggest in the world. Miles of buildings. Very, very different." Joaquim sounds wistful.

"You miss it?"

"Yeah, sometimes." Joaquim doesn't look at him. "If you drive up to the coast, you get to the beaches, gorgeous ones. Huge waves and beautiful sand and every cliché people think about. The highlands, parks, and rainforests are like nothing else. Even the air feels green and living. I went spelunking a few years ago in Jacupiranga with friends in this place called the Devil's Cave, and it was, I don't know. I don't have words for it. Have you been spelunking?"

Reid and shakes his head. "Is the sand softer?" He keeps his tone light, because Joaquim seems to be drawing into himself. Joaquim chuckles.

"Yeah. It's not manmade, so yeah." The breeze ruffles Reid's hair. "Did you know that?"

"Yeah, I researched it. I could not figure it out at first. I spend a lot of time on the small beach-ish thing by my grandma's condo."

"That's one of the things I like about this beach. It's one of the only natural ones in the Keys. It's maybe not what people imagine beaches here will be like."

"I think it's perfect."

"I suppose you'd want to be near the beach, if you're coming from Wisconsin."

Reid thinks through what he wants to say. It's not that he can't filter the information he chooses to give. He doesn't like to think about home and everything tied to it.

"Yeah. We're not close to any beaches. I mean, there *are* beaches. Just nowhere nearby." Reid says. "It's also nice and warm here. I mean, sometimes too warm—"

"Sometimes?"

"Yeah." Reid leans on Joaquim harder, hoping for another touch. Joaquim seems approachable but tentative. Reid's felt off for a long time, but he remembers the shadow of confidence he once possessed. Joaquim makes him want to slip back into that skin, or maybe it's just his skin that wants touch, *Joaquim's* touch. "I need to get new clothes, I think. But shorts are just not—"

"I should take you. We'll find you something *you* but also, you know, that's not going to smother you to death once we hit August."

"Oh, god, does the heat get worse?"

Joaquim laughs softly and honestly, and Reid likes that. His parents and Felix treat him like breakable goods. Reid kisses Joaquim's cheek. It's a silly gesture; maybe Joaquim will find it too sweet for two men alone on a beach, but Reid doesn't do impulse control all that well yet.

Joaquim closes his eyes and takes a breath and, before Reid can move, puts his hand on Reid's cheek, directing him into a kiss that doesn't pause for introduction or tentative newness. They're at all wrong angles, but Reid puts his hand on Joaquim's and slides it down his forearm and up his bicep. Joaquim breaks away; his mouth is so close he catches Reid's gasp.

"We should probably be careful," Joaquim says. Reid isn't sure if he means their surroundings or the potential for going too far. But he's right. Reid wants, and, judging by the way Joaquim's eyes don't leave his lips, it's mutual.

It's been a long time since Reid's experienced the buildup of caution, the drawing out of desire and touches. It's been a very long time since he's had someone new, someone to share the thrill of firsts with.

"Do you want something to drink?" Joaquim asks, apropos of nothing.

Reid smiles widely. "Absolutely."

Joaquim opens the cooler. He's brought a fruit salad, two forks, and three different types of pop.

"I didn't know what you might like." Joaquim says.

"I'm not picky." Reid takes a can at random. He picks at the salad. It's been a while since he's had fresh fruit; he's not the best at the grocery shopping. When he looks up, Joaquim is watching him.

"Sorry," he says around a bite of pineapple, "I don't mean to hog it all."

"It's fine." Joaquim's voice is nearly lost in the sounds of wind and water. He stares at Reid, as if he too might get lost in the wind. Reid wants more kisses and more touches, but he'll settle for raspberries and mangoes.

"This is so good." He forks up more mango.

"*So* not as good in the States as in other places," Joaquim says. He's sorting the fruit to get to the raspberries. "They do something to get them into the country. Pick them too soon? I'm not sure. They have less flavor."

"I cannot imagine this having more flavor," Reid says. They eat in silence and enjoy small glances.

"Wanna check out the water?" Joaquim says once they've eaten most of the salad.

Reid's never been one for silence; he tends to fill it with inane chatter to cover his discomfort. This beach and moment are meant for quiet. The peace has been nice.

"Yes." Reid stands. He doesn't hide his appraisal of Joaquim as he strips down to his swim trunks.

"You keeping that on?" Joaquim gestures at Reid's shirt.

"I, uh, I forgot to sunscreen everywhere. Dumb."

"Not dumb; it's fine," Joaquim says. He catches Reid's hand and pulls him toward the water. They pick their way over flotsam, wood debris, and seaweed. Rather than sand, under their feet is squishy silt. It's one of those things Reid hasn't adjusted to: the mud from the mangrove swamps that makes the ground slimy at the edge of the beach.

"Tide's out, so we're closer to the sandbar," Joaquim explains. Once out there, Reid sits and immerses himself to his shoulders. Then he lies back and floats. Above him, Joaquim smiles; the sun is bright behind him.

Eventually they go farther out. The wind dries the water on Reid's skin, leaving it tight with salt.

"Do you like snow?" Joaquim asks.

"Yeah," Reid says. "Sometimes. Have you ever seen it?"

"No. I'd like to, though. Why only sometimes?"

"Well, I like when there's a lot of snow. Right after a snowstorm. Also, in a storm, when it's snowing, everything is quiet, and you can hear the snow falling. When it's wet snow, it sticks to tree branches and wires, and everything is white. Magical." As soon as the words are out of his mouth, Reid wishes them back.

"That sounds so pretty. One of the things I love about being in the water is the quiet."

"Yeah." Reid nods. "Like that. But when it's melting or when it's only a little snow, it gets dirty, and everything is gray again. And when it's cold enough, when you walk on it, the snow squeaks. I hate that."

"What, seriously?"

"Yeah. And you can't build snowmen." Reid takes a chance, takes Joaquim's hand. They walk back toward the shore.

"I never thought of that, that snow could be different." Back at their spot, Reid shakes out his towel and dries his legs. "I wouldn't have pegged you for a snowman-building sort of guy."

Reid shrugs. "My neighbors have little kids."

"You're good with them," Joaquim says with such certainty. "You're good with Erin."

42

"Erin's awesome." Reid squints. "I don't know. Kids are just... fun. It's not that they're less complicated than grownups. But having fun with them feels a lot less complicated."

"Yeah. That's a great way of putting it." Joaquim's attention is undivided; that attention is both warming and alarming, because Reid has no idea what Joaquim is making of him. Reid has so long been a version of himself only reflected by his family and Felix.

Joaquim checks his phone and sighs.

"Time to go?"

"Yeah," Joaquim says. Reid helps him pack and searches for a recycling bin for their empty cans.

"Don't worry about it. I'll take care of it." Joaquim tucks the cans into the cooler and stands. Reid folds their towels. "We barely got to go in the water."

"It's not like we haven't done it together before," Reid says. His words sound dirtier than he meant them to be, but that's okay.

"True. Maybe we'll go swimming one time when it's not work-related." That sounds somehow dirty too, and Reid choses to take it that way. He winks at Joaquim.

Joaquim stops with Reid at his car. Reid leans back against the hot metal and, with a finger around Joaquim's, pulls him closer. Despite the cars, there's no one around. When Joaquim kisses him, Reid tilts even farther back, asking Joaquim's body to sway into his. He does and then pulls away much too soon. His smile seems to be a tease, a promise of more.

"I'll see you later."

"Yeah," Reid says, stupidly breathless.

Eight

"So," Reid catches Joaquim at the shop before he leaves to teach a class. "Delia—that's the girl I work with at Shell World—said there is this party happening on Saturday. I don't know if you're off—"

"I am," Joaquim interrupts. "It's one of my rare weekends off."

"Do you want to come with me?" Reid says. He pauses. "She said to feel free to bring people, so if you want you could bring your friends."

"That would be great," Joaquim says. He doesn't quite smile, though. *Am I not supposed to invite his friends? Does Joaquim think I don't want to take him on a date?*

"Cool. I'll text you the information when Delia gives it to me."

"Thanks," Joaquim says. He peeks over his shoulder. He's still working; Reid knows that he needs to be careful not draw all of his attention.

"I've got to go," Reid says. "I have to go work too."

They share a look. It's full of promise, and Joaquim's at work; still, Reid lets his eyes linger on Joaquim's lips. Joaquim bites them, then gives a half wave before backing away.

✶   ✶   ✶

The night of the party, Reid sits in his grandmother's empty living room and tries to center himself. When Delia invited him, he was so excited to have a place to take Joaquim and to spend time with him, he didn't think through the part where he would have to meet a crowd of strangers. And there will be drinking. Reid and lots of alcohol aren't a great mix.

Finally, he can't put leaving off any longer. He checks his hair in the mirror one more time; he re-dyed it because the roots were so long it was more black than blond. To make up for how light it is, he uses slightly thicker eyeliner.

He texts Joaquim that he's on his way and pockets his car keys and wallet. It's not quite dark, but Reid still manages to piss off some drivers while trying to find the house by slowing down at three streets in a row. Eventually he can tell he's found the place by the number of cars lining the street. He parks and walks down the street with his thumbs in his pockets. Disrupting the thick, muggy air and haze of sunset, noise and people spill from the party. Reid takes a deep breath and wades in. Despite the small size of the house, it takes him a while to find anyone familiar. Delia is in the back, red cup in hand, standing by a keg and an assortment of liquors on a wobbly folding table.

"Reid!" She folds him into a hug. He doesn't resist despite his surprise. Her breath is beer-thick, and she grips too hard. Eventually he extracts himself.

"Let's get you a drink," she says.

"Um, no thanks. I'm, um—"

"If you're looking for your boy, I don't think he's here yet. Wanna meet my people?"

"Sure." Reid struggles to tuck his whole hands into the pockets of his very tight pants. He breathes slowly, trying to relax without being obvious about his discomfort and, when he focuses on his body, he notices how tight his shoulders are.

Delia drags him around, and it becomes harder and harder to keep his anxiety in check. Joaquim isn't here, and he hasn't heard from him. *Maybe he changed his mind?* When Delia offers him a drink again, he says yes. As long as he goes slow and only drinks enough to relax, he'll be okay.

It's been so long since he's had anything to drink that the first drink loosens him up right away. He's finishing his first beer when he spots Joaquim coming in. Joaquim scans the room, and Reid takes that moment to appreciate what he's seeing. Joaquim is wearing cerulean skinny pants and a tight black shirt patterned with galaxies and stars. It's a totally different look than anything Reid has seen him wear. When Joaquim spots him, excitement lights his eyes. Nina comes in behind him, and with them a tall, lanky, brown-haired guy who must be Bobby.

"Hi," Reid says when Joaquim comes up to him. Joaquim kisses both of his cheeks and flushes when he pulls back.

"Sorry. Instinct."

"It's okay," Reid says. "Is this a thing?"

"A thing?"

"Like a Brazil thing?"

"Oh," Joaquim says. "Yeah."

"And you got two kisses, not one," Nina stage-whispers, and Joaquim shushes her before she can elaborate.

"So, Reid, this is Bobby." Joaquim gestures, and Reid shakes his hand. A wave of self-consciousness washes over him. These people know about him. Nina not only knows him as a student, but through whatever Joaquim has told her personally. The magnifying glass he perceives, their direct gazes, make his cheeks burn.

"And I am Delia," Delia jumps in, making a face at Reid that indicates he should be doing the introducing.

"Want a drink?" Reid says as they shake hands. He clenches his fingers.

"Sure," Joaquim says, and Delia leads them to the drink table. When Joaquim turns to ask Reid what he wants, his mouth is suddenly dry, and he doesn't want to stand out more by not taking one.

An hour later, he's had two more drinks, and everyone in the room is his friend.

"No, see, here's the problem," Reid says. He has one hand on the wall and an overflowing red plastic cup in the other. He was looking for Joaquim, whom he lost some time ago when Joaquim went to get a drink. Somehow he ended up with one of Delia's friends, trying to express his dislike for current home renovation trends. "If everything is open, where the fuck do you hide? Like, what if your kitchen is a mess? And whenever they put those support-beam-things in, do you really know, like, *know*-know that they'll keep the ceiling up?" His beer sloshes down his hand and onto the floor.

"Listen, man, the only tools I know how to use are a hammer and a measuring tape," Delia's friend says. He has a name, Reid is sure. He's just not sure what it is.

"Well, yeah, no, me neither. I mean, sometimes not even the hammer." Reid winces, remembering a particularly embarrassing incident when he became convinced he could build bookshelves after an eight-hour HGTV binge. "I tried to build a thing once. My dad hid the tools from me after that."

Whatshisname smiles. He's about to respond when Reid spots Joaquim coming toward him.

"J!" Reid spills a little more beer in his enthusiasm. Joaquim takes Reid's drink before he can splash it all over them.

Although he stops to spend time with Joaquim, Reid finds himself pulled to and fro in the house and these rooms, as if the people here are ocean currents. The sense of water tugging and pulling and washing over him is the best feeling, as is being the most-liked in the room.

After that, Reid doesn't remember much.

✳   ✳   ✳

THE NEXT MORNING, REID FINDS himself in his room, fully dressed and painfully hungover. Reid barely makes it to the toilet; everything hurts. He's cold-sweats hungover. All of his muscles ache, and ache more after he finishes throwing up.

Despite being disgusting even to himself, Reid ignores the shower, strips off his clothes, and crawls into bed. His phone is under the covers, and it takes him a while to find it. He has no memory of getting home. Reid shuts his eyes tight and moans, then regrets it. He thumbs through his messages and finds two from Joaquim and one from Delia.

Joaquim: *Where did you go?*

And half an hour later: *Hey let me know if you get home?*

Reid must have left without telling Joaquim. *God, how did I get home? Fuck, that's awful.* Joaquim had come to hang out with Reid, at Reid's invitation. He would rather start puking again than have to face how he's damaged the impression he had made on Joaquim. But it would be worse not to text back when Joaquim is clearly worried.

Reid: *I'm home and okay.*

He doesn't add more. Reid doesn't want to get into the "Hey, that was a blackout drunk" moment via text, or at all. But the thing is, he really, really likes Joaquim, likes the way he feels when he's with him. Reid doesn't want to give that up. Fortunately, he has experience trying to make amends for, or trying to explain, his behavior. Unfortunately, he knows how much making apologies sucks and how, sometimes, no words can change things.

What happened?

He calls Delia; it's past noon, so he assumes she's up.

"What?" she snaps.

"Sorry," he says. Either she's back to her usually charming self or she's hungover too. "You texted telling me to drink water."

"You called me to tell me this? I know. I sent it."

"No, I just, well..." he trails off.

"Honey, spit it out, I wanna go back to bed."

"Well, it's just that I don't remember what happened by the end of the night. How I got home." *God, please, please tell me I didn't go home with another guy.*

"You're a sloppy drunk. And a lightweight, too," she says. There's a rustling in the background and a sigh. "After you spilled beer all over Dylan and then puked, I made an executive decision, and he drove you home."

"I didn't—I mean it wasn't—"

"No, nothing like that. He's not even gay!"

"Oh, thank god," he says, closing his eyes and exhaling loudly.

"Aren't you in a thing? With that guy—who, by the way, is super hot?"

"Yeah, but he texted asking where I was and if I was okay, like at one a.m. So he had no idea where I was. And I don't really remember anything."

"Well, I don't know where he went off to, but rest assured, your virtue is intact. I mean, any virtue you possessed prior to last night."

He smiles at her joke, but is too tired to joke back.

"If we're done here, I'ma go back to bed and wish for a quick death, 'kay?" she says.

"Ditto," he mumbles, then slips back under the blankets and into sleep.

*   *   *

REID DOESN'T HEAR FROM JOAQUIM that day. He's been busy and he's almost finished with a specialty class, emergency oxygen or something like that. Reid can't remember just what Joaquim said, not with so much else cluttering his mind. Not having a clear sense of where he stands is rocking Reid. He's terrible at letting things unfold at their own pace.

"Don't chase," Rachel says from her spot across the room on the couch. He's doing his therapy virtually; everyone is distant and a little grainy. Nancy got new couches a few weeks after Reid left. He's only seen them through his computer screen, but the pillows look soft. Both he and Rachel always pull the pillows onto their laps. It's an inside joke. Elise often hands Reid the pillow if it's on her chair. He likes the weight and the soft, plush texture he can run his fingers over to make patterns when the changed direction of fibers catches the light. On Skype, he finds that he still needs a pillow. He's always thought the pillow was about needing a barrier, about having something between him and the ache of vulnerability in shared confessional spaces. Maybe it still is, even with the barrier of a computer between them all. But it's also the touch, the grounding of having something to hold, the weighing down.

His pillow isn't the right shape or weight or texture, though. Reid's going to buy a new one as soon as he can.

"Remember that people need space to think things through. You can't make someone communicate if they aren't ready just because you need to resolve an issue," Nancy reminds him.

Rachel is running her finger down a worksheet in her binder. "Remember to balance your needs and priorities with the other person's," she reads aloud.

"That's hardly fair," Reid says. "I don't know his needs."

"True," Nancy says. "But maybe text conversations aren't quite the place to judge the tone of the situation."

"Plus, Reid, you totally have a tendency to—"

"Elise," Rachel hisses. Reid hates that he doesn't have to ask her to finish the sentence. He's a chaser. When he panics, he chases and pushes and then retreats and panics more and assumes all kinds of things. The anxiety and panic cycle and then he spirals. It's not pretty.

"This all seems dramatically serious advice for a boy I've kissed like, once."

"You kissed him?" Elise shrieks. "You didn't tell us that!"

Reid ducks his head, wondering if his blush is visible on-screen. "Well…" Reid starts, but has no idea what to say.

"So, you *really* like this guy?" Rachel asks. She glances up at the screen and Reid meets her eyes. Rachel's never been good at eye contact; it took him weeks to realize her eyes were the most unusual hazel he'd ever seen.

Reid tilts his head. "What makes you think that?"

"Well," she says, fingers tracing the pattern of conjoined of circles on her pillow, "you swore you weren't going to get involved with anyone or try a relationship. Because, um, you know."

"Because of Felix," Elise blurts out. She takes her hair down and shakes it out. The light catches her blonde highlights. She puts it back up into a messy bun. She's forever messing with her hair when she's agitated.

"*Elise,*" Rachel says and sighs. Reid's mostly gotten over being offended by Elise's bluntness.

"Listen," Elise says. "I'm trying to help and be honest and I'm sorry if it comes off unkindly. But I care about you, Reid."

"We all do," Nancy interjects.

"And I am worried. Because things with Felix were so messed up."

"Well, I mean—I wouldn't—" Reid stammers.

"Honey." Rachel's quiet voice hardly carries through his speakers. He tilts forward. "Maybe we should have said this sooner, but your relationship with Felix wasn't good for you. And you're far away and you don't have a support system there—"

"You guys—"

"That's right," Nancy says. "Reid, I hope you know we are a support system, and that we all care for you. And that that caring might take the form of saying things you may not want to hear. And I want to invite all of us to consider or respect that we should be honest, but to be careful about pressing if we're not totally ready."

"No," Reid says. "I want to hear this. I was just surprised that no one said anything about Felix before."

"Well, I would—I thought... I tried." Rachel says.

He sighs and grips his pillow. He doesn't want to think about Felix. Not at all. When he admits that, Rachel and Elise nod, as if they understand.

"Well, we *know* you. So even though there are things you weren't saying, we could kind of tell," Rachel ventures.

Reid shrugs. "It's funny. Felix has been this huge, fucked up part of my life for a long time. So it's not like it wasn't weighing on me. How unhealthy our relationship was. How we both played a role in that. My terrible choices, his shitty decisions. Wondering if I even know how to have a healthy relationship with someone." Elise clears her throat. It's a pointed comment. Reid isn't looking at the screen, but he knows Rachel well enough to know she's sending Elise quite the look. "But I can't stop thinking about him lately."

"Because you have a potential new guy?" Rachel asks.

Reid curls and uncurls his fingers. "Maybe?"

"Do you want to follow your thought pattern?" Nancy asks.

Reid imagines the drawing he and Nancy would make, were they alone: linking circles. The first circle would be the worry thought. Then they would make another circle for whatever thought or action might be attached to it and follow the thoughts until he found the core of an anxiety that might at first seem unrelated to his situation. Not the case here.

"He cheated on me," Reid says in one rushed breath. "And I promised myself that would be the end of the relationship. And emotionally, it was."

"Was it, though?" Elise asks.

A reflexive response pushes against his lips, and he bites it back. Reid makes himself consider the *whats* and the *whys. It was the end, in a way. But if it was the end, why did I always end up back in bed with Felix, sucked back into arguments and spinning my wheels until I was so desperate to get away that the opportunity to leave everything seemed life-saving?*

"I guess yes and no? I knew—know—that I'm not in love with him anymore. But I couldn't stop caring. I thought when I came here I'd close the door on all of it."

"And it's not like that." Rachel's face is a study in sympathy.

"I just kick that door back open every time I text him," Reid says, working through the words. "And it's all tangled up. Because I really like Joaquim. I wasn't expecting to, and I don't know how to do this." Reid presses his knuckles under his eyes, forcing himself not to cry. "I'm just going to fuck all this up."

"Reid." Elise's voice is soft and kind, and he *aches* to be in the same room.

"Reid, I have some advice and some homework for you before we go," Nancy says. "First, I want you to be sure you're keeping up on your diary cards. I know you thought you didn't need them anymore, but you're in a new environment and I think it might be good to be sure you're tracking your moods to see how they correspond with behaviors."

But it was just one time.

He swallows his protest, because that's not the point. All things start with one time.

"Also, evaluate how you feel about Joaquim. If you want to pursue something with him, I would like you to reflect on your willingness to examine past relationships and their patterns. There are things you don't want to think about. I know, since we've discussed that you don't feel strong enough. But I think you're ready."

"Me too," Rachel chimes in.

"If you find that it's too painful, of course you can talk to us or contact me outside of our meetings if you're feeling triggered."

"Okay," he says softly. He digs his thumbnail into the nailbed of his left index finger. The pain is sharp, warm, and centering.

"And I'd like you to look into forming a support group or network where you are. I know," she says, interrupting him before he can protest, "that this seems overwhelming. But when we have our next individual session, we'll work it out together, okay?"

Reid nods. He misses them. He misses the soft comfort of Nancy's room. He misses hugging Rachel and Elise. It's not that their hugs are any different than other hugs. But being metaphorically and literally held by people who have walked a path no one else seems to understand, he misses that with a sharp, lonely pain like the phantom pain of a missing limb.

Nine

JOAQUIM SIGHS WHEN HE GETS Reid's text, then frowns. It's past noon. He's worried, but also on the fence about how worried he should be. Reid is a big boy after all, and, despite the kiss and the flirting, he doesn't know him all that well. *Well enough to hover?* Joaquim tosses his phone on his bed. *Why am I so invested already?*

But that doesn't matter, really, because he is.

"Talk to me, man," Bobby says from where he's still starfished face down on his bed. He had to work this morning despite his hangover and clomped into their room a few minutes ago, flopped down and groaned. "Your sighing is too intense. Also, close the blinds, will ya?"

Joaquim closes them and grabs Bobby water from their minifridge. He nudges Bobby's hand with the water bottle and then jabs harder when Bobby doesn't respond.

"Thanks." With his mouth mashed into the covers, Bobby's voice is hardly discernible. "Okay, spill. Boy drama?"

"Do you really want to hear this?" Joaquim asks, more curious than confrontational.

"Sure."

It's not a resounding endorsement, but Joaquim is bursting to bounce ideas off someone. Bobby is only a few feet away and, given his hangover, not likely to run off.

"I texted Reid last night after he disappeared—"

"He disappeared?" Bobby lifts his head slightly. He was only a smidge less drunk than Reid last night.

"Well, not like, kidnapped. Like gone. Although for all I knew, yeah." The bitterness in his voice takes him by surprise.

"I don't remember that," Bobby admits.

"Yeah, maybe he doesn't either."

"What, he didn't text you back?"

"Like an hour ago he did. It just said he was home and okay." Joaquim drops onto his bed, and the springs squeak. "But that's it! That's all I got!"

"Well, if he was drunker than me, he probably wants to die. And maybe he only just woke up."

"Okay, yeah," Joaquim concedes. "But nothing after that?"

"I repeat—"

"I know," Joaquim snaps, then closes his eyes. "Sorry. I guess I'm disappointed with how the night turned out. I didn't see him as the kind of guy to get like that at a party."

"Really? With all the piercings and the refusal to wear shorts?"

"With his personality once you get to know him," Joaquim says. "Which is not what the piercings lead you to expect."

"Book-judger," Bobby says.

"Come again?" Joaquim squints, sure he misheard due to Bobby's face still being mashed into the bed.

"You totally judged his book by the cover at first. Well, I guess we all did."

Joaquim snorts. Bobby's shoulders shake, so Joaquim assumes he's laughing at his own turn of phrase as well.

Bobby rolls over. "You seem to like me just fine, and I was hammered last night."

"I'm not saying I don't like him anymore. I didn't see that behavior coming. And I thought, um, he invited me to hang out."

"I don't know, man," Bobby sits up. "He was tipsy when we came in and he seemed nervous. It was a party; it's not like he took you to a candlelit dinner and then got fucked up."

"Yeah."

"So are you really upset that he got drunk, or…?"

"That and not telling me when he was leaving. Leaving me hanging, and then worried, and then nothing until noon!"

"I guess you should talk to him about it if you want to, if you like him that much."

"I do. Did. Do." Joaquim shakes his head.

"Well, if he doesn't text or call by the end of the day, call him tomorrow."

"Basically, wait a little and give him time." Joaquim sighs again and flops back on his bed, narrowly missing the wall with his head.

Bobby lies back, face down again; the room is cloaked in silence.

REID: *So word on the street is that I was a dumbass last night*

Joaquim squints at his phone. It's late, and he was in class all morning. Still, he's been hoping for a text all day; this is worth a moment.

Joaquim: *I don't know that I'd say it like that.*

Reid: *I would. I'm sorry. Would you believe if I said I don't usually do that?*

Joaquim pauses. The three dots at the bottom of the screen indicate that Reid is still typing.

Reid: *That I'm not that kind of boy ;)*

Joaquim wants to take the bait, because he's got a hunch Reid is trying to redirect.

Joaquim: *If you tell me you don't usually do that, I'll believe you.*

There's a long silence, too long for a text conversation at midnight when he's reasonably sure Reid isn't doing anything else.

Reid: *That's a lot of trust for someone you barely know.*

Joaquim has to think about that one, because with texts it's impossible to discern tone. Something about the phrasing prickles.

Joaquim: *Well, what reason would you have for lying? You got drunk. It happens.*

Reid: *Yeah. I guess.*

Joaquim reads defeat all over that text, which bothers him a little. He wants to tell Reid it's all okay and forgiven. After all, it's not as if Reid owes him an explanation. But his behavior irritated Joaquim. He's not sure how to approach it when he doesn't have a right to and he doesn't know Reid well enough to predict how he'll react.

Reid: *Anyway, listen. I'm sorry I left without letting you know where I was going.*

Reid: *It's embarrassing to admit, but I don't remember leaving. I don't remember much.*

Joaquim reads and rereads the texts.

Joaquim: *It's okay. Bobby said the same. It happens.*

Joaquim sends it without thinking, then realizes what a cheap platitude it is. It's never happened to him, after all.

Reid: *So, if I haven't scared you away with my bad behavior*

Reid lets that text hang, and Joaquim is pretty sure that it's on purpose. Joaquim takes the bait and the offered change in tone.

Joaquim: *Maybe bad behavior is what I want*

He types quickly and then groans. Bobby shifts in his bed across the room, and Joaquim hopes he didn't wake him up.

He follows up as fast as his fingers can text.

Joaquim: *Okay that sounded worse than I meant it to*

Reid: *;) Maybe I like worse too?*

Joaquim buries his face in his pillow.

Joaquim: *When can I see you again*

He types before he can stop himself. Irritation over the situation is washed away by the way Reid makes him smile and then laugh at their ridiculous banter. He adds the missing question mark to the sentence and waits without breathing.

*   *   *

"Okay, so," Reid says when Joaquim picks him up. He's borrowed Nina's car for the night. "What is your opinion on seafood?"

"I feel good about seafood," Joaquim says.

"I mean, I think the menu has things other than seafood. Just, um, if you were a conscientious objector to eating the fish in the sea—"

"Reid," Joaquim cuts off his nervous babbling. "I like it. I cannot wait to see where we're going, because I'm starving."

"Yeah, okay," Reid says.

"You don't have to be nervous," Joaquim says, even as he admits to himself that he's also a bit nervous.

"No, I know." Reid flashes a look that Joaquim lets himself linger in: the way it sends a curl of heat through him, the delicious ice blue of his eyes, and his blonder-than-before hair.

"You changed your hair."

"Oh, yeah." Reid runs his fingers through his hair. "It was getting more black than blond. I did it before the party."

"You don't like it black?" Joaquim asks. He doesn't remember it being blonder at the party. But the house was pretty dimly lit. "I mean, not that I don't like your hair like this. I do."

"Thanks," Reid says.

"I've never dyed my hair."

"Well, I think it's perfect." Reid winces. "That was—"

"Stop second-guessing yourself." Joaquim puts a hand on Reid's knee.

Reid squares his shoulders. "I don't know what's gotten into me."

Joaquim squeezes his knee and then pulls his hand away before he does something stupid, like move it, cup Reid's thigh, and let the imprint of his inseam burn its memory into his palm.

"All right." Reid says. The window is open and, as Joaquim pulls onto the Overseas Highway, the scratch of gravel and the roar of a motorcycle speeding past them swallow what he says next.

"I'm sorry?" Joaquim shifts closer. Reid smells good. He's put on cologne, or perhaps used a different product when he showered. It's subtle and smells fresh and light, mildly floral.

"I made a reservation at Pearson's on the Bay."

"Oh, wow." Joaquim gestures at his plain dark-wash jeans. "Am I dressed appropriately?"

"No, you look good," Reid says. Joaquim stops at a red light. Reid takes the opportunity to catch his gaze, then deliberately lets his eyes travel over Joaquim's body, slowly enough to send heat all through him. Joaquim exhales, then clears his throat when the light turns green.

"I asked," Reid continues.

"Huh?"

"If there was a dress code."

"Oh," Joaquim says, catching the conversational thread again. It's hard, when he's... well, getting hard. The weight and heat of Reid's eyes, dark-rimmed and intentionally promising, make Joaquim want to be reckless. Joaquim isn't reckless with boys. "Um, sure." He shifts, and Reid snickers. Joaquim catches his eye again before Reid winks. Joaquim risks another touch, this time a little bolder. It's his turn to turn up the heat in this ping-pong game of increased confidence and flirtation.

He wasn't planning to sleep with Reid tonight, but Joaquim is happy to go where the night takes them. Despite his initial hesitation, Joaquim senses potential for fun, for trouble, for recklessness in Reid's body. He saw it at Delia's friend's party before Reid got sloppy; Joaquim enjoyed his confidence, his easy smiles and abandon.

Joaquim orders water and peruses the beer menu. To his surprise, Reid orders an Arnold Palmer.

"No wonder you came down here," Joaquim says. His attempt to keep laughter in fails; it clearly paints his voice. "Arnold Palmer. I'm surprised we didn't come for the senior discount dinner."

"Oh, shut up," Reid says. His foot nudges Joaquim's. "I like them."

"Retirees?"

Unselfconscious and utterly lovely, Reid's laughter fills the half-empty restaurant. "I do like old people," Reid confesses, "but I was mostly referring to Arnold Palmers."

"Would it bother you if I have a beer, though?" Joaquim asks. He's not sure what Reid's deal is: He had a hard time reading Reid's apologies about getting drunk and his assertion that he's not that boy *anymore*.

"Oh no, go ahead," Reid says, taking a long sip of his water. When he puts it down, beads of condensation slip down the curved, smooth bell of the glass and onto the white tablecloth. Reid licks the pad of his index finger, a subtle but intentional gesture. Joaquim nudges him with his foot. "I'm not twenty-one."

"Oh, really?" Joaquim realizes they have many things to learn about each other. Their date on the beach was short and at least half taken up by the delicious build to a kiss that was better than its anticipation. Joaquim has never had a boyfriend whom he hadn't first known for a long time—not that Reid is technically his boyfriend.

"Is it going to be a problem if I'm younger than you?" Reid asks with a teasing lilt.

"Well, now I'm worried. *I* should have been the one to take you on a senior citizen date."

Reid's expression is brighter than Joaquim would have expected. "I'm almost twenty-one," he says.

"Ooh, I'm really robbing the cradle." Joaquim props his chin on his hands and pitches his tone lower. "Two extra years of living equals a lot more *experience* than you might think."

Reid's response is cut short when their waiter comes back. He hasn't opened the food menu.

"Um, I think we need more time." He looks to Reid for confirmation. "But I would like a lager. You pick."

"No problem," their water says, unfazed. "I'll bring that right up. We have macadamia-crusted hogfish on special today and it's happy hour until seven."

"Excellent," Reid says. "Thank you."

Thankful for the interruption to the ratcheting up of sexual tension, Joaquim peruses the menu. It's hard to focus, because his skin is sensitized; his body craves the press of Reid's fingers all over him. He tells himself, firmly, to settle down.

They remain quiet as they pick their meals, and, as soon as their waiter has taken their order, Reid turns the full force of his stunning blue eyes back on Joaquim.

"So, Joaquim from Brazil," Reid starts, then pauses. "Tell me more about yourself."

"That's it? Your first date dialogue? I'm having the strangest sense of déjà vu."

Reid tips his head and says, "Second." His voice is soft.

"You're right," Joaquim says. *Are you a second date kind of boy?* He swallows before he says it.

"So. You?"

"I'll tell you if you tell me." Joaquim goes for teasing. He bites his lip and smiles.

"You've got a deal," Reid says. In contrast with his reticence to talk about himself on their last date, Reid seems much more sure of himself, much more open.

"Well. There's the basics. Other than that I'm twenty-two. I have been wandering from place to place since I graduated high school. I didn't want to go to University. I'm bilingual, as you can tell. I went swimming with dolphins last week and it was crazy. They were very rowdy."

"What's your sign?" Reid asks.

"Sagittarius. Are you into astrology?" It seems like such a strange thing from Reid, a boy who wears trouble and anxiety, wildness and sexiness by turns.

"No, but my mother is. She always asks someone that the first time she meets them. I suppose it's a habit. Plus, she'll ask me about it when I talk about you."

Warm happiness unfurls through Joaquim's body. "You're going to talk about me?"

"Sure," Reid says. "If that doesn't scare you off?"

"No, not at all." Being talked about means being seen. Talking to each other's families means this isn't a set of quick and thoughtless dates. It's not just a prelude to more hooking up that's going nowhere, as Joaquim's experience with boys here has often been. It's too soon to call Reid a boyfriend, but he wants to find out if they're building on something that's irrefutably there.

"So," Joaquim continues, "If your mother knows, will she tell you all kinds of stuff about my sign?"

"Depending on her mood and how annoyed she is with me, yeah."

"Is she annoyed with you right now?" Joaquim asks, reading the tight set of Reid's shoulders.

"Yeah. But to be fair, she's annoyed or upset or lecturing me about seventy-five percent of the time."

Joaquim thanks their waiter when he brings their appetizer of conch fritters.

"I don't want to overstep," Joaquim says when Reid transfers some to his small plate.

"You can ask me questions, as long as you don't take offense if I say I'm not comfortable answering them or something like that."

"Of course. I'm no rude boy."

Reid rewards him with a small chuckle. "Oh my god, try this," he says around a bite of the fritter after dipping it into the aioli. Joaquim has to pull his eyes away from Reid's mouth when he licks his lips.

Joaquim tries a fritter, and the moment when he could have asked more slips away from them, a tiny melody carried like chimes on the wind.

"So," Reid says when Joaquim has shut his car door. During dinner they fell into easier getting-to-know-you conversation; but the easier the conversation, the harder it was to respond with inane conversation about favorite movies, when what Joaquim wanted most was to learn more about Reid's lips and body. "Home?"

"Yours or mine?" Joaquim says, hoping desperately that Reid wants to go to his condo. The chance of them getting privacy in his own shared room is next to none, but he doesn't want to assume that Reid wants privacy as much he does. Still, hope is free, and he's got plenty of that going.

"Dying to see my grandmother's condo, huh?" Reid says.

"Absolutely." Joaquim likes the way their laughter sounds, with the open windows beckoning the spill of muggy night air.

Joaquim is a little shocked by the condo; Reid's grandmother must be *loaded*. These gated condos on the water are not cheap. Reid leads him up a coral path to the door. The moon is so bright that the white of the coral glows brightly.

"So." Reid steps back to let Joaquim in. He's grown uncomfortable, which Joaquim regrets. Joaquim takes his shoes off. The condo is spotless. The white tile floor of the entry leads directly into a room that's part dining room and part living room. To his right is a bright, open kitchen, with beautiful cherrywood cabinets, pale marble countertops, and a breakfast bar overlooking the dining area. Not a dish is out of place; not a crumb is on the counter. Reid stands behind Joaquim as he ventures onto the plush, cloud-gray dining room carpet. On the wall in front of the sectional couch is a gigantic TV.

"Wow," Joaquim says, a little awed. "I bet you can see so much detail on this thing."

"Yeah," Reid says. He picks up and puts down some knickknacks on the glass shelves of the entertainment unit surrounding the television. "I haven't been watching a lot of TV, but when I do it's intense. No one told my grandmother that TV size should correspond with the distance to the sofa."

"I can see that." He spots the sliding glass doors that lead to a screened porch. "May I?" he gestures toward it.

"Of course," Reid unlocks the door. "It's my favorite part."

There's only one light on the porch, a peach and pink shell-encrusted table lamp with a hideous shade on a wicker end table. But it's nice, the butter yellow of a single bulb, and the rich sounds of a world alive with nature coming through the mosquito netting, the ocean sound clear in the night. It's easy to see why Reid likes this soothing space. While the condo itself is pristine, it's cold. Maybe if there were more signs of life, it wouldn't seem so austere.

Reid walks up to the screen in front of the door. His hand touches it lightly. Joaquim wonders if he realizes he's doing it.

"Hey," he says, trying for soft. Reid startles anyway. "What's up?"

"Nothing." Reid's voice is falsely bright. He runs his fingers through his hair in a rough, jerky movement. All of the ease and open invitation seems to be gone. Joaquim tests the waters by taking a step closer and then running his fingers down the back of Reid's hand. Reid shudders, and his fingers uncurl, allowing Joaquim to draw a line along his palm and to his wrist. He doesn't step closer, but reads the nervous swallow and the shaky breath Reid takes. Joaquim's job depends on being able to sense when divers are becoming nervous or clamming up. He's worked with Reid, too, and spent a good deal of time watching him.

"You sure you're all right?"

"Hey, wanna see the rest of the place?" Reid asks.

"Uh, like, your condo, or...?"

"No, outside. We can't go down to the water here." Reid gestures forward. It's too dark to see what's beyond the bit of land illuminated by the lamp. But Joaquim takes Reid at his word. "C'mon." Reid curls his fingers and laces them through Joaquim's, then pulls him through the condo. He doesn't slide the sliding glass door closed, and Joaquim turns to do it himself. Reid tugs on his hand, suddenly impatient to move. Once they're back on the coral path, he relaxes a little. He stops and turns.

"Hold on," he says, jogging the few steps back to the door. Joaquim follows. Reid rummages in a closet next to the door and comes out with bug spray. He sprays himself, muttering about the horror of mosquitos, and then holds the can out for Joaquim. Joaquim takes it gratefully. He's used to the mosquitos, but still, they're a bane upon mankind.

"So, where to?" He waits for Reid to lead the way. Reid reaches for his hand again.

"This okay?"

"Of course!" Joaquim squeezes his fingers and stumbles in the dark. Lamps line the path, but they cast more shadowy ambiance than helpful light in places, especially when they cut through a swath of woods where the moonlight can't filter through. The trees push in; spindly branches and leaves reach toward them. Joaquim falls back, but keeps a hand in Reid's. He puts his other hand between Reid's shoulder blades and follows blindly.

Ten

REID STOPS A FEW FEET from the gate to the pool. With the crunch of coral under their feet suddenly suspended and only the night singing to them, the lapping of the waves is still barely discernible because everywhere, everywhere, Reid can hear water ripple into the pool filter, its movement as loud as breathing. He's not sure why he brought Joaquim here. Nerves that were coalescing into something prickly start to make him panicky.

He opens the gate; the loud screeching noise is seventeen times more obtrusive than during the day. Reid hates how it always announces his presence. Despite wanting to go to the pool more often, he dislikes going during the day when people are there. He hates standing out so starkly; his age and hair, his piercings and tattoos and utter aloneness are all a beacon no one can ignore. He didn't come here to be the elephant in a room full of strangers. That was Eau Claire, and with people he loved.

Joaquim trips at the seam of the pressed-pebble concrete border of the pool, bumps into Reid's back, and grabs his waist to steady himself. Standing stock-still, Reid lets himself close his eyes and appreciate the pressure of those fingers and that palm squeezing him; Joaquim is still and pressed against his back. With Joaquim, he hasn't been the elephant in the room once. Every bit of attention has had to do with the *real* Reid, not his mental illness, not a silence that's trying to predict his next, inevitable disaster, not his otherness on an island full of strangers. Joaquim's attention is about desire, about friendship. It's so different, so normal, to be forgiven easily by someone who doesn't know Reid's other self, the one who ran away. Reid's used to his family and Felix holding onto his mistakes like scraps they'll use to make a quilt of proof that he will never get to be normal or even get better.

"Okay?" Joaquim says into the fabric of his shirt. His breath is warm, and his hand tightens at Reid's waist.

Reid leans back and into Joaquim. "Definitely."

"So was that the tour?" The hint of teasing in Joaquim's voice makes Reid smile.

"I don't know. I didn't have a plan. C'mon, let's sit." The pool is lit only by underwater lamps and the same border lights that line the paths. Moonlight highlights the tables, with their closed umbrellas, and the folded lounge chairs. Joaquim moves toward them, but Reid pulls him to the edge of the pool. He toes off his shoes and sits cross-legged at the edge. Joaquim follows suit.

"This is nice," Joaquim whispers. Reid nods. The night asks for quiet, for its own voice to be heard over others. Reid likes that Joaquim understands that. He puts his head on Joaquim's shoulder and trails his fingers through the water. When Joaquim kisses the top of his head, Reid squeezes his eyes shut and swallows a groan. They were moments away from a sexy night when he freaked out, and now he dragged this guy to a pool in the middle of the night and is trying to snuggle him? Not remotely cool.

"Hey," he says, pulling back. When Joaquim looks at him, Reid kisses him. It's awkward, him cross-legged and trying to turn toward Joaquim with the pool right there. He grabs Joaquim's shoulder for balance when he almost falls in. Joaquim is kissing him back, though, and his tongue against Reid's lips and in his mouth is the nexus of everything Reid can think about or want. When Joaquim breaks the kiss, Reid doesn't have time to ask why before he's in the water. When he surfaces, Joaquim is laughing like a maniac.

"Asshole," Reid says without heat. He swipes his fingers under his eyes and they come away black. "I'll look like a raccoon now."

"Aw, no, you're gorgeous," Joaquim says as he catches his breath. Reid slips under the water and scrubs his eyes to get most of his eyeliner off. There's nothing sexy about a man with raccoon eyes. He surfaces in front of Joaquim and puts his hands on his knees.

"Oh no, no way," Joaquim says with his hands on Reid's shoulders to push him back.

"I'm stronger than you think," Reid says in a singsong voice. He wraps his hands around Joaquim's and pushes back from the wall, hard. Joaquim lands on him, and for a moment their limbs tangle underwater. Joaquim almost accidentally knees him somewhere very vital. Eventually they're both standing; Joaquim is laughing, scooping his wet hair back when Reid tugs him forward by his wet shirt. His mouth is still open when Reid rises on his toes to take it. The water is warm, filled with the memory of sunlight, but Joaquim's mouth is warmer. Reid's hand is around Joaquim's neck, and when he bites Joaquim's lower lip, he's close enough to feel how that nip pulses through Joaquim's muscles.

Hands splayed at Reid's lower back, Joaquim pulls him in and, at this slightly new angle, kisses the breath out of him, kisses him differently, kisses him as if he's never wanted anything so much; hard enough to skirt the edge of pain. Reid doesn't hide the tiny, wanting noises this elicits. He tries squirming closer, but in wet clothes they're much too constricted. Joaquim's hands slip under Reid's shirt; when they almost brush Reid's ribs he pushes away and gives Joaquim a cocky grin.

"What's worse than a hard-on in tight jeans?" He asks. His fingers hook under the waistband of Joaquim's jeans. Joaquim raises an eyebrow. "One in tight, wet jeans."

As far as distraction goes, it works beautifully. It's not easy to get Joaquim out of his pants. Reid unbuttons them, and together they work to get them down. At one point Reid ducks underwater to help pull from the bottom. He comes up for air, laughs at Joaquim's face, kisses him, and ducks back under. When the jeans are finally off, he bites Joaquim's calf lightly before coming up again. He smooths a hand up the bulge of Joaquim's thigh and teases his hard-on.

Joaquim frames Reid's face in wide palms and breathes against his lips. Reid's hands are under Joaquim's shirt now, tracing his stomach and ribs and pushing him against the edge of the pool. "Shouldn't we go back to your place?"

"Your pants are already off," Reid points out. He kisses under Joaquim's ear and bites his collarbone.

"You're making me sex-dumb," Joaquim says, and Reid snorts against his skin, then starts pulling Joaquim's shirt off. "*Reid,*" Joaquim pleads. It's a whisper of protest.

"Have you ever done this before?"

"Fucked?" Joaquim says, and disbelief drips from the question. Reid rolls his eyes.

"No, fucked outside. Taken a chance. Risked getting caught."

"No." Despite his protest, he lifts his arms and lets Reid take his shirt off. Reid ducks to lick and nip at his chest above the waterline. Joaquim tastes of chlorine, and his gasp is delicious. "I've never been much of a risk-taker."

"Oh. Well, some would say your job is risky," Reid counters. He stands and looks right into Joaquim's eyes. They're bathed in shadows.

"Not like this."

"Have you ever thought about it, though?" Reid kisses Joaquim's chin and licks his lips, tiny teasing licks that lead to Joaquim opening his mouth and then groaning when Reid rubs his hand against his erection. "Doing something impulsive and dumb and fun like this?"

"Not so much for impulse, although..." Joaquim gasps when Reid's hand works under the band of his boxer briefs. "...you make a very convincing argument."

They both startle when the pool lights suddenly shut off.

"Wha—"

"It's ten," Reid explains. "Pool officially closes at ten."

With the lights off, Joaquim goes from token protester to active participant. The moonlight can't compete with the dark, so Reid takes off his own shirt. He tosses it with a plop behind him on the concrete .

"Fuuuck," Reid groans when Joaquim finds his nipples. Joaquim shushes him. With the lights off, every other sense is amplified; even their kisses sound unbearably loud. Reid's hands span Joaquim's hips, the solid curve of his hipbones, before sliding to cup his ass. Joaquim has a beautiful ass, and it's full and round in Reid's palms. He pulls Joaquim closer and squeezes.

"Are we doing reciprocity or what?" Joaquim asks, turning a groan into a breathless whimper when his erection presses against Reid. "Can we take these off?" He pulls at Reid's jeans with his fingers in the back pockets.

"In a minute," Reid says, mouth busy at Joaquim's throat, his collarbone, the curve of his shoulder. He licks Joaquim's bicep and *wants*. He keenly, painfully, wants to taste every bit of him, to collect every moment of this with his hands and mouth, to tuck this moment away: a moment when he is just a boy, being touched by someone unfamiliar with the history of his skin. He pushes at Joaquim a little harder, against the edge of the pool. "Get up."

"Uh, Reid, I think I'm already up," Joaquim says, and Reid can't hide his amusement.

"I mean up," he taps the lip of the pool and, as added persuasion, kisses Joaquim. When he stops, their lips are still touching, and their breath is indistinguishable, one from the other. "I wanna blow you."

"Here?" Joaquim's voice rises a tiny bit.

"We've covered this. We're being young and reckless." Reid slides his hand up and down and wraps it around Joaquim, who does groan then, loudly.

"Fine," Joaquim says. Reid hears the acquiescence and disbelief is his voice. "I can't believe I'm doing this."

"Shut up and let *me* do this," Reid says, laughing as he and Joaquim both struggle to get him up and out of the pool without breaking away from each other. Once he's up, Reid pulls his legs apart roughly and mouths at the wet fabric of his underwear. Joaquim's hand tangles in Reid's wet hair.

"Oh, god," he whispers.

Impatient, rushing because he cannot wait to taste him, Reid tugs the band of his underwear down. When Reid pulls him into his mouth, he has to put his other hand on Joaquim's lips to remind him of necessary silence.

"Shhh," Reid says. "You're gonna wake the geriatric squad."

"Oh my god, no old-people talk. Go back to what you were doing."

Reid bites Joaquim's stomach before taking him in his mouth. Joaquim stutters as Reid takes Joaquim in as deep as he can. Reid drops down in the water; his hands spread Joaquim's thighs farther apart.

Afterward, Joaquim slides back into the pool, loose-muscled and clumsy. In the moonlight, Reid can see Joaquim's smile. Desperately messy, edging toward begging, he kisses Joaquim again. He unbuttons his pants and, inelegant and frantic, pushes them down only far enough to free himself. Joaquim pulls him close and presses a thigh against his hard length for Reid to rub against.

"What do you want?" he whispers into Reid's ear. He nibbles at it, licks around his barbell piercing, and tugs with his teeth. "My mouth? My hands? This, rubbing up against me?"

"Fuck, all of it."

And after, Joaquim's kiss is a different sort, another new one. It's soft, less question or demand, the taste not of newness or hunger, but of coming down, sweet with the tang of afterglow. Reid doesn't remember when, or if, he's been kissed like this.

"I do not know if I can move," Reid says when they break apart. Joaquim skirts his fingers up Reid's stomach, digs them in enough to tickle, and Reid flails, laughing and pushing him away before he can feel Reid's scars.

"Nope, you can." Joaquim says, and so Reid does the only thing that makes sense. He splashes him and then ducks underwater and swims away.

Despite the delicious post-orgasm lethargy stealing into his muscles, Reid is content to swim, to let Joaquim pull him under and then up, to play a little, because it calms him. Maybe it calms them both. Maybe this is the bridge between one impulse, a tiny supernova he didn't see playing out the way it did, and the next.

There are definitely things Reid needs to tell Joaquim if they are going to go further, and there are other things he isn't ready to tell at all. He doesn't like the idea of lying, but the cost of trusting too fast, the heavy judgment of people who don't understand, hurts. In the dark, Joaquim can't see the fading spiderweb cuts along his torso, but in the light, they're undeniable.

Eleven

JOAQUIM PULLS REID TO THE edge of the pool and then as close as he can. "I have to head home soon. I'm in the shop tomorrow."

Reid's forehead rests heavy and warm on his shoulder. He sighs and doesn't say anything. He kisses Joaquim's neck and pulls away to lever himself out of the pool.

"Fuck it's dark. Where the hell are our clothes?"

Joaquim splashes out and walks carefully to the side of the pool where their clothes were tossed. Reid curses loudly.

"You okay?" Joaquim is searching for his cell phone, which he'd put on a table when they sat on the side of the pool.

"Stubbed my toe."

When Joaquim manages to get his flashlight on, he sees Reid wringing out his shirt. "There's yours," Reid says and points to another black blob the flashlight barely illuminates. Still wringing out his shirt, Reid turns and struggles to get his pants pulled up and buttoned.

Joaquim puts his phone face up on a lounge chair and begins wringing out his own shirt. He doesn't want to walk around wearing a wet shirt and he'll never get into his wet pants. At least in a shirt he might look as if he's wearing tiny swim shorts.

"Come on," Reid says. He's next to Joaquim. When Joaquim slips on his shoes and picks up his phone, he gets a glimpse of Reid. His hair is plastered down, and most of his eyeliner has washed off. Joaquim has seen him like this many times after class; now, though, he knows the secrets of his body more intimately. He's tasted the unexpected sweetness that Reid shows in small flashes. He's had Reid vulnerable, at the edge, trusting himself to Joaquim's hands. Now, though, his expression is quietly happy and tired.

Reid turns on the flashlight of his own phone as they trek back to the condo. The moon slid lower in the sky as they played, and its light waned.

"Let me get you some dry clothes," Reid says when they get into the condo. Joaquim shivers; it's so much cooler in here with the air conditioner on. He strips his shirt off and places it in the sink in the kitchen. He skims out of his wet black boxer briefs too and looks over to Reid, but he's already left the room. Naked is a lot more awkward when it's not a show.

Reid comes out, dressed in a black shirt and gray plaid fleece sweatpants. His eyes widen when he sees Joaquim.

"I, uh, didn't realize you'd left the room," Joaquim says.

"Mmm, I don't mind." Reid pulls him in and slides his free hand down to Joaquim's ass. "You are gorgeous," he says, and then his blue eyes, bright and hot, are locked with Joaquim's. Joaquim wants so badly to take this boy to bed again.

"You're very tempting," he says. Reid's smile is wicked and sharp.

"A boy can try." He kisses Joaquim, and then hands him the clothes. "The pants might be a little short, since you're taller, but they're a bit long on me." Joaquim slips into the pants and shirt. The pants are fine, but the shirt is a little tight.

"It must all be in my torso," Joaquim says, tugging the hem of the shirt. When he moves, it rides up and a strip of skin is exposed.

"Hopefully no one will see you go in," Reid says.

"Well, I haven't done what Nina calls 'the walk of shame' yet, so maybe it'll help my rep." Joaquim winks, and something in Reid's face changes. Joaquim isn't sure what that means. A glance at the clock tells him he must go, though.

"All right, I don't want you to turn into a pumpkin or anything," Reid says.

Joaquim puts his shoes on, and Reid hands him his phone and wallet, which he would have left on the counter otherwise. He's exhausted and a little disoriented. He kisses Reid at the door and then again after he tries to pull away.

"I'll see you later?" Joaquim asks against Reid's lips.

"Definitely."

Reid opens the door and, when Joaquim turns to offer him a last smile, catches Joaquim by the hand and pulls him close for a rough kiss. "We're okay, right?"

Joaquim frowns. The naked insecurity is at odds with both the kiss and the last few hours they've spent together. "Of course." A hug seems to reassure Reid. His tight shoulders soften, as does his grip on Joaquim's shirt.

⚹   ⚹   ⚹

MOST OF JOAQUIM'S SHIFT AT the dive shop is spent lost in daydreams. He's alone for the morning: no customers and none of his coworkers come in to bug him. He breaks the no-phone rule for the first time since Bobby got them all in trouble and tries to keep an ear out for Mike.

Joaquim: *Morning!*

Perhaps not the most eloquent opening salvo, but he's tired. He has to wait a while for a response. Of course Reid didn't have to get up at the butt-crack of dawn the way Joaquim did. He has to work at ten, however, so Joaquim assumes he'll be up by nine. It's eight, but he can't help himself. Not only was last night amazing, but Reid's sudden vulnerability as they parted has stayed with Joaquim. Reid's moods are very changeable and fluctuate so easily. *Once we get to know each other better, I'll be able to read him more easily, right?*

Eventually, his phone buzzes. He has it on silent, but against the counter the vibration is startling. Joaquim'll have to keep it in his pocket.

Reid: *You mean, *good* morning, right? ;)*

Joaquim: *For sure. I'm tired, but fantastic?*

Reid: *Unsure?*

Joaquim: *Nope just searching for other adjectives.*

Reid: *Too early for adjectives. Too early for everything. Wanna stay in bed. Think of you.*

Joaquim smiles. It's an easy opening for a dirty comment. But he's definitely not going to start something that'll end in sexting right now.

Joaquim: *I'm tempted to say that's sweet, although for all I know, you are being spicy.*

There's a long pause, and, after he rereads his own text, Joaquim groans.

Reid: *Sorry, I couldn't stop laughing long enough to text for a bit there.*

Joaquim: *Oh good. For a second I thought you would never speak to me again, that was so cheesy.*

Reid: *Not at all. I need laughter.*

Joaquim frowns, unsure what that means. He dithers, then types.

Joaquim: *Everything okay?*

Reid: *Of course. I just mean in life. Everyone needs more laughter.*

The bell that signals the front door opening startles him.

Joaquim: *G2g customer*

He pockets his phone.

"WHAT IS THAT SMILE?" NINA says when he sits down for lunch. He hoped the picnic table near their rooms would be empty, but he found her lying on a bench and staring at the overcast sky.

Now she sits across from him, arms crossed, gaze unwavering. In the sunlight, the green of her eyes is brighter. He bites his lip, unsuccessful in suppressing his smile.

"Nothing," he says, but it's useless, trying to keep his voice neutral.

"Oh my god, you got laid!"

"Shhh! Nina, the whole complex doesn't need to know!" Joaquim is laughing, though. He unwraps his sandwich and makes himself take a bite.

"Wow, dry spell over," she says. She grabs the pickle that was separately wrapped.

"Stop," he says, though he doesn't mean it.

"This boy must be special, getting in your pants on the second date and all." She moves to the side when he makes an attempt to get the pickle back.

"Nina, are you slut-shaming me?"

She rolls her eyes. "Honey, you are the farthest thing from a slut. Plus, I hate that phrase."

"I know. I'm just messing with you."

"Plus, you needed it. Not that you couldn't have gotten laid about ten thousand times since you and Rory broke it off."

Joaquim winces at the mention of his ex's name. "I'm picky, okay?"

"And this boy is the one—"

"Nina," he warns. He's not sure what she's going to say, but her opinion probably won't be flattering. She wasn't very impressed with Reid after that party. "I like him, okay? You spent time with him before the party. You liked him just fine then. You haven't gotten to know him better."

"And after two dates you have?" Skepticism doesn't suit her, or maybe it's just irritating.

"Listen, he was in my class; I've spent a lot of time with him. Please don't make me tell you it's not your business." In an attempt to lighten a conversation that has become too serious, he swipes what's left of the pickle and eats it despite her protest. "You'll never get details that way."

JOAQUIM: *NINA NEEDS ME TO take her dive tomorrow*

Reid: *You're kidding*

Joaquim: *Nope. Ugh. She has a double ear infection. This keeps happening to her.*

Joaquim waits for Reid to respond, but he doesn't see the little dots that indicate a response. He watches his phone, unsure why Reid isn't replying. He goes back to the TV show he was watching and waits for the phone to chime.

An hour later he's wondering if he should message Reid again to make sure everything is all right. Maybe he got called away, but it's unlike Reid not to send him a *hold on* or *brb* text. Joaquim doesn't want to nag, but he also doesn't want Reid to be upset with him about something he can't control—or in general. They have talked briefly about the terms of his internship and how much it can restrict Joaquim's freedom, but not in detail. It would be way too hard to type all that right now. And if Reid is mad, that conversation might seem insincere.

After another hour, when Joaquim is in bed and trying to fall asleep, he texts again.

Joaquim: *Hey everything all right? You never responded.*

Reid: *It's fine*

Reid responds immediately. Joaquim waits for more about their plans for tomorrow, but gets no other texts. When he tosses his phone on his nightstand, it's with annoyance rather than the nagging worry and confusion that had been dogging him. He actively resists the urge to send another text, because if Reid is upset, things can only escalate. Joaquim hates fighting via text. Seventy percent of what is said gets taken out of context.

The next morning, he still has no texts from Reid. Bobby is going with him on the dive, and they're loading the boat together while he subjects Bobby to a one-sided monologue about the situation.

"Dude," Bobby finally interrupts, hefting an air tank. "You're killing me. Call him."

"I don't want—"

"Yeah, yeah, in case he's mad. But how is not figuring out if he is going to help? You're mad, but aren't sure you should be mad. You're upset in case he's upset, because you didn't want to upset him. You're annoyed with the whole thing, but don't know what he's actually thinking. Man, that's way too many feelings over things you could be wrong about."

Joaquim is silent as they check their personal gear. "You have a point."

"Thank fucking god."

"Hey!" Joaquim exclaims as Bobby walks away.

"No offense," Bobby says, and Joaquim swallows an angry follow-up. Bobby's not the one he's mad at. And he's not a guy he'd go to for this advice anyway; he happens to be the only one around. They don't have time for Joaquim to make a phone call now, but he shoots off a text.

Joaquim: *Hey can I call you later?*

He doesn't get a response before he has to leave, but maybe by the time they're back he will. Reid has the whole day off, which is why they made plans, so who knows what he's gotten up to for the day. Maybe he'll drive up to Homestead and shop, since he's been complaining about his clothes being too hot for this weather.

The first of his divers comes in, and so Joaquim turns off his phone and stores it in his locker.

It's not the best dive Joaquim has ever been on, and he's in a pretty bad mood when they dock. One of their divers was seasick, the currents were strong, and another of his divers could not figure out his buoyancy. Stubborn divers who get it wrong but won't listen irritate Joaquim intensely, especially when their behavior ends with damaging the reef—which wouldn't have happened if they paid attention to the pre-dive briefing and allowed Joaquim to help with their weights, which they insisted they knew how to adjust. Joaquim was unfamiliar with this group, and while he's pretty good at maintaining composure and getting to know people when in diver mode, he went into the dive annoyed and upset. Nothing that followed helped, especially the vomiting part.

When they're finally through and Joaquim goes to shower, he retrieves his phone and has a message from Reid.

Reid: *Sure*

Joaquim frowns, grips his phone hard, and practices deep breathing. *Oh my god, what is with the one word texts?* He doesn't text that or anything else. Instead he pockets his phone and slams the locker shut.

Once he's showered and in his room before his class, Joaquim flops onto his bed and calls Reid. After five rings, Reid picks up.

"Hey, you," Reid says.

"Hey." Joaquim clears his throat. "Is every—"

"I'm sorry I—"

They both pause, and Joaquim jumps in despite the awkwardness. "You don't have to apologize."

"No, I… I wasn't trying to be rude. I promise. I had a hard night and I was looking forward to seeing you. Sometimes when things… get a particular way, it's better for me to step away." The last is said so softly Joaquim struggles to hear.

"A particular way?"

"I don't, I'm not—" Reid stammers.

Something is definitely off; it's clear in Reid's voice, and Joaquim senses that it goes beyond a canceled date.

"You don't have to talk about it now if you don't want to," Joaquim says.

He probably shouldn't have said *now*, but he can't bring himself to take that back. He wants to know, even if it takes a while for Reid to trust him. At lunch with Nina last week, amidst a semi-abridged version of the details of their pool escapade, Joaquim told her that he doesn't want to get too invested in the relationship, because he doesn't know how long Reid plans to stick around or what Reid plans for his future. Despite what he told Nina, he's in. Time will tell if he's too far in, if he'll get hurt. Nina was right: although he thinks he knows Reid and their connection, there's a lot he doesn't know. *How many secrets do we hold? Don't all relationships start this way?* The unfolding of a relationship should be the slow exposition of secrets and selves as trust thickens and matures.

"Joaquim?" Reid says, interrupting what must have been a long silence.

"Sorry, no, I was thinking," he says. *Honesty will benefit us*, he hopes. Joaquim wants honesty between them without having to push, and acknowledgment that they need to keep learning so they aren't pretending or ignoring things. With a foundation of honesty, Joaquim hopes that it, and trust, will always be on the table so that in moments like these communication will feel beneficial. Necessary even.

If the time comes.

"Okay." Reid sounds so unlike himself; Joaquim badly wants to be able to see him, to get a read on him in person.

"I'm sorry about today."

"It's okay," Reid insists. "You're busy; it's okay."

"I know. I wouldn't have canceled if I had any choice. This internship—I really don't get a choice sometimes."

"You mentioned something like that before," Reid says. "Can you explain? Not because I am, like, doubting you or anything. But I don't know the details about how this works."

"I would love to." Joaquim sighs. "But I have to go to my next shift."

"Okay," Reid says; no sadness or upset laces the words. If he's upset, he's very good at hiding it. He doesn't sound as quiet as he did when they first got on the phone.

"But, um. I really wanted to see you." *It's too soon for* I miss you, *right?* "Are you around Monday?"

"I am after work, at seven. Are you able to do that?"

"Yeah," Joaquim says. Relieved that their schedules line up so soon, he grins at Bobby, who has walked in the door. Bobby shoots him a look that plainly communicates he thinks Joaquim is a weirdo, but Joaquim ignores that. "I don't have an early shift Tuesday, so that'll be great."

"Awesome." Reid's voice is rich, as if infused with happiness.

"I'll call you later, maybe?"

"I'd love that."

"If it's not too late for you."

"No. I'll be up late tonight anyway."

"All right then."

"Bye," Reid says. His voice is sweet and quiet.

Twelve

After he hangs up, Reid tosses the phone onto the bed beside him and resumes his examination of the ceiling. It's one of those popcorn ceilings that drives him crazy when he looks at it too long. Reid simultaneously wants to run his fingers over it, letting the tiny sharp edges press into his skin, and also to scrape at it. Watching it disappear slowly, becoming clean and smooth, would be utterly satisfying.

Reid realizes that this is not how his compulsion will play out. And that he can't, because it's his grandmother's condo, not his. Finding a sensory outlet definitely would have been helpful last night; maybe if he'd accepted his compulsion to feel those sharp edges, those small hurts, he wouldn't have slipped up last night. It's been five months since Reid last cut; five months since his last relapse. It's the longest Reid has ever gone without self-harming, and although it's been a struggle, Reid can't help but wonder if he'd taken the positive strides he's made for granted.

Tonight is therapy night. That's one of the reasons he and Joaquim were going out during the day, though, of course Joaquim didn't know that. For the first time in a very long time, he doesn't want to show up for therapy. He can't ignore his relapse. Reid must reach out and utilize his support systems.

On paper, there's no good reason to skip and many compelling reasons to attend. He's let them down, though. He's let himself down. The community of support they can offer him won't be the same as it would be if he were there in person. Reid hates to cry in front of people.

Therapy is the only space he makes an exception for, and not because he wants to. He promised himself, when he committed to getting better, that he would teach himself to be vulnerable in spaces where he's safe. The computer monitor is a cold buffer; the vulnerability of crying while so alone frightens him.

Reid sighs and rolls onto his side. Out of direct sunlight, the old wallpaper his grandmother never replaced looks dingy. Its vertical stripes, thick with pink flowers, have taken on dusty rose and cream tones with greens that edge toward brown. The pattern of vines between the overblown peonies running up to the ceiling is painfully familiar. He's traced them with his eyes for hours now, between bouts of sleeping. The only time he got up today was to shower. He thought it might help wake him up. Instead the shower made his lethargy worse, and he stared into the mirror at his side, touching the small, thin cuts over and over for a long time, trying to center all of the not-right inside at the point of slight pain outside. Touching the fresh cuts was like touching a memory, like a haunting that seemed to pull him together, pull in everything that was skittering out of control.

It went on too long—he doesn't know how long. Long enough that, by the time he roused himself from reading the braille of his failure obsessively, the mirror was completely steamed over, and he wasn't able to see himself.

He finished his shower as fast as he could, put on an undershirt and a long-sleeved shirt, and crawled back into bed under his own comforter, the one from the empty twin bed, and the musty-smelling blankets from the hall closet. His wet hair left the pillow damp. He clutched his fingers together under the pillows and tried and tried and tried not to think.

Then Joaquim called him. Initially, answering was hard, because what could be said? Reid wasn't mad at him. Logically, none of this had to do with Joaquim in the first place—in any place—but finding normal, finding evenness, finding the will to fake okay was impossible, impossible, impossible.

Improbably, by the end of the call, Reid is smiling. He's still tired, so tired. But his mood has lifted enough for him to think more seriously about therapy tonight. If he calls in from bed, they'll understand.

One of the most frustrating things about trying to explain his lows to his parents, particularly after a rapid and intense cycle, is how *tired* he is. It's not the kind of tiredness that he can shake off, it's an exhaustion that comes from a place he can't understand. Many of his problems seem to stem from places he can't understand and does not control.

What would Nancy tell me to do?

Reid rolls over and trains his eyes on the ceiling again. He imagines pressing his palm to its rough surface. Pressing the heel and then the tips of his fingers to feel how the smaller points would dig in. The way it would hurt without hurting.

Sit up, Reid.

He sits up. His hair is a wreck: flat and matted on the left side of his head, dried in stiff clumps elsewhere. His phone chimes. It's not Joaquim, and there's no one else he wants to talk to. Reid sits slumped for a long while, eyes on the geometric mauve and baby blue patterns of the comforter. It's almost more hideous than the wallpaper. But there's something soothing about the lines he can trace over and over. Nancy has pillows like that, with concentric beige and bronze circles he followed and followed with his fingers for the hour and a half they were together each week.

Get out of bed, Reid.

He sighs, peels back the heft and warmth of his blankets, and slowly stands. He's stiff from hours spent in that bed. He wobbles a little and puts a hand on the doorframe when he pauses there. Eyes slipping closed, he leans on it and has to fight going back.

I can do this. I can.

It's been a day since he's eaten, and, though he's not hungry, eating is an important part of his self-care plan. He's never struggled with food or body issues, but he has struggled with taking care of himself when he's low. At Sycamore Grove, the therapists told him to work recovery like sobriety. He scoffed. Months later, when he was home again, Nancy offered him a different perspective on "one day at a time," breaking it down to whatever increment of time would work. Reid's worked them all: day-to-day, minute-to-minute. Right now, he's on the moment-to-moment plan, the one in which the only thing he can think about is the thing he is doing at that very moment. He cannot let himself think past it.

Break an egg, Reid.

And so he does, into a pan on the stove that he remembers too late isn't turned on. He does so, leaving it on medium, and struggles not to turn it off and leave. He watches the egg whiten and bubble and stirs only enough to break the yolk. Reid combs his fingers through his hair to try to order it. It's hopeless. He has no one to worry about today, other than his DBT group, so he could theoretically let it go.

Eventually, Reid breaks a second egg into the pan. They'll cook all mixed up, which isn't good. But he hardly has an appetite. This is a thing he must do because they told him to.

THE SUN IS SETTING AND Reid sits on the screened porch with a half-empty plate of eggs on his lap. He's drowsy, but the salty air has helped him stay up. Sounds of kids playing on the beach down the tiny cliff make him smile. More likely than not, they're visiting a grandparent, but it's nice to hear young people.

Other than the tall green spikes of Joe the aloe poking into the blue curtain of sky, his view of the water is uninterrupted. Soon the sun will set and those blues will part for her impressive show. Reid has to show up to therapy. He has to. Once he sat on the porch, the only other command he had to give himself was to stay awake. Each minute, his plan is a continuous reminder that he *must*. He made promises to other people, but they're less important than the promise he made to himself, the promise that he'd work his hardest to be as healthy as possible.

Working recovery when he's not well is vital. Reid's relapsed before. Climbing out of a deep hole is much harder when you've let yourself stagnate in it, let your muscles atrophy and hope disintegrate. His group is the hands reaching in for him.

Reid closes his eyes and shakes his head. That might be the cheesiest self-help line he's come up with. And he comes up with good ones. Nancy loves them.

When it's time to get up, he puts the dish in the sink, and then, halfway out of the kitchen, comes back to put it in the dishwasher. He has no idea how he'll feel for a while. Will he feel this low? If so, letting things pile up will only make him worse. Reid has stringent rules about maintaining order in his surroundings. That gives him a sense of control.

In his room, he finally checks his phone. He finds texts and calls from Felix and one from his mom, who calls every day. His mother has a keen sense for when Reid isn't doing well and a brand of caring that is equal parts patronizing and loving. He's not ready for that. And Felix? Felix has texted him consistently ever since Reid left home. In weak moments, when Felix's texts become worrisome, Reid breaks his own promises and texts back to check in, to make sure he's okay. Because physical distance alone isn't enough; physical distance isn't a boundary between two people who were so enmeshed, so unhealthy together, for so long.

His therapy group encouraged Reid to sever all ties with Felix several times, but Reid can't. Doing so would feel like betrayal. Felix, in whatever fucked up, and at times damaging, capacity, was once a person who kept Reid together at his worst. They kept each other together in turns.

And hurt each other in turns. Felix hurt him as well, irrevocably.

Reid ignores those texts. He also has a text from Joaquim from hours ago, asking how he's doing.

Reid stares at it, wondering what tone to read it in. Caring? Checking in? Wanting to exchange pleasantries? Worried because he could hear something wrong? Joaquim is in the dark, but Reid could not disguise the tone of his voice when they spoke. If he were in Joaquim's position, he would be curious and perhaps concerned.

Rather than read them or delete any of the texts, Reid tosses his phone back on the bed. Group is in twenty minutes. There's not enough time to shower again, but he can do something about his hair. In the bathroom he tries to stick his head under the faucet, but it's a tiny sink. He settles for splashing water over his head haphazardly, then combing the weird angles and clumps out. When he runs his hands through it briskly, messing it up again, it's more him. It's a mess, yes, but the kind he wants.

"Reid, are you okay?" Elise asks when Rachel pauses. Reid looks up from where he's been playing with the braided black leather bracelet he wears sometimes.

"Yeah," he says. "Just listening."

"Hmm," Rachel says. She's on the left side of the screen, not where she usually sits. But Jess has come to group today and is sitting in her spot.

"Reid, you said you were going to go on a date with Joaquim last week," Nancy says, "How did that go?"

He makes himself smile. "Really great." Anxiety curls heavily in his stomach.

"Tell us more," Rachel pleads, laughing. "It's been so long since I was on a date, I don't even remember what it's like."

"Well, I can't tell you everything." Reid wiggles his eyebrows.

"Oh my god, Reid, you *so* can," Elise says.

"Anyway," Reid continues. His face is bright red. He remembers Joaquim's tongue in his mouth, his taste lingering and sharp. Yeah, no. Not sharing that. "We went to dinner, kind of the usual. He makes me laugh. But..." He goes back to fiddling with his bracelet.

"But?"

"Well, we came back here after, and I was showing him around and... the thing is that I *wanted* him to come over. So I invited him. But as soon as he was here, it felt all wrong. I don't know why. And then I started to get anxious."

"And what did you do?"

"You didn't sleep with him anyway, did you?" Elise asks.

"*Elise!*" Rachel hisses.

"What? I ju—"

"I took him on a walk." Reid doesn't want to know where Elise is going to go next. "I felt better outside. We went down to the pool, and I thought I could tell him. Some things, not everything."

"How did that feel? How did that go?"

"Well." Reid bites his lip. "We never got to the talking part."

"Reid! I'm scandalized!"

"Oh, shush, Jess, stop being melodramatic," Rachel says.

There's a lull. Everything is so tangled, his current anxiety and shame and the unexpected anxiety and wrongness he felt as soon as he invited Joaquim in. That anxiety and wrongness had dissolved quickly; being outside, being in the water, being with Joaquim, Reid was someone else for a moment, for a few hours.

"Reid, honey, tell us what's going on."

"I don't know. I like him. But it was impulsive. Maybe a little reckless. I promised I wouldn't be that guy."

"Reid, we're young. You like him, and it sounds like he likes you, right?" Rachel asks.

"Well, yeah, but he doesn't really know me. And he'll find out; no one wants to deal with all of this. I don't just have baggage. I *am* baggage, you guys."

"Reid," Nancy starts.

"No," he interrupts, "I am. Even Felix—"

"Come on, Reid, not Felix, you cannot let him keep—"

"But I was a part of his problems, wasn't I? I made everything worse with all of my fucked up—"

"Reid." Elise tries to cut in. He can't stop, though.

"If this keeps going, I'm going to get in deeper. And I could hide it. I can now, but not forever. He'll see." He stops talking; he hopes they get his meaning even when he doesn't want to say what he's done.

"He'll see?" Jess asks. With her inconsistent attendance, it's possible she missed the story of Reid's relapse struggles. Explaining them now would be exhausting, and Reid's tired enough.

"Reid," Nancy hops in. Her voice is soothing, or maybe it just seems so because, after a year of working with her, she's the most stable part of his life. "Are you safe, right now?"

Reid nods. While he traces the woven strands of his bracelet he thinks, *If only this is what my life was like.* Yes, there are many strands, and it's a complicated pattern. But Reid has no pattern. He's a mess.

"I'll be okay," he promises. Every time he falls back into it, he feels worse when he promises he won't do it again. "Maybe I'm just on a slow-and-steady plan," he says. He presses his lips together to hide the way they tremble and then clears his throat to hide how thick it's become. He will *not* cry. "I need to… I don't really know how. I just, um. It was a really sudden and fast cycle."

"Do you have an idea what might have triggered it?" Nancy asks.

"No. There's so much, but not anything I can pinpoint." It happened soon after Joaquim canceled their plans. Reid often experiences displaced triggers, one thing setting off an episode that's unrelated to the event.

"It's not nothing, Reid," Rachel says. Of everyone she understands the most, because she and Reid have been caught in such similar struggles.

"Well, for now, an action plan sounds like a good idea, right?" Nancy says. Of course he agrees. He's so mixed up, though; so often he doesn't know where to start.

"First, I am going to encourage you again to go back to diary cards. Maybe you can identify some patterns. They've been helpful for identifying triggers in the past, right? You're in a new environment. Maybe they've changed. Maybe they're harder to recognize."

"Yeah," Reid says. *New location, new triggers.* He hadn't thought of it that way. This should have been obvious.

"I want you to talk to Dr. Michaelson, even if it's just an email, so you both can be prepared to talk about options for medication changes if you continue to experience rapid cycling or mixed states. Remember that we are both available in emergencies at all times."

"Me too," Rachel chimes in. Reid shakes his head. He's not in any immediate danger, unless stupidity and inability to hold himself together like a normal person are a danger. He says as much.

"Reid, I want you to listen to me," Nancy says. "You *are* a normal person. We all are. We all have brains that work differently, that's all. You guys have been handed challenges. But you are worthy of happiness and health and *help*."

Thirteen

"Hey," Joaquim says when Reid opens the door. He moves to kiss Reid's cheeks and then stops. Reid is still over the threshold, and his eyes are tired. His smile is bright, though, and he comes to Joaquim, kissing him quickly on the cheek and going adorably red. He's wearing a vibrant blue graphic T-shirt with almost invisible palm fronds printed on it. Joaquim's never seen him wear anything this colorful. Despite the pop of color, this boy, reckless and teasing a few days ago, is now all downcast eyes circled with exhaustion.

"Hey, yourself," he says. He locks the door and turns to Joaquim. "Where are we going?"

"I thought we could have lunch. There's a place down in Islamorada with Cuban food. Unless you don't like it?"

"Never had it," Reid says, giving him another smile. "I'm open to any and all new foods."

"Any?" Joaquim says, opening Reid's door for him.

"Yeah. I'm pretty food-adventurous. I've eaten things I hated, but at least I can say I took that chance."

Joaquim settles into his seat and turns the radio down when he turns the car on.

"You don't have to do that if you don't want to," Reid says. "I want to hear what you like."

"Oh?" Joaquim leans his head on the headrest and turns toward Reid. Now their eye contact shifts their almost-shy, not-sure-where-we-stand energy to confidence, heat, knowing.

"I want to know you," Reid says. He takes Joaquim's hand, but then lets go. "Sorry."

Joaquim takes Reid's hand. Nina's car, which he's borrowed again, doesn't have air conditioning; though the windows are down, it's very hot. Reid's hand is warm. Reid startles a bit when Joaquim kisses him, but meets him halfway for the second one and kisses him back. Joaquim's stomach grumbles, which is a shame, because with Reid's lips on his, he's tempted to ask if they can go inside. Reid's desire to know Joaquim isn't one-sided, though. Joaquim doesn't just want this boy; he wants to learn him, too.

"All right, let's go. Nature is calling you toward the Cuban food." Reid laughs and leans back; his posture is looser, and his tension has uncoiled in the wake of touch. *Maybe that's what he needs, sometimes.* In the water, in their classes, and on dives, Reid is one of his most unflappable divers. Out of the water, Reid is someone else completely.

"How much time do you have today?" Reid asks over the wind rattling in through the windows.

"Nina took my shift as a thanks for taking her dive. We're not supposed to do that, but Mike is cool with us. The rules are sometimes…" Joaquim breaks off. He doesn't want to complain when he's been given a great opportunity. Before Reid, he's seldom had reason to complain other than exhaustion. He's coming to resent the moments he could be with Reid but has to work instead. Silence lingers before Reid turns the radio up, loud, to be heard over the wind.

Lunch is delicious. Reid has a lot of questions about places on the islands he can go, the ones Joaquim knows of because he's been here long enough to explore and discover. Joaquim has friends to explore with, so he wonders how lonely Reid must be sometimes. Loneliness is a familiar language, a longing for family and home Joaquim can't shake. It's *saudade*; a word with no good English equivalent. A lovely aching nostalgia for something that's still with him. His family and home will always be there for him, even if it's far away right now. He's happy, but often his life is so different and new it seems not quite his own. Like Joaquim, Reid has displaced himself. His reasons are a mystery, but something motivated Reid to leave behind a whole life. Joaquim did it for adventure, for experiences, for living life while he is young and unencumbered.

"I'll take you anywhere that sounds interesting," he promises. "When I'm not being overworked."

"That sounds nice." Reid takes a huge bite of his Cubano. He can't talk because his mouth is so full, but he waves his hand.

He swallows, too fast, and Joaquim says, "Hey, don't hurt yourself."

Reid clears his throat. "That made it sound like I think it's nice that you work too much for us to do stuff. I just meant, um, discovering things with you."

Although that ends up sounding vaguely dirty, Joaquim doesn't say anything. He bumps Reid's feet with his. On the table, Reid's phone vibrates. In their quiet moment, it's jarring. Reid glances at it, and a look Joaquim can't read crosses his face. He tosses his phone facedown on the table without responding and takes a deep breath with his eyes closed.

"Everything okay?"

"Fine," Reid snaps, and then his shoulders fall. "Sorry, I don't mean to bite your head off. There's people back home I don't want to hear from."

It's a vague answer, but likely Joaquim isn't going to get much more. Reid is slippery when answering questions. Right now isn't the time, but soon Joaquim has to ask more. He likes Reid; this is could be going somewhere very special. But not without Reid's trust.

They talk about their last dive. Reid's class is over, so he's planning to slowly accumulate dives. Reid doesn't make a lot at Shell World and he tells Joaquim that his grandmother paid for his class.

"I'm living rent-free, so I can save pretty fast. I am trying to save most of it. For whenever..." Reid looks out the window. His arms are tightly crossed around himself.

"I like your bracelet," Joaquim says, redirecting the conversation.

"Thanks! My niece Morgan makes stuff like this. This one used to have a charm but it fell off." He makes a face, scrunching his nose.

"Hey, do you wanna get out of here?" Joaquim says. They've been finished for a while. If they're going to linger over conversation, he can think of more atmospheric places to do it.

"Yeah." Outside the sky has taken on a different blue. She's preparing for her sundown show, her nightly performance: brilliant colors and light acquiescence to night.

When they exit into brutal heat, Reid turns to him. "Want to see one of my favorite places?"

"Yeah," Joaquim says. Any part of Reid's story, he'll go along with.

When Reid leads them back into his grandmother's condo, it's as spotless as it was before. Remembering how anxious Reid seemed last time they were here, he follows Reid directly through and out onto the small, scruffy yard beyond the porch. In the daylight he can see the view. With the sharp drop-off, all he can see is the bay; no beach, only the gray and turquoise and deep blue, almost black patches. The ocean is changeable today as clouds skitter above in fast patterns. He hopes it's not cloudy when the sun sets. He hopes Reid lets him stay that long. He very much wants to watch the sunset with Reid.

Reid carefully gathers towels he has on the porch and bug spray, which he hands to Joaquim. Reid pauses at the top of the path and drops a light kiss on Joaquim's lips, then nods toward the water. "Watch your step."

The steps down can hardly be called steps, as uneven and overgrown as they are.

"I should probably clear these. But I like the way they look."

"Um," Joaquim says, caution in speech only a reflection of his movements, "Aren't there groundspeople? There usually are at places like this."

"Oh." Reid turns at the bottom and offers Joaquim a hand on the last step. The towels are tucked under his arm, and he doesn't let go of Joaquim's hand. "Yeah. Duh."

Joaquim doesn't say anything. Despite this place, which is one of the most expensive condos in Key Largo, Reid doesn't seem spoiled. Joaquim would bet he has no idea how much the condo costs.

"Come here," Reid whispers and pulls Joaquim close for a kiss. Breathing softly, they hardly move, touching gently with only their lips. Joaquim pulls Reid's lower lip between his carefully, then kisses him in the same way, then again, like raindrops and promises.

Joaquim pulls away regretfully. He wouldn't be averse to going right back up to the condo with Reid, but he senses Reid's reluctance. Joaquim wants to share whatever Reid does, and, right now, Reid wants to share this space, a place that's important.

It's not the prettiest beach on the Keys, but it's very private. He supposes everyone in Reid's condo unit can access it, though.

"Hardly anyone comes down here," Reid says, as if he's reading Joaquim's mind. "I've met everyone in this building, though. They either think I'm adorable or weird; maybe it's because I'm young and pierced up. And I'm Monica's grandson. I bet most of them have been subjected to stories about me. Hopefully just the good ones."

What are the bad ones? Joaquim bites his lip and helps Reid settle the towels for them to sit on. The sky is a lighter blue, and the sun slides down inexorably. Sunset is still an hour away.

They sit, shoulder to shoulder and thigh to thigh. Reid lets out a sigh. It means either longing or homecoming comfort; Joaquim can't tell. When his head rests on Joaquim's shoulder, hair tickling his neck, Joaquim can't help but smile. But Reid pulls away suddenly.

"Sorry."

"Why? Why do you pull away?"

"I don't know," Reid admits. "Felix used to hate that. He used to say I'm too touchy and sappy."

"Felix?"

"Yeah, my ex." Reid fiddles with the laces of his shoes, Converse with fluorescent rainbow laces. They seem out of character and are obviously new.

"I like your shoes," Joaquim says. He doesn't intend to change the topic. But he has.

Reid flashes him a smile.

"Do you want to talk about it? Or, is it okay if we do?" Joaquim ventures. "I don't want to pry, but I do want to get to know you."

"It's fine." Reid says. "He's the one who texted me at lunch."

"You guys are still in contact?"

"Yeah. I don't want to be, but he doesn't seem to get it."

"Have you asked him to stop?"

Reid's laugh is hollow. "It's complicated. I have, but he's got his own issues, and I feel guilty."

"You sound unsure." Joaquim leans on Reid, hoping the closeness will translate as safe space.

"No. I'm sure. It's hard really, to describe why I feel guilty. Things with Felix... he's been in my life for a long time. Not always as my boyfriend. But as a boyfriend too. He's been through a lot of stuff with me, and the other way around." Reid draws his fingers through the sand, leaning away from Joaquim. "Sometimes I think he knows me best, that no one else will know me like he does."

"And?" Joaquim prompts, because it's clear Reid has more to say.

"Mostly now, he doesn't know me at all, just another version of me. I don't know if I ever was who he thinks, but I'm definitely not now. And I don't want to be."

Clearly there is much more to Reid's story than he's telling; Joaquim isn't sure it's something he is ready to hear.

"Me coming here, some of it was because of him. I want to be someone new. He says he gets that, but he doesn't, because he won't let me go. And he tells me things that only I could know. Should?"

"I'm not sure I understand."

"He doesn't have anyone else. How can I leave him alone when he needs someone?"

Joaquim thinks about that. *Is he good for you?*

He doesn't ask.

"*Are* you someone new?" he asks instead. Reid's eyes, meeting his, are such a rare pale blue. The sky mimics them, but doesn't manage. Joaquim wants, badly, to draw him into a kiss. He doesn't care; he wants Reid however he his, whoever he is. But this transformation is important to Reid, clearly.

"Sometimes." Reid says. "With you, often."

Joaquim gives in, puts his forehead against Reid's shoulder, and kisses him through the soft cotton of his shirt. Reid shifts so that his arm is around him, pulling him closer.

"I'm being pretty vague. You probably have questions, but— "

"You can take your time. Only when you're ready."

Reid doesn't answer with words, but with his body, which sags into Joaquim's.

"I have a question about jellyfish," Reid says suddenly, and Joaquim grins at the randomness of the segue.

"Well, I'm no expert, but go ahead."

"Come in the water with me? Not far, just out a little way?"

Joaquim stands and pulls Reid up. They toe off their shoes. "Lead the way."

They wade in slowly: Reid rolls up the hems of his floods, exposing the soft skin of his strong calves. He shoots Joaquim a smile, and the sun is a halo behind his head. Joaquim picks his way around the plants and jellyfish; the silt is slimy and clouds the water when he stirs it up with his feet.

"Okay. So what are these?" Reid bends over to point to a jellyfish. "At first I thought they were plants, but they're jellyfish."

"Upside-down jellyfish," Joaquim says. He stops Reid as he's about to touch one. "They sting."

"Yeah, but it's not bad."

"Remember? Don't touch the wildlife," Joaquim reminds him with a wink.

"Good point."

"Anyway, that's what they are. Um, Cassiopeia, I think? Their official name I mean. There are different species." He squints. "There are tons of them here."

"Right? Not as many on the other beach. But that one is a little more cleaned up. Meant for swimming I guess."

"Do you swim here?" Joaquim asks. This would not be a spot he'd pick.

"No, I just like being out here. It's private. I like the way the water sounds."

Joaquim checks to be sure he won't step on anything and carefully takes a step toward Reid. His hand is wet from grabbing Reid's in the water, but that doesn't stop him from framing Reid's face gently with his palms. When Joaquim kisses him, Reid responds by tilting his head, sighing beautifully into Joaquim's mouth, and swaying against him. Joaquim runs his wet hands down to Reid's throat. Reid's pulse thrums under his thumbs, and then Joaquim runs them over his shoulders and down to Reid's hands.

Fourteen

IT'S HARD FOR REID TO resist pulling Joaquim upstairs into the bedroom and against him.

But there are more things to say. And sunset is a while away; it's too bright out, and Reid can't think of a good excuse to keep his shirt on. Although Joaquim's body clearly asks for more, as does Reid's, Reid takes Joaquim's hand and pulls him back toward the towels. He tugs him until they're lying down.

Joaquim doesn't resist or ask questions, nor does he hide his excitement. He has Reid by the hips, and arousal is unmistakable where they're pressed together. Reid thinks back to Joaquim's reticence in the pool and pulls away.

"What happened to the shy boy who didn't want to do it where he could get caught?"

"I think you broke him," Joaquim jokes. Even his eyes smile, scrunched a little at the corners; for a fleeting moment Reid is so *intensely* happy. Joaquim's joy is palpable and stunning, and right here, in this moment, Reid is only a boy being kissed, being wanted, washed clean, and sheltered from everything that's haunted him all the way from Eau Claire. He traveled the country to run away. Sometimes, he thinks it worked. Sometimes, all he has is the faith that it will. Right now, he has the certainty of possibility.

"Can we…" Reid folds his arm under his head. Eyes intent on Reid's, Joaquim does the same. Reid has never met someone with eyes the color of Joaquim's: so dark he wouldn't call them brown. He can barely tell the pupils from the irises.

"Can we what?" Joaquim traces Reid's eyebrows with a sweet, light, curious touch.

"You'll think it's dumb."

"I promise I won't," Joaquim says seriously. Maybe this trust is as reckless as anything else, as dumb as so many impulses Reid follows. But it's there.

"Can we linger?"

Joaquim regards him for a long moment. His face is kind, contemplative, with no judgment. Measuring the moment, maybe reading it. Him.

"I would love that." He scoots closer and runs that same finger over Reid's lips. Reid kisses it. Reid can't think of a time anyone has let him do this, has *wanted* to linger, or wanted Reid *long enough* to linger. Felix wanted him plenty, but not in all the ways Reid wished for.

Perhaps he's stalling. But Reid's been learning the value of asking for things he wants and needs, rather than ignoring them.

They lie quietly. Joaquim kisses him carefully. He charts the territory of Reid's neck, then pushes aside the collar of Reid's shirt to kiss his shoulder. He lies back when Reid pushes his shoulders and lets him return the favor. Reid savors the caress. When the sun begins to put on her show, he scoots down and turns toward it. He pulls Joaquim's arm around him; with his other arm, Joaquim props his head on a bent elbow, and they watch the sun set in comfortable silence.

THE GLOAMING IS WRAPPED AROUND them when Reid finally moves. His secret self, the one that's ached for romance like this his whole life but has never thought he deserved it, overflows. But this also seems to be the hell hour for mosquitos that spray doesn't deter, so he turns over.

"Want to come up?"

Joaquim lights up. "Yeah, I'd love to."

They're just shy of the porch when anxiety begins to curl inside Reid. He *has* to talk to Joaquim now, before things go further, about Felix and what happened. Well, about the one thing.

"We need to talk first," Reid mumbles as soon as they're past the screen doors. Joaquim's hands frame Reid's hips; he doesn't drop them, but squeezes.

"Okay."

"Want some water or something to drink?" Reid stalls frantically, refusing to turn and look at him.

"Yeah, sure," Joaquim says slowly.

Reid fills a glass with ice, and the loud grinding of the machine and the clatter of ice cubes into the glass are too sharp, too intrusive after the quiet of their interlude. Reid hands the glass to Joaquim and then hops up on the counter. Sand is still on his feet and now on the floor. He'll have to vacuum before it spreads.

Reid's fingers tangle. He presses the edge of his thumbnail into the soft cuticle of his forefinger.

Little hurts, Nancy calls them. They're a transition as he learns to cope, learns not to need self-destructive behaviors but to recognize the limits of his coping skills and find less dangerous ways to stay calm.

"The thing is that I've... in the past I... I can be impulsive, sometimes."

"Okay," Joaquim says. He hops onto the counter across the kitchen. Reid glances up, then back at his hands.

"Maybe the other night was a little impulsive. I didn't ask if you—I mean, we didn't use a condom, and I should check—"

"I'm totally clean," Joaquim interrupts him. "You don't have to trust my word. But it's been a long time since I've been with someone. I've always been safe and I've been tested multiple times."

Reid holds in a deep sigh at the very last minute.

"I'll admit," Joaquim slows his speech, "that night was pretty impulsive for me too. That's not..."

"Usual?"

"Yeah."

"Okay." Reid takes a breath and then another. "Well, I need to say. . . I need to be careful. We do."

Joaquim is quiet as the implication sets in.

"I didn't know that Felix was cheating on me. That he wasn't being careful. I only found out recently. I've been tested, but I'm just shy of three months. I mean, they said chances are slim, but I need to tell you that."

"Okay," Joaquim says, and Reid can't believe it's that easy.

"Really?"

"So we'll be careful." Joaquim shrugs. "There's a lot we can do that doesn't have to be risky. I don't care how we're together." He hops off the counter and crosses to Reid. He cups Reid's knees and puts his forehead against Reid's. "I hope you'll give me a chance. That you want to be with me too."

"I really do." Reid laces his fingers behind Joaquim's neck.

"Reid." Joaquim pauses, and Reid can sense the weight of words being measured. "I'm honored that you trust me, after what's been done to you."

Reid closes his eyes. He has to, because this is not the time for tears. There's trust, and then there is trust with his hurting, sensitive self. He swallows and then surges into a kiss. He spreads his knees apart and pulls Joaquim between them. He doesn't want to think about anything else, not Felix, or how it felt to be betrayed, or how confession leaves him so raw. He wants the heat he tamped down on the beach. He wants Joaquim's hands and his body; he wants to know Joaquim, and know his body more and more every time they're together.

Joaquim puts his hands under Reid's shirt and bites his lip; he kisses Reid in a dirty way, so different from before. When he pulls at the hem of Reid's shirt, Reid pushes him back and hops down.

"Come on," he says, then shows Joaquim the way to the bedroom. He pulls him onto the bed before Joaquim can turn on the lights. It's a twin bed, small for them both, which means he gets to keep Joaquim closer. With the curtains drawn, it's dark enough for safety, and when Joaquim tries to pull his shirt off again, Reid gladly lets him.

✳   ✳   ✳

THE WEEK AFTER THE FOURTH of July, Shell World is dead slow. Everyone who rushed down for the holiday must either be recovering from the parties or abandoned ship and went back to the mainland. Reid hasn't seen a customer all day, and he's resorted to sorting tiny bins of shells into piles of similar color and shape. There's only so much tiny-shell sorting one can do before becoming cross-eyed and impatient, and, after four hours of boredom, Reid is ready to walk out and find another job just to have something to do. He's also begun fantasizing about pouring the shells onto the floor and walking on them to hear the crunching noise they'd make.

The thought crosses his mind that this *is* all there is to do, which isn't right. He could do plenty of other things if he wanted to. He could work in a restaurant or a bar. That might be fun; he'd have more people to talk to at least. But Reid gets overstimulated easily. He should learn to get over it. He can't live his life avoiding things he's not sure how to cope with. That's why he's struggled to hold jobs. Well, that and the other reasons.

Reid tries not to think about those. Nancy used to tell him that was okay, that he didn't have to think about them until he was ready. *What if I'm never ready? What if I never want to be ready?*

His phone chimes and he pulls it out, ducking behind the register in case Shel comes in. All day, Joaquim has been texting him when he can: sweet things, semi-dirty ones, funny ones. Joaquim is turning out to be a boy of many faces, now that he and Reid have gotten closer.

Felix: *Guess where I am?*

Reid's stomach falls quickly when he sees it's not Joaquim, but Felix.

Felix: *Reiiid you really can't ignore this one, you're gonna love it!*

Reid rolls his eyes. He's been semi-successfully ignoring Felix recently. Joaquim plays a large part in that, he'll admit. It doesn't seem right to keep talking to his ex when he's starting something new. And Joaquim makes him so happy; it's so uncomplicated right now. *Why shouldn't I enjoy that?*

Reid: *Where are you?*

He sighs and hits send as the strung shells that serve as door chimes clatter their hollow signal. Reid hates that noise, but figures it's better than bells.

"Surprise!"

Reid drops his phone and jerks back. He hates when people jump out from behind things or come up on him unexpectedly. Worse, it's Felix. *Felix.* What? Reid's heart thumps so hard it takes his breath.

"What in the actual fuck?" Reid grabs the counter. One night two weeks ago, when searching for any excuse to end a text conversation he let himself get sucked into, he told Felix where he works. *Why did I do that?*

"Aw, don't be like that," Felix kisses Reid's cheek over the counter. He doesn't have time to jerk back, but he wants to. He barely resists wiping the kiss from his cheek. Instead, he bends to retrieve his phone. His hands are shaking.

"Felix," he manages. "What—"

"I thought I'd come see you!" Felix says. His eyes are bright, and he's vibrating with energy. Anxiety buzzes in Reid's fingers; it's hard to tell, with Felix, what's behind his behavior.

"You couldn't have called?"

"Uh, duh. No. You don't answer your phone." Felix taps on the screen, and Reid snatches it away before Felix can grab it.

"Felix, I'm at work," Reid says. "I can't just—"

"I know!" Felix picks up and puts down impulse-buy items from the counter. "I wanted the code and key to get to your grandma's condo so I don't have to wait until you're done. When are you done?"

Oh, as if Reid will give him either of those things! He checks his phone. He has two hours to go. "Let me text my friend. Maybe she can come in early."

"Sweet." Felix hops up on the counter, and Reid pushes him down. "I work here, man. Come on. Try not to break things or get me fired."

Felix holds his hands up. "Okay, okay. Calm down." As he walks away, Reid has a chance to take a breath. Felix's hair is an even brown. Reid's never seen its natural color before. He looks good. Healthy. Reid dials Delia and, when she doesn't answer, texts her.

Reid: *Srsly. SOS. Need help if you can*

She responds within five minutes, during which time Reid watches as Felix systematically searches all the kitschy goods engraved with names for one with *Felix* on it. He's messing up all of the stock, but Reid's too busy freaking out waiting for Delia to respond to intervene again. Felix keeps darting looks in his direction. Reid remembers him looking drawn, with his brown eyes pooled in shadows from sleepless nights. Unlike Reid, whose skin is naturally very light, Felix has always looked washed-out from refusing, for long periods of time, to leave his room in his parents' basement. If Reid were to measure their moments, how much of his life was wasted there, curled unhappily on Felix's bed, watching him play video games and keeping himself occupied with dumb cat videos?

Great, now Joaquim is texting him. He ignores those in favor of Delia's text.

Delia: *What's up, how big an emergency?*

Reid: *My ex showed up out of nowhere and wants the keys to my condo and I've been ignoring his calls for days now and I don't know what to do can you come take my last two hours?*

Delia: *WHAT?!?!*

Reid: *Yeah.*

Delia: *That's insane. You didn't know he was coming?*

Reid: *Of course not! Did you miss the part where I've been ignoring him?*

Delia: *Good point. I'll be there in 5. You owe me.*

Reid: *Anything. Tx.*

"Okay," Reid says after one long exhale. "My coworker is coming in. We can go home together."

"Home?" Reid sees that Felix got his other eyebrow pierced.

"Yeah," Reid says. He tries to back down; the defensive edge in his voice will only set Felix on his own defensive spiral. He has to be the calm one. His phone chimes and this time it's Joaquim, again. *Fuck.* What should be do?

His first instinct is to lie, to make up some excuse, or not answer—what he's been doing with Felix for a while now. But Joaquim lay on the beach with him for hours and let Reid direct the tempo of their night. Joaquim promised to do right by him and looked him in the eye, even when Reid admitted to something that shamed him deeply. Felix lied; Felix put him at risk. But Reid knows he shouldn't have been with Felix in the first place. All Reid does is backslide. He puts in months of work to get out of bad cycles, only to fall back into them, usually with Felix.

Delia comes in, in a whirl of black clothing and overbearing perfume. She's about as happy as ever, which is not very, and gives Felix one long, unimpressed glare.

"What's your problem, sweetheart?" Felix isn't the sort to back down. At Felix's height, it's not hard to intimidate. Reid's seen Felix get out of trouble by simply entering someone's space.

"Okay, time to go," Reid pushes Felix toward the door before there's bloodshed, because that shit definitely won't work with Delia. She shakes her head at him when he peers over his shoulder. He's not sure if it's because she's pissed, or if it's a warning.

Felix talks nonstop the whole way to the condo. About nothing. It's all Reid can do to tell him not to shut up. Instead he presses his lips together and lets Felix's voice wash over him and then off his skin. He tries. His skin crawls and his stomach is in knots. Felix doesn't know about Joaquim, but Reid knows *Felix*. He knows what Felix will expect to happen, what always happens.

Reid shoves his way into the condo, takes his shoes off at the door, and heads straight for the kitchen. He rubs at his temples, where a headache is gathering. The sky over the bay is dark; the tumult of clouds tumbles toward them. The barometer must be dropping. Storms coming in always give him a headache.

"Take something for it," Felix says, putting a hand on Reid's shoulder. He twists out from under the touch. He picks up Felix's bags and takes them to his grandmother's room; no way he's sharing a room.

"This is where you sleep?" Felix drops onto the bed and bounces.

"No, I sleep in the other one."

"We're not sharing?" Felix grabs Reid's hand to tug him closer. Reid tugs his hand back.

"Felix," he says on a quiet sigh. He tries to put everything into the word, to will Felix to understand without asking. Reid wants the word alone to carry both kindness and endings. But Felix's eyebrows knit, and his shoulders set.

"You always do this, Reid!"

"*I* always do this?" Reid's kindness instantly dissolves. "I didn't ask you to come! I told you why I left home. I need to get away from…" he bites back the word *you* before it can leave. It wouldn't be fair to say it because, although he's a huge portion of the problem, Felix alone isn't why Reid's run away.

"C'mon, Reid," Felix says, standing up and stepping closer again. Reid forgot how much taller Felix is, what it felt like to be so tiny in someone else's hands. Joaquim is taller than Reid too, but Felix is bigger-boned, broader. "You know how this is gonna end. It always does. This wouldn't hurt as much if you didn't fight it."

Reid stares at him; disbelief courses through his body in cold waves. He stumbles back. His phone rings. It's the stupid ringtone he picked for Joaquim. Late into the night, long after Joaquim left, Reid kept himself up, curled in the delirious pleasure of having been with someone and not leaving (or being left) ashamed and sick at his own inability to say no. He recalled every moment, and the way Joaquim said his name, urgent and low and slipping around a moan.

And then, stupidly smitten, he spent thirty minutes picking out a ringtone.

"Who is that?" Felix's halfhearted gesture indicates he doesn't care. Reid narrows his eyes and steps into the hall.

"Hey," he says. Damn, his voice is unsteady already.

"Hey, you," Joaquim says. The warmth of his tone helps assuage a bit of that cold anger Felix brings out in him.

"Sorry, something c-came up." Reid presses his lips together hard and goes into his room. He shuts the door on Felix, who has followed him. His eyelashes are damp. *How strange.*

"Are you okay? What's going on?" Joaquim's voice goes from warmth to concern so quickly and oh—*Why am I crying?*

"I just, um," he clears his throat, but it's hopeless.

"What do you need, Reid, can I come—"

"No, no," Reid says quickly. That'll only make things worse. "It's..." He does not want to lie to Joaquim, but if Joaquim knows Felix is in his home right now, he'll either want to come over or ask for explanations Reid doesn't have. "It's a Felix thing." It's a small truth to settle on. But his breathing is going funny, and Felix has opened the door, wearing the strangest face. "Can I call you later?"

Joaquim is quiet. "Are you sure?"

"Yes, I promise. I'm fine."

"Okay," Joaquim says. He clearly doesn't believe him, but he accepts Reid's repeated promise to call him. When Reid hangs up, he has to turn away from Felix. His shoulders are shaking; in fact, his whole body is shaking, worse than at the store when just his hands shook. *What is the problem?* Sure, he doesn't want Felix here, and he's pissed and upset, but Reid knows an overreaction when he sees one, and right now he's not just seeing it. He's living it.

"Who was that?" Felix asks. Reid doesn't have the wherewithal to figure out his tone.

"Felix, why are you here?" Reid clenches his hands into fists and faces Felix. "I can't, I can't—"

"Hey, hey, breathe. Reid, *breathe*, man." Felix puts his hand between Reid's shoulders, and he can't pull away because he really does have to try to breathe. Reid puts his head in his hands and breathes, eyes on the carpet. He deciphers the pale gray threads, reads patterns. Once he's calm enough, he shifts away from Felix's hand, which is rubbing soothing circles on his back, and wipes his eyes. The heels of his hands come away black.

"You don't want me here," Felix says flatly when Reid can finally meet his eyes. Reid turns and, at the mirror in the bathroom, takes his contact lenses out slowly. He takes his time washing his face, leaving it naked and, when he puts his glasses on, young and vulnerable. He pushes past Felix and straight onto the porch. He doesn't bother with lights, but sits on one of his grandmother's hideous wicker armchairs.

Felix follows, pauses, and sits across from him. There's only the sound of Reid's breathing, whistling a little through sinus passages swollen from crying. He becomes aware of the sounds of night and then, last, of Felix's breathing.

"Felix," he starts. He has nothing else to say, no defense against this boy, whose indrawn shoulders make him look young too. This boy who's finally dropped the bravado, who wears his own vulnerability in his eyes and his hands and feet, which pigeon-toe in, shoelaces untied.

It's the shoes that firm Reid's spine: shoes he's seen countless times, tripped over in the middle of the night on his way out the door, and re-laced when Felix's fingers shook too hard to do it himself; shoes Reid bought with him one day when they'd gone on a sudden, pricey, stupid shopping spree; shoes that remind him of the hundreds of reasons this won't work, and the hundreds of reasons he needs to put a stop to it, for both of them.

"I'm sorry. You shouldn't be here. It's not good for me."

"For you?" Felix's eyes go hard. In the dark, they're the same black-brown as Joaquim's. But Reid knows every nuance, every line of Felix's face. Knows how his eyes look like melting chocolate in the sunlight. How bright they are sheened with tears. How his pupils swallow all color when he's on the verge of orgasm. Reid knows so many sides to this boy. Too many, because that knowledge makes it so much harder to hurt him.

"For me." Reid squeezes his hands between his knees and tries to remember everything Nancy's taught him to say and the scripts he's written, tries to form his own arguments so that Felix can't break through them. They are—*were*—always so entangled, it's all too easy to get tripped up.

"What about me?" Felix says softly. "I was on a bus for like thirty hours—"

"I didn't ask you to."

"But I needed it," Felix says. "*I* need you."

"I'm sorry, Felix," Reid says. "I am. But I have to. I can't take on any more. I have to worry about me first. I have to take care of me."

Felix snorts. "When you said that, when you were leaving, I didn't tell you what a selfish asshole you were being, because I didn't think you meant it."

"But I did," Reid says. The quieter he gets, the louder Felix argues.

"I didn't think you—you were supposed to come home!"

"I can't, Felix. I can't." Reid doesn't want to beg, but the part of him that's inexorably beholden to Felix does. He stands, and Felix stands. "I have to take care of myself. I'll never get better if I don't."

"Reid, you're not fooling anyone," Felix says, stopping him with a hand on his wrist.

"Who is there to fool?" Reid rolls his eyes. "That's the best part. No one gets to judge how I'm doing here. No one has to know."

"And that's good for you?" Felix always was fast, and Reid doesn't see the movement coming, but before he can move away, he's got a hand up Reid's shirt, pushing it up to reveal his abdomen and chest. Sucking in a huge breath, Reid pushes him away, hard, and pulls his shirt back down. Felix whispers, "Reid."

"Can you go?" Reid said, voice hoarse. He wraps his arms around himself. All of the high ground, all of the stock phrases he's stored carefully in an emergency cellar—they mean nothing now.

"Where?" Felix says, raking his hands through his hair. "I have nowhere to go."

"I don't know. A hotel? Until you can go home?"

Felix turns away.

"Felix," Reid says. He has to get him out of there. He *has* to.

"I don't have any money. I don't have anywhere else to go."

Last Reid knew, Felix was living with a few roommates in a shitty apartment near the University of Wisconsin-Eau Claire campus. The place had always smelled of yeast and unwashed men. Reid's parents didn't like Felix around, but Reid always let him in anyway. He hated that apartment.

"How much trouble are you in, exactly?"

"None."

Reid raises an eyebrow.

"Okay, just a little. I lost my job. My mom said I couldn't stay with her again."

"You can't stay here," Reid says flatly. "I'll give you money. We'll figure something out tomorrow. Somewhere for you to go. But you can't be here."

"Reid, baby," Felix tries.

"Don't." He should sound stronger, but he can't. "Don't do that. It's over, Felix. Really, *really* over. I'll help you if you need. But not like that."

Felix takes Reid by the wrist again. He wraps his fingers around it as if he is taking Reid's pulse, the thrumming rush of blood pushed by his scared and rapidly beating heart.

"Have you found someone else?" Felix asks. It's not a dare. At least, if it is, it's Felix daring himself to ask, not Reid to answer.

"Yeah," Reid says. He pulls his wrist away. "And I trust him. He won't hurt me. You and me, Felix, we're no good for each other."

"And if I promised you can trust me now—"

"I could never believe you again. How do you not get that?"

Felix finally drops his wrist. He shrugs and turns into the apartment. "Look, I promise I'll leave you alone. I'll stay in the other room. I swear. I just... I really don't want to be alone in a hotel somewhere I don't know."

Reid has fears, and lots of them, but he can name each and every one of Felix's as well. They push into his chest, and there isn't room for them all. He can't do that to Felix; because these fears, they speak loudly and with the weight of history under and over them.

"Fine." He goes to the closet and pulls out a towel for Felix. "I have to make a phone call."

Felix takes the towel. He steps into the bathroom and closes the door.

Reid takes a breath and then another. He rubs his eyes under his glasses and thinks, hard, about what he wants, and what's best for them both, about what it'll take to make the best of this situation.

Fifteen

JOAQUIM PICKS UP THE PHONE the second it rings, before he's checked to see that it's Reid.

"Hello?"

"Hey," Reid says. His voice is steadier than it was before, but lower. Sitting on his bed, Joaquim exhales and bunches the scratchy navy fabric of his blanket with his free hand.

"Can you talk? Is everything okay?"

"Um. No." Reid clears his throat. "I mean, no, everything's not really okay. But I can talk for a few."

"What's going on?"

"Joaquim, if I asked you for a big favor, could you, um—"

"Anything," Joaquim promises immediately. He's heartened to hear a small laugh.

"Don't say that without knowing if someone is about to ask you to stash a dead body, man."

"Good point," Joaquim says. If Reid can joke, surely things aren't too bad.

"I... please don't be mad, okay?"

"Why would I be mad?"

"Felix is here," Reid says, "I didn't ask him to come; he just showed up."

"Okay," Joaquim says, then adds, to calm him, "It's okay, Reid."

"Could you maybe come over?" Reid says then. "I don't want to be alone here with him."

"Why is he still there?"

"It's complicated," Reid says. Joaquim squints hard at the wall and starts to answer. *How complicated can it be after what Felix has done?* But he also remembers how often Reid has said that about his relationship with Felix. From what little Reid has told him, it sure seems so.

"Please. I don't know how to—"

"I'll come," Joaquim says. He'll need Bobby to cover for him. Nina will probably lend him her car and if not, he'll Uber. He's not sure what Reid needs. Does he need him to help get Felix to leave? Not to be alone? But Reid's remarkable vulnerability is hard for Joaquim to turn away from. While he's made himself vulnerable with Joaquim before, it's always been controlled, in small doses. This isn't that.

"Thank you." Reid breathes. He starts to speak and cuts himself off. The phone is muffled, and then Reid is back. "Text me when you leave?"

"Okay," Joaquim says. He's planning to leave right away, anyway.

Ten minutes to travel, five to get ready, five to procure a promise from Bobby and a car from Nina, and five to text Reid and ask for the gate code. Twenty-five minutes alone is all it takes, and yet, by the time Joaquim gets there, the composure Reid had on the phone is utterly gone. His eyes are slightly swollen under glasses Joaquim's never seen; his hair is a mess, and, with his arms tight and defensive around himself, his shoulders look bony. He's so young, and very real.

Before he's crossed the threshold, Joaquim pulls him out into the damp night under the wide open, star-scattered sky and holds him. If he had doubts about what the right moves were, they evaporate when Reid tucks his face into Joaquim's neck. He keeps his arms around himself; Joaquim holds him tight, thinking that between the two of them, maybe they'll hold this boy together.

"I'm sorry," Reid says into Joaquim's neck. "This is a little intense, isn't it?" He doesn't pull away. Joaquim's hands support this new shape of Reid's spine, tight and drawn in a language he hasn't had time to learn yet. Reid's breath hitches, once, and he pulls away. He turns away and wipes his eyes with one hand, trying to disguise the action.

"No, hey," Joaquim says. He puts a hand on Reid's arm and slides it down to his elbow. "It's all right."

Reid offers him a watery smile.

"Does he know I'm here?" Joaquim asks. He'd like to know what he's getting into.

"Yes. I have no idea. I don't know how he'll be. To you." The dark hides whatever crosses Reid's face, and Joaquim thinks that, no matter what, he must find a way to balance whatever harm is being done. No matter what happens, or how vile this man in Reid's home is, Joaquim must be calm.

"He's not violent in any—"

"No! No. Just difficult."

On Joaquim's worst dive, a married couple got into a huge fight. Neither tried to hide it; their yelling affected all of his divers. Anxiety and discomfort were palpable, and it took every ounce of Joaquim's composure to keep them together. In the water, many of them fell apart. Partners weren't communicating. Half his divers damaged the reef in some way. He had to ask the couple not to dive together, if they chose to dive at all, which was excruciating. The wife chose to dive and had fire in her eyes whenever she looked at her husband as she prepared. Joaquim partnered with her. Once in the water, her anger disappeared, replaced by a complete inability to remember basic skills. She panicked halfway into the descent, and nothing Joaquim did could reassure her. He understood how getting back into the boat right after going in must have tasted of defeat. Joaquim didn't know what went on after that; he had divers to attend to. Leaving her in Claude's hands, he went down to try to mitigate the damage his other divers were doing to the reef.

On the way home, the couple seemed to have worked things out. They sat together quietly by the bow with her head on his shoulder, her water-darkened blonde hair a riot in the wind. But the flavor of his divers' anxieties, of his own failure in holding everyone together, that stayed with him. Later, Tammy told him that he was great. He kept his composure, and that had gone a long way toward helping his divers.

Joaquim lists all the things he can remember from that day, how he kept calm and didn't crack. For Reid's sake, Joaquim will be anything he needs.

Felix is surprising. Like Reid, he sports piercings and lots of tattoos. His hair is plain brown, drying in tufts; it's probably lighter when completely dry. Despite the tattoos, and other than his height, he's unassuming. He's still wearing his shoes. *How rude!* Reid is so clean. Everything is always in order. The rudeness is either passive-aggression, defiant anger or inattentive carelessness.

Joaquim slips his shoes off. Instinct tells him he needs to follow Reid's lead.

"Felix, this is Joaquim." Dispiritedness tinges his voice. Joaquim risks putting a hand between his shoulder blades. Reid doesn't move away. Felix regards him for a long, assessing moment. Face blank, brown eyes unreadable, posture virtually unchanged, he's utterly still. Joaquim's own breathing has slowed to match the moment. Felix reads *defensive*, but something else too. When his mouth moves with his lips pressed together, Joaquim can see it. Sadness. *What did this boy come here expecting from Reid? Surely he had to know this wouldn't work?* Whatever push and pull they were tangled in at home, Joaquim figures that a cross-country trip away and rarely answered calls or texts would all speak for themselves.

"Hello," he says eventually.

"You're not from here," Felix says. Joaquim blinks. "You have an accent."

"Yes."

"He's Brazilian," Reid says. Felix's non sequitur must have signaled something, because some of the tension in Reid's body unravels under Joaquim's hand. Joaquim moves into the room, but sits on one of the heavy wood stools at the breakfast bar, keeping the dining room table between them, unwilling to sit on a couch. Joaquim isn't sure of his place until Reid looks at him. His eyes are wide and ask plainly for help. Reid sits next to him and doesn't miss Felix's sharp breath. Joaquim was skilled at reading people even before he became a dive instructor. It's a gift to his profession and it's only increased with his training.

"That's cool," Felix says, hollow-voiced. His empty eyes follow the movement of Reid taking Joaquim's hand. The action clearly hurts Felix somehow, but Joaquim isn't here for this man at all. Regardless of how palpable his emotions are, Joaquim can only focus on what Reid has told him, and the naked truth that this man not only hurt Reid, he also risked his health with lies.

The air conditioner kicks on. Even from outside its clatter and whir intrude on the silence. Cold air whooshes out of the vents, and Joaquim cannot think of a single thing to say. Reid and Felix stare at each other, speaking in a way Joaquim cannot begin to understand. He's not meant to and he doesn't want to. He wants to hold Reid, to hear his history, and to know how to best treat him. Joaquim knows enough, though, to recognize that Reid needs to work this out on his own. Reid's a grown man. A troubled one, maybe, but nonetheless, Joaquim's place isn't to fix things for him. Reid leaving Wisconsin to try to overcome his troubles speaks of strength and character.

"I'm going to bed," Felix says. "I hung the towel over the shower curtain; I wasn't sure where else to put it."

"Thank you," Reid says. Felix doesn't close the bedroom door with a slam, but with a click that makes Reid wince. "Well, at least there's the towel," he says quietly, to himself.

"The towel?"

"He knows how I am about, um, keeping things clean." Reid glances at Joaquim; he nods to keep Reid talking. "When he's really mad, he makes a mess on purpose."

The shoes weren't an oversight, then.

"I know it's weird, the clean thing. Or maybe it seems like it. It's just a thing that makes me... it helps." He stops talking and won't meet Joaquim's eyes. Joaquim stands. His hands on Reid's shoulders are meant to calm, to ground, to indicate that he's here, in this moment with him. The fabric of Reid's well-worn white undershirt bunches between his fingers. Reid looks down, winding and unwinding the drawstring to his plaid pajama pants around his finger. Reid seems so afraid—as if Joaquim can't tell that there's more to say, as if Joaquim might run away.

"I'm not leaving," he says. Reid's eyes widen. He pulls Joaquim forward by his hips and rests his forehead against Joaquim's sternum.

"There's a lot I should tell you. You say you aren't leaving, but if I did… it's more than you might think."

Joaquim kisses Reid's head. "And you're scared?"

Reid nods. His hair is a waxy mess. Joachim can't run his fingers through it, so he settles for running a palm over it and then cupping the back of Reid's neck. "I'm right here. And it's okay not to tell me anything right now."

"Thank you." Reid looks up. He stands and kisses Joaquim lightly. "For letting me keep you a little longer."

What does that mean?

"Can you stay?" Reid asks. Joaquim shouldn't, but he can't say no, not with Reid a barely held together mess of secrets and vulnerability.

"Yeah."

He follows Reid to the bedroom. Reid strips down to his undershirt and underwear. His shorts are striped neon, and, when Joaquim laughs, Reid's eyebrow does the thing—the *I don't get it* thing.

"I like your underwear." Joaquim strips down to his boring, unadorned black briefs. Reid shrugs and smiles. He pulls back the blankets, and Joaquim grabs the extra pillow from the other bed. Neither the pillow nor the men fit well on the twin bed, but Reid doesn't seem to mind the closeness.

"Tighter," he whispers when Joaquim spoons him from behind and wraps an arm around his waist. It's hot, but Reid pulls all the covers over them. "I like the weight," he says. He's half asleep, as if something has leeched the fight right out of him. In minutes he's asleep. Joaquim rearranges the covers so that he's not sweltering to death but is still holding Reid.

*   *   *

MORNING COMES VERY, VERY EARLY with the slam of a door that startles them both. Joaquim nearly rolls out of bed when his body jerks awake. Only Reid grabbing him keeps him in the bed.

"What the fuck?" Joaquim groans, covering his face.

"Felix," Reid says. His voice is hoarse with lingering sleep. He tucks his face against Joaquim's back and sighs. "He's an early riser. And passive-aggressive."

It's enough to make Joaquim light up with amusement, even when his body aches from sleeping so uncomfortably. "Time 'izt?"

Reid rolls to reach his phone on the nightstand behind him. Joaquim takes the opportunity to roll onto his back. Reid, having retrieved his phone, snuggles up to him and puts his head on Joaquim's chest. They both smell a little sweaty. Although Joaquim feels sticky and vaguely gross, he likes it on Reid. He smells like closeness, like familiarity. Joaquim shifts until they're comfortably plastered together. He likes this too: Reid's softness laid bare for him.

"Six-thirty," Reid says. His sigh is heavy.

"Fuck, I have to go soon." Joaquim makes no move to leave. "It's probably a good thing he's being an ass, because I forgot to set an alarm."

"You have to work today, huh?" Reid's palm is flat on Joaquim's stomach, as if to keep him there.

"Class. You gonna be okay?"

"Don't worry. We'll have more time for each other soon enough, right?" Reid says. Joaquim hums. He's not through with his internship until September. "Do you need to shower before you go?"

"Do you mind?"

Reid sits up. His hair is a riot, and his eyes are a little puffy, but his smile is sweet. "Not at all. I'll get you a towel." He locates his glasses on the floor. "I must have knocked them off while we were sleeping."

"You are lovely," Joaquim says, as surprised when the words come out as Reid's face shows he is.

"Shut up. I'm a mess," Reid says. Joaquim stops him from turning away with a palm to his cheek.

"I like your glasses." He sits up, propped on one hand. His eyes flicker to Reid's lips, and he traces Reid's cheekbone and his ear before kissing him under it. Now when Reid's hand touches his chest, the touch manifests his intention to keep Joaquim there for a very different reason.

"Do that some more, and maybe I'll believe you." Joaquim hears the teasing in Reid's voice. He kisses him again and then kisses down his throat. Caught and suspended in sleepy desire, there's nothing but them. Joaquim can keep Reid here, forgetting the world outside this door. Once they open it, Felix and whatever host of problems he's brought into Reid's life will be unavoidable.

Reid rolls on top of him and catches Joaquim's lips with his own; every kiss tastes like desperation, every touch demands escape, and, although Joaquim doesn't have the time, he's dizzyingly hard in minutes. Reid's body rolls easily against his, a sensual rocking and receding that's impossible not to get lost in. Joaquim breaks out of another kiss, a bruising kiss, and gasps Reid's name. Reid is impossibly here and real in his arms, but not nearly close enough. Joaquim fumbles with Reid's clothes and Reid impatiently pushes his hands away and pulls their underwear down with fumbling hands. Reid is fire in his arms, whimpering and shaking, and, caught in it, Joaquim comes in seconds.

"Fuck," he pants while Reid rolls off of him. "I think I may have been a little too loud."

"Who fucking cares," Reid says. From his laundry basket, he grabs a shirt, which he tosses to Joaquim. He strips his own shirt and grabs another; Joaquim can't read his expression since his back is turned.

"Reid, you didn't do that on purpose, did you?" *Because that would be pretty fucking passive-aggressive of you.*

"No," Reid says, sitting on the bed next to him. His face is nothing but open, even a little hurt. "I wouldn't do that. Well, maybe in the past. But not getting sucked into that dynamic with Felix is something I've worked on. I promise. That was just… that was all you." Reid meets his eyes. "You make me forget so easily. It's like there's nothing but you."

Joaquim doesn't speak. He lets Reid touch his cheek and hopes, very deeply, that Reid can see on his face how much that means. *Reid—oh, this boy; so much, too much, and so soon.*

"You need a shower," Reid whispers.

"You do too," Joaquim points out. Reid shakes his head.

"I think that might be a little too much. For him. Salt in the wound and all."

"Shit, sorry. I wasn't even thinking—"

Reid kisses him. "Don't worry, I know. Let me get you a towel."

Sixteen

FELIX IS NOWHERE TO BE seen when they emerge from the bedroom. Coffee is brewed. It's either an olive branch or yet another passive-aggressive move. Reid doesn't much care, because there is coffee in his mug and he's still warm from his morning with Joaquim. The shower starts, and Reid takes his coffee out onto the porch. He's tempted to walk down to the water to see if Felix is there. Other than wandering the condo grounds, he can't think where else Felix would go. It might be too much to hope he's actually left.

Alone with the morning and his coffee, Reid acknowledges something he would never tell Joaquim: He doesn't want Felix to be gone, not on the lingering notes from the night before and this morning. No matter how much he changes, he's tied to Felix. It's something like love, something like guilt, something sown in deep history. Maybe one day they'll be ready for a goodbye that's more than geographic space and the silence between texts. Some part of Reid can't help but hope for a healthy friendship or a peaceful resolution. Rachel insists that this is why he can't be free of Felix, that Reid is holding on for the impossible.

Felix appears, ascending from the beach. Reid can't quite reconcile this shadow Felix, the ghost of so many aches, with the one with plain brown hair and a green shirt and hideous tan cargo shorts. He doesn't greet Reid when he opens the screen door, but he does sit with him. They respect the quiet together. Reid doesn't hide that he's watching Felix; he doesn't turn away when Felix catches his eye. Evaluating his reactions, Reid is relieved by the utter lack of attraction this boy has for him now. He doesn't want Felix in the least.

What he does want is for Felix to stop coming back to him. He wants them to be at rest. Felix may not be resigned, but he might be at peace with Reid's decision to break things off. Calling Joaquim last night served many purposes. Reid needed that grounding; later, he'll examine how quickly he acknowledges the way Joaquim provides that. It also sent a clear message to Felix: *This is over. I've moved on.* Perhaps it's not the nicest way to handle things. Maybe he used both Felix and Joaquim to set himself apart. Reid hopes, though, that for once, or finally, both he and Felix will feel the seismic shift in their relationship. They can learn how to build from there.

In the condo, Joaquim emerges from the bathroom. His hair is still wet, messy, and black. Reid turns to offer him a smile; uncertainty is written across Joaquim's face. Reid crosses to him.

"There's coffee," he says, quietly. "I can put some in a to-go mug for you."

Joaquim evaluates him before nodding. "That would be great." Reid can't say what Joaquim has gotten from the assessment, but he doesn't seem upset with Reid.

Felix stays on the porch.

"Will you be okay? How are you going to get him to—"

"Don't worry," Reid interrupts. "I can handle this."

Joaquim's face clearly states that he doesn't trust this. Reid swallows a seed of frustration. He'd been a mess when he called Joaquim last night. Of course Joaquim is worried.

"Listen," he continues. "I was a mess last night. He took me by surprise. And yeah…" He checks to make sure Felix can't see him. "…I don't want him here. It's not good for me. But I can handle this."

Joaquim's eyebrows draw together. "What do you mean it's not good for you?"

Fuck. Think fast. "Would your ex showing up out of nowhere be good for you?"

"Okay. I see what you're saying. I'm not trying to make you feel like you can't handle this. Please just call if you need me?"

"You have class today, right?" He's not sure why he doesn't want to promise. *Yeah, sometimes I fail, but everyone does, right?*

"Yeah, and a night dive."

"Don't look upset. That's awesome. A night dive sounds so cool." Reid touches the line between Joaquim's eyebrows lightly and rises on his toes to kiss him. "Call me when you're done, okay? I wanna hear all about it."

When Joaquim gathers him in, Reid lets himself go, puts his head on Joaquim's shoulder, and sighs. He smells like Reid's bath products; it's not bad, but it's not Joaquim's smell.

A thump and a cleared throat announce Felix. "Sorry, didn't mean to intrude. I just wanted more coffee."

Like hell you did. Reid steps away from Joaquim slowly. He wouldn't have minded that hug lasting longer, but the clock tells him Joaquim is dangerously close to late. Felix's face is disarmingly neutral, almost blank. Reid recognizes the face Felix wears when people hurt him and he can't expose himself by showing pain. He *won't.*

A small pang bursts, but Reid has to swallow. *I'm not doing anything wrong. I set limits.* Over and over he's read about the dynamics of their relationship. Changing codependence with someone who refuses to do so as well is hard. Reminding himself that Felix was unable to respect what Reid asked for doesn't mean Reid has to feel guilty or upset.

"Go ahead," Joaquim says, graciously. He puts his own mug down and, at the door, tugs his shoes on.

"No, here." Reid presses the to-go mug into his hands. "You'll give it back when I see you again."

Joaquim looks at Felix, who is blatantly staring at them. Reid's sigh comes from deep in his belly. "Come on."

Out on the small patio, the sun is brighter. Reid doesn't drop Joaquim's hand, but tugs him into his arms, hugs him, and gives him a small kiss.

"Careful, you'll scandalize the old ladies," Joaquim says, lips smiling against Reid's. Reid cups Joaquim's face. His eyes are warm and even in the sunlight. His lips, with their perfect cupid's bow, and his lovely brown skin tug at Reid; he's beautiful and charming and, right now, inexplicably, his. He kisses Joaquim again, more slowly.

"I don't give a fuck," he whispers.

"I'll call you," Joaquim says as he opens his car door. Reid nods, already backing up, hand on the doorknob. The sunlight is so clean; the sky is scattered with puffy, perfect white clouds. Even when Joaquim's car has gone around the corner and is hidden by the trees, Reid lingers. Tension presses through the door behind him. He doesn't want to go back to the anxiety and fear and that stupid ache Felix inspires, not when he's found something like this. Reid's struggles still exist here, in this place, in so many ways, but nothing here has been touched by home; his secret history is tucked away, unknown. It's been easier to manage, even at his worst, than his life in Eau Claire.

Felix is on the couch flipping through the channels.

"Where's the History channel?" he asks. Felix has a penchant for war documentaries. Fondness mixes with everything else inside Reid.

"I have no idea," Reid says. He sits, too, but in an armchair, nowhere close to Felix. "I almost never watch TV, to be honest."

"Really?" Felix raises an eyebrow, and Reid shrugs. Felix might be the only person in Reid's life who knows how intensely Reid can binge-watch TV shows. He used to tease Reid incessantly about some of them, but in Reid's room he was happy enough to curl up, watch along, and let the semi-dark hold them. They never had to talk, then. They could exist together in a temporary bubble. But something always popped it: Reid's parents, or the incessant ring of Felix's phone as his parents called him, or they themselves, with the stupid fights they'd have.

"I like how quiet it can be here," Reid says. "The sound of the water."

"This doesn't seem like you, Reid. What about concerts? There can't be any good places to see live music here."

Reid shakes his head. It's strange, having someone else remind him of who he is. Reid's always loved concerts, loved getting lost in a crowd of people absorbing and experiencing the same moment, the same sounds. Reid used to go and see musicians and bands he'd never heard of. Here, he hasn't missed that at all. Reid doesn't want to lose such pleasures. He just doesn't want them right now.

"Don't you get lonely?" Felix curls a leg up on the couch and turns toward Reid.

Reid wishes Felix would mute the TV. "Maybe, sometimes." Reid has to think about it. Even loneliness tastes better here. "I have a job, though. I took diving classes—"

"That how you met him?"

"Yeah," Reid says, working hard to keep any fondness out of his voice. "It's not just that. I don't have to explain myself to anyone here. Or, I didn't." Reid doesn't mention his slips; talking to his group doesn't count. Felix wouldn't understand. He doesn't think he needs therapy. He always told Reid that their problems weren't remotely the same. Reid can't argue with that. After all, no one ever hospitalized Felix or sent him away. Reid understands that their need for help isn't mutually exclusive. Just because Reid's the more obvious mess doesn't mean Felix isn't a mess as well. Felix absolutely refuses to acknowledge this.

"Which means you haven't told him anything," Felix concludes.

Reid's face flushes. He picks up a throw pillow. Its fringed edges feel good running between his fingers.

"How on earth are you keeping cutting from him when you're fucking him?"

"Shut up," Reid snaps. "That is *so* not your business."

"You fucked him this morning when I was right here! God, that was such a dick move, Reid."

"Okay," Reid says. He takes a few deep breaths, trying to remain calm, even when a familiar anger eats at him. "That's fair. I didn't—it wasn't on purpose or anything. For you to hear." What more can he say? Any explanation would be unkind. Even less kind. *I couldn't help myself? It's so good, when I'm with him; nothing's ever been like this?*

"What the fuck ever." Felix picks up the remote to snap the TV off and tosses it back on the couch. His movements are jerky, and his eyes are bright.

"No, really," Reid says. "I'm not trying to hurt you, Felix. I promise. When I told you I was leaving, you didn't believe me. You told me I couldn't do it and that I wouldn't make it."

Felix looks away.

"But I *did* do it. I am doing it. I am moving on and I'm sorry that you can't do the same."

"I could if I wanted to," Felix says.

Reid almost scoffs but controls himself in time. "Felix, two people have to want to be in a relationship for it to work."

"I don't mean that. God, don't patronize me!"

"I'm not trying to! But I don't know what else to say. Dude, I wish this could be easier for you. For us. But it's not."

"You said we would still be friends." Felix's voice cracks, and no matter how Reid tries to harden his heart, it isn't.

"And then you kissed me, and then we fucked, and after that you said being together was inevitable. That's how it always went. How else could our relationship ever go, when we couldn't let *each other* go?" Reid asks.

Felix presses his fingers under his eyes, catching tears before they fall. Reid wants so much to hug him. Hurting Felix is like hurting himself. They're too tied together, still, but Felix can't stay here long. He wasn't lying when he told Joaquim that Felix wasn't good for him.

"Look, Felix. I wish I could have it both ways. You in my life. Me getting better. Us being friends. But right now, it can't be that way."

"Are you going to tell him?" Felix asks again. Reid blinks, thrown off by the sudden redirection of the conversation.

"Tell him what?"

"That guy—" Felix jerks a thumb toward the door. "Seriously, can you honestly say that you'll ever tell him everything?"

"What's your point?"

"How will it ever be real with someone when they don't really know you?"

"I don't see how this is your business," Reid says again. He's been wondering that very thing ever since their first date. He's worked pretty hard to hide everything from Joaquim. But this morning, in the sunlight, Joaquim's kiss is his to keep. Reid knows in his heart that if he wants to keep more than that, he'll have to reveal secrets.

"Don't." He stops Felix as he's about to speak. "Don't you dare tell me I can't. I'm so tired of everyone telling me what I'm incapable of, of them not trusting me, not thinking I know what's best for myself. This is *mine* to figure out, Felix."

"Do you really think I don't believe in you?" The question seems genuine.

"I think you *think* you do. But you act like you don't. And your actions speak louder. They hurt more."

Felix stands suddenly and pulls his phone out of his pants.

"What are you doing?" Reid stands too.

"Getting an Uber. Getting out of here."

Reid gets to his feet and puts a hand on Felix's arm. Felix shrugs it off.

"It's okay, Reid. I guess this..." He gestures around them, and Reid has no idea if he means this place, Reid living here, or their current situation.

"This?"

"I don't want to lose you completely either. I don't, I'm sorry if I made you feel like that. I am. I'm trying to figure out my shit too."

"You are?" Reid asks. They've never gotten to this point in any conversation.

"Yeah. And I wanted to do it with you. But that's not right, is it?"

"Wanting to be with me?"

"Thinking it had to be with you. Assuming that's what you would need, is me to help you."

Reid can't say anything, because Felix is right to leave. Months ago, Reid would have jumped at the chance to work things out together. Months ago, he didn't know that there was no way for them to get better with each other.

"I guess," Felix says, and this time he doesn't catch his tears fast enough, "I wasn't listening to you. But I am now. I'm going to show you that I can do this."

Reid catches Felix's wrist and, against his better judgment, hugs him. He won't take it further than that. To his surprise, Felix doesn't try to persuade him. Felix inhales, as if to capture a memory, to remind himself of things that are familiar. Reid lets him. Despite the pain of having to hurt Felix, of having to keep cutting the cords between them, Reid finally feels in his gut what's been there all along. He's free. It's freedom that's come with a price, freedom he has to keep working at.

Happiness is his to capture, and he can't have it when he's tied to Felix. He hopes that Felix understands that now, too. It isn't only that Felix isn't good for him. Reid isn't good for Felix either.

Felix packs what little he's brought with him while he waits for his ride.

"Where will you go?" Reid asks.

"I'll figure something out. Don't worry."

"How could I not?" Reid asks. "I still care."

"Yeah," Felix smiles. It's small and forced. "I'll text you wherever I end up and let you know I'm okay."

"Do you need money?" Reid asks. Felix presses his lips together, and Reid rushes to assuage the offence. "I have extra. It's not a big deal; just…" All the work he's done, will this undo it? "…let me do this one last thing for you. Please?"

Felix puts his bag on the stool at the breakfast bar. His back is turned to Reid, who can't read his face, but sees the line of his shoulders rise and fall as he takes deep breaths.

"Okay," he says, almost whispering. "I don't want to, but I have to. I don't have any. Don't wanna have to earn it in any of the bad ways."

It's a terrible joke. Reid goes to the bedroom and takes out the envelope where he keeps money. It's not the most responsible place for it, but he's been lazy about opening a bank account.

"Here." He doesn't offer any more and he doesn't offer to give him more if Felix needs it.

He does hug Felix again when he leaves; he kisses him on the cheek and looks into his eyes when he says goodbye. When the door of the black sedan idling in the lot slams shut, Reid knows the goodbye is somewhere deeper, in a space where he finally trusts himself, perhaps not perfectly and in a small measure. It's there, though; he'll hold on to that for a long time, because it's trust, but also hope.

Seventeen

Joaquim cannot get Reid off his mind all day. His preoccupation affects his work, and Mike has to pull him aside more than once to remind him to get his head in the right space. He takes a moment on his lunch break to text Reid and then his sister. His workmates are nice enough, but the more intense his relationship with Reid has gotten, the less comfortable he's felt talking to any of them, even Nina. Joaquim always misses his family and carries homesickness with him. It aches, usually faintly, but constantly. Today it's more intense.

Joaquim: *Can we talk tonight? It'll be late.*

He's eaten most of his lunch before Sofia replies. Reid hasn't responded either.

Sofia: *Sure. All okay?*

Joaquim: *Sure, I guess.*

Joaquim frowns.

Joaquim: *IDK. Boy issues.*

Sofia: *LOL, finally.*

His issues aren't really the laughing kind, but he doesn't want to explain over text. His lunch is over anyway.

Joaquim: *I'll call when I'm done for the day. Night dive. Te amo.*

Sofia: *You too.*

Joaquim tucks his phone away and tosses his paper plate into a nearby garbage can.

"You okay?" Bobby asks, mouth full.

"Fine," Joaquim responds. Something makes Joaquim want to protect Reid and protect how they will think of him.

AFTER THE LATE DIVE, JOAQUIM is pleasantly tired and less weighed down by the events of last night. He's still worried about Reid, but mostly he's curious. He tries calling him, but gets no answer. He doesn't get a text back either.

Joaquim: *Seriously, are you okay?*

He texts again half an hour later, after he's showered and put on his most comfortable sweats. He's on his bed, cross-legged, trying not to stare at his phone and will it to buzz. Finally, he gives in and calls Sofia.

"Oi, irmão," she says.

"SoSo." Joaquim rests his back against the wall. He hasn't talked to her in a while. He's been too busy with work and with Reid.

"Boy troubles, hmm?" Sofia is disarmingly direct. "Quim, you've been holding out on me. There's a boy?"

"Well." He clears his throat. "It's new."

"How new? And already troubles?"

"A few dates new. It's complicated." He leaves out the blistering-hot sex part.

"Isn't that the definition of boy troubles? It's not like you to do boy troubles, carinho."

"I really like him." He means it too. He's in too fast and too soon, but he's connected to Reid. So close to love. Too close.

"Tell me about him, then."

"We met when he did a dive class. He's new to the Keys. He came to take care of his grandmother's condo." Joaquim isn't dumb; Reid's story is a cover. That condo development has groundskeepers. "He's sweet but complicated. Sometimes he's open, but he's unpredictable. Moody sometimes."

"Not everyone is as laid-back as you," Sofia points out.

"True. Anyway, the issue is more that his ex showed up yesterday. Out of nowhere. He's done stuff to hurt Reid. It was an ugly breakup."

"And he just showed up? Where is this boy from?"

"Wisconsin," Joaquim says. "I know, right?"

"That's a long way to come to show up on your ex's doorstep. What's the story?"

Joaquim only knows the little that Reid has told him, a story he's hesitant to share. "Last night, Reid called me. He was a mess; it was, I don't know… Is it weird that a part of me likes that he called me then?"

"No. Not if you really like him. That means he trusts you, right?"

"That's what I think." Joaquim closes his eyes. "But this morning, this guy, Felix, was still there. And when I asked if Reid was going to be okay, because he wasn't last night, he got upset with me. Not like, yelling. But he was definitely upset."

"Did you leave it like that?"

"No, actually." Joaquim stops. Reid's rapid shift in demeanor and the knowledge that he was leaving him alone with Felix is what had stayed with Joaquim. "He was happy? Sweet. When I left. He hasn't answered my calls or texts, and he said we'd talk tonight. But SoSo, there's more to his story with this guy. I can tell. But he hasn't told me."

"Hmm."

"I don't know what to do. I want to know if that guy is still there. I can't tell if I'm jealous or worried or confused."

"Can't you be all of them, bebê?"

"I guess."

"Quim," she says, and her voice is warm; he closes his eyes and absorbs it. He wishes he was with her, laid out on her bed and talking about his problems while she sits on her spinning desk chair making fun of him and giving him advice at the same time. "It sounds like you really like him anyway. You can't make him call you. Yesterday, he let you in, right?"

"Yeah," Joaquim says.

"Remember that part, then. If there's more for him to tell, you have to wait and hope he tells you. I know you're serious about this, even if you haven't said so. And if *he* is serious, he'll tell you."

Joaquim thinks this over. Reid is complicated, but he's special. There are many, many sides to this boy, and he's barely scratched the surface. And he can't help it; he does want more: more of Reid, more of his story, more between them.

"Obrigado, lindeza," he thanks her.

"It's late for you," she says. "Email me tomorrow with an update, okay?"

"Okay," he says. It's so long until he will get to visit her. "Beijos."

"Pra você também."

He puts the phone down and checks the clock. It's late, and he still has no response from Reid. Complicated, he told Sofia, but the truth is that he is too—or at least his feelings are, because right now he's a mess of annoyed, worried, and crazy for a boy who won't answer a fucking text.

Joaquim plugs in his phone and brushes his teeth. When he comes back, Bobby is in the room. Joaquim has no idea where he's been, but he's too tired for small talk. He curls up in his bed after turning his light out. Bobby is gaming; he turns off his light too, but the clacking of his keyboard follows Joaquim into bed. It's hard to turn off his brain; he swallows more annoyance.

*   *   *

JOAQUIM WAKES TO HIS PHONE buzzing. It's early—6:37 a.m. according to his clock—but he checks his texts anyway.

Reid: *I'm so sorry*

Reid: *I fell asleep. I must have been more tired than I thought*

Reid: *Pls don't be mad*

Joaquim squints at the phone. He can hardly blame Reid for that; he was tired too.

Joaquim: *I was worried, are you okay?*

Joaquim stares at the message, then remembers Reid telling him he can take care of himself. Concern is still okay, right? After forty seconds of internal debate, he sends it anyway.

Reid: *Fine*

Fuck, are they back to one word answers? Last time this meant Reid was upset.

Joaquim's alarm is set for eight, because he is working the shop today. If all he is going to get from Reid is one-word answers, then Reid is going to get the silence of Joaquim going back to sleep. He silences his phone and burrows back into the covers for another hour of sleep.

He doesn't check his phone until he's on his way to the shop. He has a string of texts from Reid. *Fuck.*

Reid: *Sorry my mom called. Could not get her to stop talking*

Reid: *This is why I avoid phone calls*

Reid: *Well, not yours.*

Reid: *Hello?*

Reid: *Damn you're getting ready for work prob*

Reid: *Listen, I just want to be sure u know I'm really sorry abt last night. When's ur nxt day off? Wanna do sth fun? Go to a club and hang out nxt day?*

Joaquim smiles at the last one; after the intense heaviness of the last few days, that sounds nice.

Joaquim: *Sorry I fell back asleep*

White lies intended to not drag misunderstandings into the light are all right, right?

Joaquim: *That sounds great. Wanna go on Sunday? I have Monday off.*

Reid: *Yes!*

Reid: *That sounded way too enthusiastic didn't it?*

Joaquim: *No, it was the perfect amount.*

Joaquim gazes stupidly at his phone before pocketing it and clocking in at the register.

*   *   *

THE DAYS BETWEEN MAKING PLANS and their date are interminable. Joaquim has a lot more boring shit to do than usual and fewer dives, which is a fucking shame; they're the best way to pass time. In all fairness, he could hardly call diving passing time, since it's his favorite thing to do. His only distractions are texts and phone calls with Reid, usually recalling memories of the times they've been together.

After three days without seeing Reid, Joaquim wants to call him and tell him how much he misses him, but anyone in the dorm could hear him, so he settles for texting.

Joaquim: *Is it weird to say I miss you? I'm craving kisses ;)*

It dawns on him that this would be the opening salvo for sexting rather than texting; he goes into the bathroom. *The scene of the crime.* He texts Reid, shaking his head at himself even as he rubs the palm of his hand against his dick through his pants. He's never sexted before, so he can't be blamed for poor understanding of the logistics of typing and jerking off, and therefore accidentally coming all over the floor. He types with shaking fingers after he's come down.

Joaquim: *That was amazing, but I feel bad for everyone else*

Reid: *Why? Were u loud?*

Joaquim: *Fuck I hope not. No, I came on the floor in our bathroom*

Reid: *OMG no. Laughing so hard right now.*

Joaquim: *Fuck off ;)*

Reid: *Sorry, not sorry. Worth it?*

Joaquim is trying to clean the floor while Reid texts him.

Joaquim: *Hell yeah*

Once all is clean, and Joaquim is put together enough, he makes his way back to his room. That was awesome and weird and complicated, but doesn't remotely replace having Reid with him.

He texts again before he can think it through.

Joaquim: *I miss you*

Joaquim's heart rate spikes again, but for a completely different reason.

Reid: *I miss you too*

⚹   ⚹   ⚹

"OH MY GOD, HI," REID says when Joaquim slips into his car. "You look fucking amazing."

"Thanks," Joaquim says. His return compliment is cut off by Reid's mouth. Reid's hand comes around his neck and pulls him in and the kiss is hungry, mirroring Joaquim's own insatiable desire for Reid. Joaquim pushes into the kiss and grabs Reid's thigh. Surprised by the feel of skin, he looks down.

"You're wearing shorts!"

"Shut up and keep kissing me," Reid demands and makes a breathless sound Joaquim could live on when Joaquim slips two fingers under the hem of said shorts. "Or just keep—"

"Reid, we're in the parking lot." Joaquim pulls his hand away reluctantly. Reid's eyes flutter open. He adjusts himself in his shorts and sends Joaquim a flirtatious sideways look that brings his breath up short. "Let's go have some fun before I tell you to fuck all this and take me home."

"The idea has merits." Reid's eyes and smile are so bright. The sunset lights his hair; with his ice-blue, dark-lined eyes, Reid is otherworldly—nontraditionally beautiful, beautiful in his contradictions. "But I wanna dance."

"Lead the way," Joaquim says, buckling himself in. "What?" he says when Reid doesn't start driving.

"You need to tell me where to go, loser," Reid says, a smile crinkling his eyes.

"Get on the highway and head toward Isla Morada," he says. When Reid complies, Joaquim puts his hand back on Reid's thigh. He doesn't grab or stroke, but keeps his palm there like a promise and a reminder.

"Fuck," Reid says under his breath, and Joaquim smirks.

Eighteen

JOAQUIM IS SENSUAL AND LOOSE on the dance floor. Under his calm and quiet, he is at ease with sex and his own body. Reid loves that. That ease only comes to Reid in spurts and more often when he drinks. He's not drinking tonight; he's pretty sure he could if he wanted to, despite being underage. He has no desire to fuck up the night, to blur any of the moments when their bodies press together and Joaquim's smile is brighter than anything else in the room. Joaquim's fingers hook through the belt loops of Reid's brand new shorts; under Reid's palms and through the thin material of his tank top, Joaquim's nipples are hard. Reid rolls his body against Joaquim's. He expects a response, but not Joaquim biting his lip, hard. Harsh breath is so hot between them.

"You play dirty," he says into Reid's ear, then slips a hand into the pocket of his shorts and pulls him closer.

"Isn't dirty the point?" Reid says back. It's so loud in the club they're nearly shouting; in this bubble, just them in a sweating, throbbing, dim and glitter-lit moment, it's like whispering. He wants Joaquim to take him hard and bruising-delicious. Asking to get out of the club is on the tip of his tongue; but when he sucks a kiss onto Joaquim's neck and catches a smirk on someone else's face dancing behind him, he realizes how much he loves the taste of anticipation.

"Please tell me you'll fuck me tonight," Reid says.

"Oh, yeah," Joaquim stays, all wide smile and heat.

The music changes, and so does the crowd's dancing. Reid pulls back and grabs Joaquim's hips in his hands when he turns away. Joaquim has his arms in the air; he's beautifully lost in this moment. Reid closes his eyes, and the air is thick and heady; he is safe in this space, and it's fucking fun. He chooses to lose himself to the moment. He's never felt this way. Promises he brought from Eau Claire, about the new boy he'd make himself, are tangibly achievable if only he turns off his mind.

And so he does.

"COME ON," JOAQUIM PULLS THE back of Reid's tank top when Reid doesn't get out of the car fast enough.

"Joaquim," Reid protests. "I bought some stuff; I wanna grab it." Joaquim's hands are on Reid's ass as he bends over to retrieve the grocery bag in the backseat. Desperation followed them from the club all the way home, especially with Joaquim's hands all over him *while driving*. Reid's car is a two-door, so he has to pull the driver's seat forward to get the bag. When he stands, he lets Joaquim press him against the car and kiss him.

"Trust me, you want me to grab this," Reid says when Joaquim pulls away. He takes Joaquim's hand and pulls him to the condo. Joaquim is biting and sucking at the back of his neck as Reid unlocks the door. And while he senses that Joaquim would do this anywhere in the condo, including at the front door, Reid pulls him to the bedroom.

Joaquim shuts the door behind them. Reid wants to joke about it—who's going to catch them?—but then he turns the lights on and pushes Reid against the door. His hands are already at the button of Reid's shorts. Panic cuts through Reid's desire. He doesn't want to lose this, the wave of easy wanting, of not over-thinking, of *being*.

He turns the lights off.

Joaquim stops, and Reid stills.

"Please?" Reid is asking for more than just having the lights off: he's asking for the absence of questions, for Joaquim to keep touching him as if he's unbroken, is not fragile, and has beautiful, unmarred skin.

"Sure," Joaquim says. Reid kisses him hard and asks with his touch for Joaquim to take him back to where they were. The bag he's been holding falls to the floor.

"Reid, what's in the bag?" Joaquim asks against the skin of Reid's neck that he's marking up pretty well.

"Lube. Condoms. Fuck, *oh*—do not stop," he begs when Joaquim starts to pull away. "Fuck me like you mean it, J," he speaks into the darkness, into the space where it's just the two of them and unbreakable pleasure.

"I always fuck like I mean it." Joaquim's got Reid's shorts off now and helps get Reid's shirt off.

"Don't be gentle." Reid strips Joaquim without finesse. When Joaquim pushes him toward the bed, Reid gives in easily. He closes his eyes and lets Joaquim saturate his senses. His touch, unhesitating, searing, and intimate, curls deep inside. It's almost like time loss, riding the pain and pleasure of being manhandled and owned; Reid bites his arm to muffle his cries.

"Stop. I want to hear you," Joaquim says. Reid turns his head and moans.

"Don't stop," he says, "even if it sounds like you're hurting me, you're not."

"Tell me if it's too much," Joaquim says.

Nothing could be, not with you. Reid bites his lip, grabs the comforter under his fingers tightly and gives himself over to his body completely.

*   *   *

REID WAKES BEFORE JOAQUIM AS the sun is coming up. Unless he's in a low part of a mood cycle, Reid's body clock is always set early. Some days he makes himself fall back asleep. It's always fitful sleep, but the choice is the best part. Here, he's the one in charge of all of his choices.

Today he's grateful for his sleep rhythms, because he's stark naked and plastered against Joaquim's overheated body. He eases away so as not to wake Joaquim. The floor is littered with their clothes; he grabs the first shirt he finds and his own underwear and puts them on quickly. Joaquim must have questions now, but, with his body aching deliciously and his skin marked from Joaquim's fingers and teeth, Reid wants to put that conversation off.

As silently as possible, Reid pulls clean clothes from his drawers and works his way to the shower, hoping the whole time that Joaquim isn't the kind of guy who'll pop into a shower with someone without asking.

Joaquim is still asleep when Reid comes back to the room. He's only half covered by the sheet and, in the light, Reid appreciates the time to *look*. Joaquim's skin is beautiful, warm brown, smooth and tempting from ankle to shoulder. His ass is perfect, round and tight. Reid wants—wants so badly—but rather than wake Joaquim with touches that might lead elsewhere, he lies next to him and runs fingers through Joaquim's hair.

Joaquim wakes slowly, sleepy-eyed, lashes fluttering open and then closed again. He hums and wiggles closer, encouraging Reid's fingers to keep playing with his hair.

"Morning," he says, his voice sleep-scratchy and low.

"Hey," Reid whispers. "Wanna go to Sue's for breakfast?" Sue's Diner is one of the few places Reid patronizes consistently.

"Sure. In a minute." Joaquim's eyes close again. He wraps an arm around Reid and burrows into him.

"You're very sweet half asleep, you know?" Reid says.

"No, I didn't. Good to know, though." Joaquim's voice is muffled against Reid's chest. "Another tool in my arsenal."

"Arsenal?"

"Evil plan to bring you down."

"Down where?" Reid jokes.

"No idea. Just want you is all."

Reid runs his fingers through Joaquim's hair again. "Don't worry. You've got me."

Joaquim is still sleepy at the diner until he gets coffee into him. "You're way too awake in the morning," he informs Reid, as if this is news.

"Can't help it. I'm usually an early riser," Reid says. He scans the menu, even though he always orders the same thing. Reid likes habit. He's had a hard time establishing structure and schedule since he came to the Keys, but little moments like this, knowing exactly what he wants and knowing he'll get it, help him.

"Usually?" Joaquim doesn't look at the menu "I'm never an early riser unless forced."

"It's not too bad. I get to see a lot of sunrises."

Joaquim doesn't respond, although he does take in Reid's appearance. It's not uncomfortable, but Reid is hyperaware that Joaquim is sussing him out. Their waitress comes to take their order, breaking the moment apart.

Reid's phone rings while they're giving their orders. Reid silences it and, after the waitress leaves, checks the caller ID, and rolls his eyes.

"Do you need to call them back?" Joaquim asks.

"No, it's my mom," Reid says.

"You gonna call her later?" They have plans to spend the day together, since it's Joaquim's day off.

"No. Well, not today. I'm on a mom break."

"Really?" Joaquim tears himself away from the coffee he's been doctoring very intently. Reid isn't sure if his tone implies censure, confusion, or genuine curiosity.

"You get along with your mom, don't you?" Reid asks.

"I get along with my whole family." Joaquim takes a sip of his coffee, shakes his head, and reaches for more creamer. Reid thinks Joaquim might be drinking creamer with some coffee in it, not the other way around. But what does he know? Coffee makes Reid jittery; it makes him feel too much like being in that space between rapid mood swings.

"I miss them a lot," Joaquim says. Chin in hand, elbow on the table, Joaquim shares vulnerability so easily. Is this trust a deliberate choice, or has Joaquim never had to guard his secrets? Vulnerability isn't something Reid does well. It opens the door for people to hurt you or take advantage of you.

"Do you get to see them?" Reid says.

"Yeah. Holidays and stuff. In a few months, I'm going home." Joaquim's expression draws Reid's inexorably; it's reflexive, and Reid has no desire to break the connection.

THEY LINGER OVER BREAKFAST LONG enough that the sun is bright and hot when they emerge. In the car, Reid slips on sunglasses; they're too big and ridiculous but only cost four dollars.

Joaquim pokes fun when he sees them.

"I lose my sunglasses a lot." Reid shrugs. His cheeks heat up. "So I usually don't care what they look like. They were cheap."

"They're delightful," Joaquim counters. He opens the window to let out the built-up heat. Comfortable in the moment, they don't speak; the only noise in the car is the radio.

"Oh my god, I love this song!" Reid turns the volume up when the B-52s' "Love Shack" comes on. At the stoplight, he has to laugh, because Joaquim is dancing, arms up, and picks up the lyrics immediately.

They sing together, and Joaquim knocks on the dashboard at the bridge; they fall into the call and response easily, with none of the self-consciousness Reid would feel with anyone else.

Watching Joaquim, Reid's chest tightens. It's good. He's easy, unfiltered happiness, unselfconscious joy—things Reid wants badly. Joaquim turns to him and smiles.

I love you.

Reid inhales sharply. He yearns for the things Joaquim can bring to his life. Possibilities have hurt Reid so many times, but Joaquim is a bet he's beginning to think he can place. Reid's mood mirrors Joaquim's happiness on the way home and, when they pull up to the gate of The Largos, he almost regrets that the ride is over.

"Hey, can I get a glass of water?" Joaquim asks as he toes his shoes off at the entrance. As if everything is normal, as if Reid isn't holding a bright bead of happiness, stringing it with others—beads that have been few and far between until recently.

"What? Is everything all right?" Joaquim asks when Reid doesn't respond.

"Yeah," Reid says and shakes his head. "Of course. Maybe I'm a little tired."

"You're the one who woke up at the ass-crack of dawn." Joaquim pokes Reid's side as he reaches for a glass. He giggles and squirms away. "I can get my own glass, you know."

"Hush. Wanna go sit on the porch?" Reid doesn't have anything planned for the day, but being here with Joaquim is enough.

"Yeah." Joaquim takes the glass of water and thanks him with a kiss.

"I'll be right out," Reid says. He lets Joaquim assume he's going to the bathroom. He needs a moment to gather himself. Reid's never been in love like this. *Am I supposed to tell Joaquim? Wait?* He's a mess, and Joaquim probably has questions; after the Felix fiasco and last night, he has to. *And if I'm in love, I should trust Joaquim, right? But if I trust him, would I be asking myself that question?*

Reid makes the bed, then picks up their clothes. He folds Joaquim's and leaves them in a neat pile at the end of the bed. He straightens anything out of place in the bathroom. He stalls as long as he can with his heart pounding so hard it throbs in his ears.

Right. Okay. He can be in the moment and he's going to enjoy this. He'll enjoy it, but because he really wants to be with Joaquim he'll have to own up. Asking Joaquim to be in a relationship with him without disclosing his history, his problems, his struggles, would be tantamount to lying. He'd be asking Joaquim to be with a version of Reid that isn't real. And then *it* wouldn't be real. And Reid so very badly wants real.

CRADLING A SWEATING GLASS OF water in his palms, Joaquim is curled loosely on the chaise lounge. The ocean view and the silence are mesmerizing. He doesn't startle when Reid gently takes the glass and sits in the curved open space Joaquim's body makes. Joaquim's hair is soft under his fingers. Their skin tones are so different; against Joaquim's dark hair, Reid's skin is actually a warmer cream than he's noticed. Usually Reid bemoans how pale he is; in the past, when he was in the sun, his skin didn't take on a tan or healthy glow. It tended to burn and then fades to nothing. He hasn't been in the sun as much as he has this summer since he was a kid.

"Mmm," Joaquim says, sleepy contentment nestled into his voice. "That feels nice."

"Tired?" Reid asks, his voice low. "You can nap."

"No." Joaquim shifts so that his head is on Reid's thigh. "I'm always so busy; I feel like the time I get with you is so short and fast. I want to be with you today."

"Good, because I want to be with you too."

"It's gonna be hot today," Joaquim says after a few moments of silence, during which Reid runs his fingers up and down the skin of Joaquim's arm. Already the air is sticky, and no breeze comes through the screens. "We should go swimming."

Reid doesn't freeze; he doesn't let his fingers stop their slide. "The air down there is as warm as up here," he points out, stalling.

"No, I mean the pool."

"You don't think we'll scandalize the old people?" Reid cups Joaquim's bicep, marveling at its solidity and its truth. He's so real; everything about this boy is real, and he's opening a door Reid can't close, a door he doesn't *want* to close, but isn't yet ready to open wide.

"A little scandal never hurt anyone."

"That sounds nice," Reid says, and, damn, his voice is obviously unsteady.

"Reid?" Joaquim sits up, almost knocking Reid off the chaise lounge.

"Um, so," Reid clears his throat and tries to take a breath because he's a bit dizzy. "I, um. *Fuck*."

"Okay, you are officially worrying me." Joaquim puts his hands around Reid's arms to steady him. Or at least, Reid thinks it's to steady him. Maybe he's about to shake sense into him. If only that ever worked.

"I have some things to tell you."

Joaquim regards him. "Bad things? Like, us things?"

Reid takes a moment to puzzle that out. "What? No. Not at all. I mean maybe bad things, but not about us. Actually, it could be good. Um—" he cuts himself off and shakes his head. This is weird. They don't fit on the chaise together. It's pretty old and made of wicker, and he doubts its ability to hold their dual weight. And if he's going to do this, it has to be somewhere safe.

"Can we go down?" He gestures toward the beach.

"Sure," Joaquim says quietly. Reid collects towels.

Joaquim follows him down, one hand careful on Reid's shoulder, and he treasures that connection, because its continuance is an unknown. He wouldn't blame Joaquim for leaving after this, because Reid is a lot to take. Reid exposed, a package with all of his burdens, is too much.

They settle on the lonely beach, and Reid sits cross-legged, facing Joaquim.

"I'm sure you've noticed. Well, you had to have last night. About…"

"You don't want me to see you?" Joaquim guesses.

"Yeah," Reid says. He has no idea where to start. "There's a whole lot of things that I need to explain. But I want to say up front: I've never said them to someone who doesn't already know me or about my shit. So I can't promise I'll make sense. I don't have a script for this, because I wasn't planning to tell you right now."

"You would have had a script?" Joaquim asks. His hands are on Reid's knees. Reid puts his hands on them.

"It's something we learn to do in the therapy I do," Reid says. He examines their hands, clasped together. "I do a skills-based therapy called DBT. Dialectical Behavioral Therapy."

"That's... I don't know what that first one means."

"I don't either," Reid admits, daring to smile a little. He runs a hand through his hair when the wind tosses it onto his face. His hand is shaking. A lot. "That's why I call it DBT like everyone else."

"Don't be scared," Joaquim says quietly. He takes Reid's hand and impossibly, sweetly, kisses Reid's cheek. "You brought me down here to tell me you're in therapy and you're freaking out about it. Why?"

"Well, it's more than just the therapy."

"Okay." Joaquim sits back and waits out Reid's breathless moment.

"*I'macutter,*" Reid says, as fast as he can.

"You're what?"

Reid thinks he started with the wrong bit, but it's too late now. "I'm a cutter."

"What does that mean?"

Reid's head whips up. "Have you seriously never heard of this?"

"No, I mean, I have," Joaquim says. "I just meant, for you."

Reid does not, absolutely does not, let himself cry. The burning in his eyes is so pressing, he squints. He's unintentionally squeezing Joaquim's hand hard, too hard. This moment is shaped by Reid's uncertainty: *How do I tell him? How will he react? Who will Joaquim think I am when the telling is done?*

"I want you to know." Reid's whole body is shaking. "I wouldn't tell you this if I wasn't serious about you. I should have said this first probably. But I—you're just—I want to be with you."

"I want to be with you too," Joaquim says. He doesn't stop Reid from squeezing his hands. He doesn't move away. Concern and confusion pass over his face.

"Don't say that," Reid begs. "Not until you've heard me out. I'm not saying that to get promises out of you, because you shouldn't make them until you really know me."

"Reid," Joaquim says. His voice sounds helpless and small.

"It means that sometimes I cut myself. Or I did. I mean, I'm in recovery."

"Recovery? Isn't that, like, an addiction thing?"

"Well, yeah. But self-harm can be an addiction. Or like one."

"So you don't do it anymore?"

Reid sighs and curses his own weaknesses and failures. "So, the reason I never let you see me is because I cut…" He puts his hand over his ribs, on the right side. "…here."

"And there are scars."

"Well…"

"And not just scars," Joaquim guesses. The sadness in his voice is almost unbearable; because Reid feels it, keenly, for himself. This is the first time Reid has been normal in someone's eyes, the first time he's been unmarked by mental illness and the stories and histories that follow him in everyone's memory and perception. And in this moment, he's tearing that apart. In this suspension of terrible vulnerability, he's unmasked and unable to decode Joaquim's response in either his voice or his demeanor.

"When you say recovery, then… I don't get it. I mean, you're saying that you've cut, um, recently?"

"Well, right now I'm back to counting days. Weeks actually."

Joaquim is quiet for a very, very long time. Reid doesn't try to fill the silence. What could he fill it with? Excuses?

"Will you tell me more? What does… I haven't ever known someone who, I—"

"Take a breath," Reid advises. Calm comes and then ebbs, washing over him in small bursts. He wills it to come, to wash over him. He always does. Underwater, he's in a perfect silence, tucked into a perfect calm, and nothing can touch him. He wishes he was there now.

"It's not about wanting to kill myself." That's definitely a story for later.

"But it's about wanting to hurt yourself?"

"It's… the whole thing is hard to articulate." Reid thinks of Nancy and what she'd advise: that he advocate for himself, draw healthy boundaries, understand his limitations. "Because I really like you. And to me, telling you is making a promise, to let you know all of me. But sharing it all… I am not making ultimatums. But it's excruciating."

"Wanting to hurt yourself?" Joaquim is completely lost. Reid doesn't blame him. His anxious babbling isn't helping either of them.

"Telling you this. What if this is a deal-breaker for you? Because if you don't want to be with me—"

"Reid, no—"

"No, please listen. If you're unsure or worried, I would rather you take some time to consider whether this is something you can do. Be with me."

"I don't understand; this doesn't mean I don't want to be with you." Joaquim looks at Reid, and the urgency in his voice is mirrored in his eyes and the set of his mouth.

"Joaquim, I have a lot of baggage. I come with a lot. I've never had a relationship where I wasn't someone else's baggage. I've definitely never had a relationship with someone who didn't already know about my problems. I don't want you here because you're beholden, or guilty, or like you *have* to stay because I'm fucked up."

"I don't," Joaquim says.

"Joaquim." Reid shakes their joined hands a little and tries to smile. "I'll tell you everything, if you want to know, if you want to be with me. But please don't make me do it all at once. I realize I'm asking a lot when I've just dropped a bomb on you." He presses a hand to his chest, suddenly conscious of his short, tight breaths. "I'm not sure my heart can take it right now."

"Hey," Joaquim frames Reid's face in his hands with tender care in his very gentle touch. "Breathe. It's okay." He kisses Reid's lips and whispers their mouths together. "It's okay. I can wait. I want to wait."

"Really?" The burning in his eyes cannot be stemmed; the tears that well up distort everything he sees, and so he closes his eyes. The tears spill over, and Joaquim catches them with his thumbs. The next kiss Joaquim bestows is longer, somehow sweeter. Another brilliant moment, another beautiful bead to add to that string of memories he'll force himself to keep even in the worst moments—which will come. The shape of his life was predestined by darkness. The darkness always cedes to the light, and he always emerges—thus far, at least. Reid's journey in the last two years has been in learning to trust and wait for the light, rather than give in to the dark.

Reid unabashedly snuggles into Joaquim's arms. He must be terribly uncomfortable in the position they're in, but Reid can't bring himself to move and Joaquim does not complain. Reid can hear his heart, though, beating as fast as Reid's. Only his demeanor is calmer, steadier. Reid wonders if this means Joaquim is better at handling shit or if he's pretending.

"So, what do you want to do next?" Joaquim asks.

"You mean today?" What a strange transition to a request for stage two of their day off.

"No, I mean, you? What will help you right now? To feel comfortable, or safe, or whatever?"

Reid sits up and watches the water. To his left is another impressive aloe plant. His grandmother always used to make him break off a piece when he needed aloe for a sunburn. He doesn't remember the plants being this big.

Now that he's out of Joaquim's arms, anxiety whispers at him. Reid's not fool enough to think it'll go away on its own.

"I wouldn't mind swimming."

"And you're okay with that? I mean, you didn't want me to see it, right?"

"Well, no, I didn't. But I always swim with a swim shirt on anyway. Too much sun exposure makes scars heal more prominently." Reid musters as much matter of fact information as he can. "But I knew if I wore one you'd have questions. And after last night, this seemed inevitable."

"Would you have tried—"

"Tried what?"

"To keep it a secret if you could?"

Reid wonders what Joaquim is really asking. If Reid trusts him? If he's only told Joaquim because he's backed into a corner? This is important, an opportunity for Reid to get this right. Cards on the table, scared but open and willing, Reid goes for honesty.

"No. I didn't want to anymore. Maybe if things were different between us, if I didn't feel so..."

Joaquim doesn't help him, but watches and waits patiently. Reid clenches his hand in the sand. Rough and heavy, the texture is a small balm, a centering.

"I really like you." *I love you.* "And I want this. Do you—I—do you want this to go somewhere? Serious?"

"I've been there, Reid," Joaquim says. His voice is unbelievably steady. "So, yes." He touches Reid's knee.

"Well." Reid swallows. "No time like the present, then. Let's go upstairs. We can go swimming. Wait, do you have swim trunks?"

"Reid, I always have swim trunks," Joaquim smirks. Reid doesn't carry swim trunks around all the time, but apparently this is a habit of Joaquim's.

"Then let's go," Reid says. He stands and offers Joaquim a hand.

Upstairs, Reid fiddles with the towels and then puts Joaquim's water glass in the dishwasher though Joaquim isn't finished with it.

Joaquim takes his hand. "Why are you so nervous?"

"Okay. So. Come into the bedroom." Reid turns without waiting, trusting Joaquim to follow. He's shaking so much it's hard to think. Without dithering more, he takes off his shirt. His back is to Joaquim, so he doesn't see his approach. Startling at the touch of Joaquim's lips at the nape of his neck, Reid shivers at his fingers sliding down his back, to his waist.

"You don't have to do this."

"I *do*. Just try not to make a big deal about it." Reid cringes. *What a stupid thing to say.* Joaquim exhales in what might be a laugh, or perhaps frustration. Hell, it could be anything.

Man up. Fuck this.

Reid turns.

Nineteen

JOAQUIM LOOKS RIGHT INTO REID'S eyes. Out of his depth, ridiculously, stupidly out of his depth and terrified that he'll do or say the wrong thing, Joaquim can do nothing else but be sure Reid knows that Joaquim is here with him. Right here, in this moment. Not running away. Reid's eyes flick away; the weight of eye contact is perhaps too much.

Thinking it may ground Reid, Joaquim puts his hand on Reid's shoulder. Joaquim, too, needs the connection of his skin on Reid's. Promising himself he'll keep an even expression on his face no matter what, he steps back a little to take him in. One tattoo on Reid's side in particular grabs his attention. Joaquim bends to examine it more closely. The font is like handwriting, a little messy and tilted.

"I can't believe that's what you're looking at first," Reid says. Joaquim glances up; there's a trace of a smile on Reid's face, and he looks less worried.

"I don't understand, though. Why would you want to suffer? How does that lead to hope? What are the words from?"

"A Florence + the Machine song. I'll make you listen to it sometimes. I'll explain the story too, one day."

Joaquim's curiosity burns, conflated with confusion. He feels utterly lost. He traces the tattoo and then looks at Reid's other side. He bites his lip, breaking his own promise, but perhaps that's better than the gasp he holds in. Across Reid's ribs, on the front of his torso, are ladders of scars, some almost invisible, some thicker and scar-white. Wrapping around his ribcage and under his arms is a spiderweb of more scars. They're thicker and, unlike the others, which are perfect straight lines, these are haphazard, a mess. They are overlapping, and they tell a different story. Reid's hidden histories are written on his skin; his body holds many secrets.

Joaquim can't begin to know them; Reid will have to hand them to Joaquim, trust him with the gifts of vulnerability and intimacy and trust. But these tattoos, and scars, and the recent cuts tell a story anyone could see.

"I'd like that," Joaquim says. He swallows and doesn't try to say anything else. Anything else would be inane, superfluous, or dumb. Reid twitches and then pulls away.

"Let's go, then." Reid pulls open a dresser drawer. All of the clothes within are neatly folded and stacked. He changes into swim trunks and a swim shirt before Joaquim has gotten his bearings. Reid turns and raises an eyebrow at him, a silent hurry-up. The topic is closed, clearly. Joaquim respects that. If he had stories to tell that looked anything like Reid's, he would need a lot of time and care to share them.

"ARE YOU SURE YOU DON'T mind scandalizing the old ladies?" Joaquim teases Reid, who has taken his hand as they cross a parking lot toward the coral path that leads to the pool.

"I relish the opportunity," Reid says. He's in an improbably good mood; his smile is in no way fabricated; his movements are light and unrestricted. Joaquim would rather dwell in this strangely infectious happiness than worry. Reid shared something huge with him today, and is still here: a beautiful, bright boy despite everything else. Joaquim hasn't a clue what that everything else is, but he knows that this moment is both precious and very, very important.

So he doesn't worry. He risks a kiss to Reid's cheek and lets Reid take them to the pool.

The pool deck is empty except for one older lady, who has a cooler at her feet, a drink at hand, and what appears to be Rummikub on the table. Her bathing suit is the sort of monstrosity only retirees seem to favor, covered in blue and pink flowers that manage to clash. Oddly enough, she's wearing pink slippers.

"Reid, dear," she calls out.

"Hi, Mrs. Smith." Reid tugs Joaquim behind him toward her. "How are you doing?"

"Excellent," she says briskly. "Elise and Kathy decided it was too hot to come down today. What can you say to that? It's the Keys. Of course it's hot. Does your young man play?"

Reid goes a delightful red at this, and Joaquim has to hide a smile. He also doesn't let Reid let go of his hand, because this is gold and very endearing.

"I'm not sure."

"I do, actually," Joaquim says, eliciting a wide-eyed look from Reid and a small cry of delight from Mrs. Smith. "Hi, I'm Joaquim." He extends his hand, which she takes easily.

"You can call me Betty. And, as I've said, so can you, Reid."

Joaquim sits at the table; she begins to set up the game, taking out three tile holders without asking either of them if they want to play.

"I'm sorry, it's just that you've been Mrs. Smith to me for so long—"

"I've known Reid since he was little. Maybe five or six the first time he came to visit Monica. His hair was much lighter then."

"It's lighter now," Reid points out.

"Not the same thing, dear." Betty is only half paying attention to him; mostly she's focused on getting the game started.

"I don't really know how to play," Reid tells Joaquim. "They keep asking me to play, but I don't remember how, and then things get so competitive they stop explaining things."

"I'll help you," Joaquim says, ridiculously charmed that Reid is a pet amongst all these older ladies. Is this something Reid does in his free time? In the shade of the umbrella, Reid's taken off his sunglasses, so Joaquim can look right into his eyes.

"All right, all right, enough flirting, save it for later," Betty says, causing Joaquim to laugh and Reid to choke.

IT TAKES MORE THAN ONE game, and Joaquim learning not to show his amusement when Reid makes mistakes (although he does file away how hot Reid's intense competitive looks are for a later date and time), before the three of them manage to play a true, winner-take-all game. It is a rather hot day, and Joaquim finds himself envying Betty's cooler. She offers them drinks, and he discovers that her cooler is full of beer she's been pouring into an insulated tumbler.

"No thanks," Reid says politely; the face she makes in response is less than impressed, but also fond.

"I wasn't offering it to you, dear. I know you're not old enough."

Joaquim accepts a beer and shoots Reid an apologetic look. Reid's expression is sly, lined with mischief and mystery, and Joaquim wonders what he's up to.

Reid wins their last game in a stunning turn of events and celebrates by taking off with a holler and cannonballing into the pool. Betty laughs over the noise.

"For all the worry he's brought Monica," she tells Joaquim quietly, "I've always told her that there's a happy boy in there." Her eyes linger on Joaquim. He sits back to sip his beer, content to stay with her and watch Reid fool around in the water. He's floating on his back, starfished and smiling with his eyes closed. "He seems happier than he was. Thank you."

"Who, me?" Joaquim gestures toward himself with his beer. "How do you—"

"Oh, I just have a feeling. Besides, only nice boys play Rummikub with an old lady on a hot day when there are better things to do," she says with a knowing smirk.

Joaquim has to look away, because the suggestiveness in the statement is too embarrassing from a woman who could be his grandmother.

"I had fun," he insists, because he did.

"Thank you." She packs the game away neatly, with a practiced economy of movement that tells of repetitive action and years of habit.

He wonders how long she's lived here. *How far back do the longstanding daily games of Rummikub go?* "Now go have fun. Make him smile more."

THEY PLAY AROUND IN THE pool. They race each other, and shockingly, Reid wins. Then they take turns seeing who can hold his breath longest. Joaquim comes out of that one a clear winner. When he comes up for air, Reid splashes him the moment after he takes a breath; Joaquim tackles him into the water on a whoop of laughter.

"You're such a little kid," he says when Reid wriggles away. Reid wipes his face off and pushes his hair back.

"Takes one to know one," he teases and ducks under the water. Joaquim only has a second to prepare before Reid pushes forward, grabs his ankles, and tugs him under too.

By the time Reid calls a cease-fire, the pool deck is empty. Betty must have gone off in search of air conditioning, which is probably good since they've not only gotten louder, rowdier, and more immature; fingers have also begun to wander.

"Oops," Reid says, all innocent wide blue eyes, when he grabs Joaquim's ass while "wrestling."

"Oops, my ass," Joaquim says, and then laughs at his own turn of phrase. Reid swims closer; they're both breathing hard, but when Reid pushes up against him and grabs his ass again, very deliberately, the hitch in his breath is entirely different. Reid's smirk is confident, his hands on Joaquim's body unhesitating.

"Do they put special chemicals in this pool?" Joaquim wonders. Reid bites Joaquim's neck, and plasters his body against Joaquim's.

"I think you bring it out in me," Reid says. Joaquim smiles: he hopes so. Not because he's possessive or jealous, but because the time he spends with Reid can never be replicated. No matter where their lives take them, Joaquim never wants another moment to taste like this one: Reid's sweet mouth wet and open against his, his own heart pounding hard as Reid kisses him into acquiescence.

"Wanna go—" Joaquim mumbles, sun- and water-drunk, dazed and ridiculously turned on.

"Absolutely." Reid doesn't hesitate to hop out of the pool. He gives Joaquim a hand out and then tosses him a towel. Joaquim thinks of the picture they make: two men attempting to hide obvious arousal with towels while walking across a condo complex occupied by mostly retired folks so that they can fuck—loudly, he hopes, and multiple times.

As if by mutual agreement, they don't talk on the way home. Instead they speed walk—as well as you can in sandals on coral—all the way home. Before the door has closed, Reid's on Joaquim, tearing the towel from around his waist, clawing at his wet swim trunks.

"Fuck, *fuck* get this off now," he says, mouth already busy at Joaquim's chest. *God, it's amazing.*

"If you need motor coordination from me," Joaquim gasps against Reid's wet hair, "you have to stop that."

Reid stops, but only for as long as it takes to wiggle Joaquim's trunks off.

"Reciprocity," he says, hands at Reid's waist. His fingers are already at the hem of his swim shirt when he notices Reid's gone still. "What? What's—?"

"If—" Reid's face is naked and uncertain. "When you see me, will you still want me like this? Because I can't do pity—"

"Reid," Joaquim says. "Shut up." He pulls Reid's shirt up without hesitating, and then pushes roughly in to kiss him. Joaquim has the dizzying sense of being caught between desires. How he handles this is vitally important to Reid's trusting him in the future, but he also wants Reid so badly nothing else seems to matter. Nothing would make him want Reid less. Under his fingers is the thrum of Reid's pulse, fast and hard. Reid is gasping into his mouth when it hits Joaquim, so very clearly, that he loves this boy. Pulling away, Joaquim rubs his thumb over Reid's lips and looks into his eyes. Reid's smile is tentative, but the resounding truth of Joaquim's feelings for him are anything but.

"Okay?" Reid asks.

"*So* okay, you have no idea," Joaquim says. "You know what would be better?"

"Hmm?" Reid's distracted, with his lips on Joaquim's neck and then on his shoulder. He runs his fingers over Joaquim, trailing delicious fire into his skin and muscles. Joaquim gasps and almost loses his train of thought.

"Taking your pants off, and you fucking me."

"Why don't you work on one, and I'll work on the other," Reid says, breathless and amused, squeezing Joaquim's ass, the touch a tease and nothing more, but somehow enough, electric and bright.

Together they get Reid naked; he almost knees Joaquim in the process. The floor is a wet mess from their bathing suits and a tripping hazard, too, from the towels. They somehow make it to the bedroom without injuring themselves. Reid pushes Joaquim unceremoniously onto the bed, climbs onto him, and kisses him until he can hardly breathe. His skin, his cock, his heart all throb with love, with longing, with urgent wanting.

"Please tell me you're going to fuck me soon," he says when Reid shows no inclination to do more than tease him half to death. He's stationed himself at Joaquim's hipbones, having made his way torturously down from his neck, leaving bite marks and kisses along the way.

"How do you want it?" Reid asks, propped between Joaquim's legs. Reid sits up straighter and runs his palm up Joaquim's thigh and then down, encouraging him to spread his legs farther apart, which Joaquim does without hesitation.

"You mean, how do I want you?" Joaquim asks, gasping as Reid's touches become bolder, more intimate.

"That too," Reid says, and Joaquim gets his meaning.

"I want to see your face," he says. Joaquim loves being fucked, yes, but he loves being fucked in particular ways. He likes being able to see his partner, to anticipate and to reciprocate. He prefers lovers who are gentle and, though Joaquim has never been shy with sex, he's always found that hard to articulate in words.

Once Reid has the lube and is touching him with one slippery finger, Joaquim reaches out and draws his own fingers down Reid's arm, slowly and carefully. Reid's eyes meet his and the direct understanding, the frank assessment of needs they each have and want to meet, makes it hard for Joaquim to breathe.

Reid kisses Joaquim very gently, drawing it out, and slips his finger in at the same time. When Reid inhales, Joaquim exhales, closes his eyes, and opens his body. It is much easier to do with a lover who has read you right. Joaquim has always thought of sex as a litmus test in relationships. It's not the end-all or be-all, but a lover who isn't patient enough to take the time, when that's what he likes, isn't worth his time. Reid's not only patient, he also seems to love it. He teases Joaquim with a finger and with his lips. He pulls back and eases Joaquim's legs as far apart as they'll go, until Joaquim himself takes them in hand and pulls them back and away. He's deliciously exposed, and is so rewarded when Reid uses the index finger of his free hand to lightly touch his rim after carefully sliding a second finger into him.

Joaquim tries to keep his eyes on Reid, who is so painfully beautiful, whose eyes are riveted by Joaquim's body. He wants to be ready, right now, to watch Reid's face while they fuck.

"Hey," Reid says, and kisses the inside of his knee. "Relax."

"I am," Joaquim says.

"No I mean, there's no rush," Reid says. His fingers move in, and in, inexorably pushing pleasure into him; little pulses of it run warm through his pelvis. "Let me enjoy you, J."

"Reid, you are so backward," Joaquim says, and then gasps, loudly, when Reid twists his fingers. "Oh *fuck*, fuck that's so—"

"Hmm." Reid's grin is smug and warm. He bites Joaquim's knee, reaches for more lube and a condom with his free hand, and works Joaquim's body until he's pliant and open, begging and desperate for him. When Reid is finally there, pushing into him, it's as if his whole body is orgasming, as if pleasure is pulsing from his skin inward. He's sweating and gasping and shaking before Reid's even all the way in.

"Stay close," he gasps and puts his hands around Reid's neck. Reid has one hand wrapped around Joaquim's thigh, which is pulled up around his waist, and is propped on the other next to Joaquim's head.

"I will," Reid says. His forehead against Joaquim's is sweaty, his moans low and urgent, and from the moment they begin moving together, Reid never quiets. He feeds small moans and gasps to Joaquim as they move in response to Joaquim's requests for *more*, for *harder* or *wait*, or *yes, please*.

"When I come, go slow," Joaquim says, and Reid stills above him. "I want to feel everything, Reid."

"Fuck, you—oh god, that's so—" Reid tries to speak but can't.

"Kiss me, oh, *oh*, I'm about to—" Joaquim says, breathless and aching at the precipice of release, and then Reid's lips are on his as he rocks Joaquim through a wrecking orgasm.

"Don't stop," Joaquim begs, even when his orgasm has come and gone, because it's so good, so deliciously good. Post-orgasm, everything is different, and Joaquim's body has always taken a different pleasure from this, as if his pleasure is centered in his partner, as if what his body can give is as good as what it's been given. He can watch Reid unabashedly and focus on remembering all the tiny details: the way Reid bites his lip before he comes, the way his eyelashes flutter during his orgasm, the way he holds himself so tightly that the muscles of his arms grow taut. Joaquim wraps both legs around Reid and tilts his hips and makes his body as available as possible so that he can drink in every moment of Reid's orgasm as if it were his own.

After he comes, other than to collapse on Joaquim, Reid doesn't move for a long time. He's heavy, and they're both ridiculously sweaty, but Joaquim doesn't move either. Reid feels so true. There's no precision to the movement of his body now; they're both basic in this wreckage, both recovering and being.

"Hey," Reid finally says, flopping off Joaquim and onto his side.

"Oh my god, hi," Joaquim says, gasping in a deep breath and wiping sweat from his forehead.

"Sorry, I was probably—"

"Finish that apology and I'll make you get back on," Joaquim threatens.

"Huh?" Reid puts his head on Joaquim's shoulder.

"I don't… I make no sense right now. Ignore me."

"Mmm, don't wanna ignore you." Reid sounds half asleep; Joaquim does too. Everything smells of sweat and sex and, while it's nice, in its way, Joaquim is also aware that they are growing stickier by the minute and that's gross.

"Hey, wanna shower?" he asks.

Reid hesitates. It's not obvious, just the smallest pause in the pull of his muscles as he inhales. "Yeah," he says quietly.

Reid gets up to turn on the water, leaving Joaquim behind. Joaquim's legs are wobbly, and he's focused on trying to figure out how to walk without making a fool of himself. Then he realizes why Reid hesitated. *Right.* Acting normal with Reid has been easy up till now because he's been so very much in the moment, unable to see or focus on anything but Reid. A shower is different, or it must feel so to Reid. A shower is being naked in a different way.

And it's not as if Reid's given Joaquim an instruction manual. *Can I look? Should I not? If I avoid looking at his scars, does that signal that I don't care? That I'm pretending not to care? That I care too much? Fuck.*

Honestly, Joaquim wants to *be* with Reid. He follows Reid to the bathroom. He steps into the shower. The look Reid sends over his shoulder to Joaquim is hopeful and tired and a little wary. It triggers the sure knowledge he had when they came in from the pool.

Right. He's in love with this boy. And there's no manual, but maybe if he takes care, Reid will let him in enough to tell him how he needs that love shown.

Twenty

"Tell me about your sister," Reid says later that night. They're squashed into Reid's bed again. Reid likes the closeness; he likes that Joaquim has no choice but to snuggle with him so he doesn't have to ask for it and seem needy or pretend he doesn't want to cuddle. A little more room might be nice, though. For the first time, Reid considers moving to his grandmother's bed. But only if they're not having sex there—because, no.

"Sofia?"

"Do you have another sister?" Reid drapes himself over Joaquim's chest and smiles down at him. The only light in the room is the faintest glow from the window. Joaquim's face is glints and shadows. Reid ghosts his fingers over Joaquim's lips and a sense of comfort spills, glowing, through him.

"Nope, just Sofia" Joaquim says after kissing his fingers.

"So?"

"Well, she's beautiful. And protective. She makes dumb choices about boyfriends."

Reid snorts. "Because she has them, and you hate them all no matter what?"

"No, because they are dumb choices," Joaquim responds. "I swear she picks guys who are projects. No job. No education. No motivation. Needs a haircut. It goes on and on."

"Hmm." Reid refrains from laughing.

"She's always there for me, though. She was the first person I came out to. Only family member I am out to. I've always been able to tell her anything."

Reid sighs and puts his cheek on Joaquim's chest. "I wish I had a relationship like that with someone."

"Not with anyone in your family?"

"No. I mean, I guess maybe my grandma." How to say that he never felt like he fit in? No one excluded him. His family loves him. But Reid's always stood apart. Before his diagnosis, Reid was out of step, confusing and isolated, angry and unpredictable for no reason. After his diagnosis, they had a million reasons to explain him, none of which changed the fact that Reid would never be like them.

"It's complic—fuck."

"You don't have to tell me," Joaquim says; Reid's unsure if he's imagining a slightly slowed cadence in his voice.

"No, I do. I realize I say that things are complicated, like, every time you ask me a question." Reid props himself up. "I don't think I'm sheltered, really. But all of this history? Everyone in my life knows that part of me. They only know me through the context of my mental illness for other reasons."

"Okay." It's obvious Joaquim isn't sure how the threads of this conversation are connecting.

"You're the first person I've been close to in a long time who saw me as anything other than Reid-with-problems, who doesn't define me by my 'crazy' or the stupid shit I've done. It makes me nervous, because I love that. I don't want that to end. I want to tell you stuff. But it's—I just…"

"I get it," Joaquim says, covering Reid's hand with his own. "Or, I think I do."

"I'm not like, giving away family secrets or exposing my root—"

Joaquim snorts and mimics Reid's tone. "Your *root*?"

"Shut up," Reid says, poking Joaquim's side. "It's from a movie called *But I'm a Cheerleader*. It's a cult classic; just really campy queer fun."

"Campy queer fun?"

"I love that movie!" Reid says. "We'll watch it. Anyway, not the point. I don't want to change in your eyes. I feel like someone new. I could tell you about my parents. And I will. It might not change things. But I'm scared."

Joaquim holds his breath, telegraphed under Reid's palm flat on his sternum. "I don't ever want you to be scared with me, Reid. I understand why you are. I'm scared too, but only because I've never known anyone with—like you. I mean—"

"It's okay," Reid stops him stumbling through an explanation.

"I don't want to say or do the wrong thing. But I want to know you so much. I..."

"Yeah?"

"I think... *Ikindofloveyou.*"

"What?" Reid's body flashes hot and then cold.

Joaquim groans. "It's really soon, and I've probably scared you off, but I can't help it."

"Babe." Reid kisses Joaquim gently. "I think I kind of love you too."

Joaquim kisses him back with lips flavored not so much with sexual intent, but more than passing sweetness—a little like a promise, with warmth and passion.

Reid pulls back and puts his head on Joaquim's chest. His finger circles Joaquim's navel. "I never fit in. With them. My family."

"Oh?"

"They didn't exclude me. But I always knew something was different. I knew I was different. Some things seemed to just come for people. They knew how to react to situations appropriately, to manage their moods. I tried. I tried to learn how to act like everyone else. And then I tried to fake it, because it became clear I couldn't, but not being able to was disruptive."

"Reid—"

"No, let me finish," Reid says, but gently. "I always knew there was something different about me. But I didn't have the tools or words to figure it out. None of us did. And so it snowballed. Some of my history," Reid gestures vaguely at his body, "Comes from that. But really, that's a part of a complicated set of circumstances: feeling alone, not having coping skills to pair with mental illness."

Joaquim is quiet long enough that nervous buzzing begins in Reid's stomach.

"You don't have to explain it all to me now. It sounds complicated. But will you trust me enough to try? At some point?"

"Yeah," Reid says. He forces his body to relax, bit by bit. "So, with my parents. History… it's there. I recognize that we could have a closer relationship. That partly it's on me, for keeping distant. Maybe one day I'll be in a place where I can work on that. I'm still working on other aspects of recovery. Here, I don't feel that separateness, like I'm the odd one out. Like I'll only ever be 'crazy Reid.' I don't want to feel that. Here I could be someone new."

"Could?"

"Well, now you know."

"Reid," Joaquim shuffles them precariously in the tiny bed until they're face-to-face, noses almost touching. "You'll never be 'crazy Reid' to me. You're the same man I fell for. I—" Joaquim cuts off suddenly.

"What?"

"Nothing. I knew I didn't know all of you. You can be an enigma. But I wanted to. I want to. That hasn't changed, and neither has what's under everything."

"The core of me?" Reid bites back the sarcastic urge to point out that he's been keeping some pretty core stuff from Joaquim.

"No, of us. Connection. How drawn I am to you, how you fascinate me. Your sweetness—"

Reid scoffs.

"Your secret sweetness that you think you should hide." Joaquim has him there. "Your unpredictability. I love that. I love that you make me feel free, sometimes reckless, in a good way. You and I, we make a good pair."

Reid closes his eyes. He kisses Joaquim with shaking lips; his breath punches out of him as his heart pounds. He's wanted to hear words like these for so long, but never thought himself worthy. And when he recognized he might be worthy, the possibility that he could or would ever hear them still seemed a foolish wish.

"You're not out to your family?"

Joaquim sighs. "Can I borrow a phrase? It's complicated." He smiles when Reid laughs softly. "It's more like… we've never talked about it. I assume they know. I don't want to make a huge thing of it with them. But maybe it's cowardice."

"Hey, no." Reid's fingers are cool and gentle on Joaquim's skin. "Everyone does this their own way."

"I guess. They'll notice sure enough when I tell them about us."

"Wow, you're going—you've never told them about a guy before?"

"I've only had one serious boyfriend. It didn't feel like this. I kept waiting for the right time. But the fact that I never found it says a lot."

Reid is quiet, processing the weight of implication. Everything they speak of tonight is a different proof of love. It's humbling and frightening and utterly exhilarating. "You haven't seen them in a while. But you'll see Sofia when you visit, right? She's still home?"

"Yeah, she's in university there."

"What will she do after? Travel?"

"I don't know. She doesn't have the wanderlust."

"You do, right?"

"Yeah. I've been lots of places. I didn't want to go to university. I want to see the world."

Reid holds his breath; anxiety blooms in his chest. "So where to next?"

"What?"

"When you're done with your internship and stuff."

"Oh." Joaquim clues into the direction of the conversation. "I have no idea. I like it here, though. If I can get a job once I'm done, I'd like to stay for a while."

But what if you don't?

Reid barely curbs the impulse to ask. It wouldn't be fair to ask Joaquim to stay, or to insinuate he should, or to make a big deal of this when he himself has no idea what his future holds. A lack of defined direction could be good for them, give them flexibility. But not knowing how something will end, not having a road map, is one of Reid's anxiety triggers. It's always been a low-level trigger. Since he's begun working on turning his life around and managing his mental illness, Reid's learned the importance of structure in his life. It supports him, gives him focus, keeps him present. But perhaps his anxiety in times of chaos has worsened as a result.

Recovery is a constant practice, a balancing act, and exhausting.

Joaquim's lips are on his neck, though; if this is the promise of what Reid could have in the future, it's worth it. His thoughts are too heavy, and this boy in his bed is too bright a promise.

"Let's play a game," he says.

"Uh, like a board game?" Joaquim pulls back. "In bed?"

"No," Reid swats at him through his laughter. "Twenty questions." He's perfectly aware that he's dodged a lot of Joaquim's questions so far. But if they're both going to act like there's more to Reid than his issues, Reid wants him to know more.

"Um, okay."

"Favorite food?"

"Ugh! I suck at these. I love food!"

"Nope, not how it goes." Reid bites Joaquim's chest lightly, making him squirm.

"Wait. Are punishments involved? Because I'm happy to break the rules—"

"Yes. Every time you do this wrong I tease you, but don't follow through."

"Oh my god, that's terrible," Joaquim says. "What's your favorite food?"

"Beef stroganoff, but only the kind my mom makes."

"That's not what I expected."

Reid kisses him. "I'm full of surprises," he whispers against Joaquim's lips.

Reid learns that Joaquim is bad at answering questions on the spot. By the time Reid's gotten to fifteen questions, he's marked up Joaquim's neck and chest with love bites. He's busy sucking the tips of Joaquim's fingers into his mouth and nipping at them lightly while Joaquim curses and moves restlessly, barely able to form answers, much less questions of his own. In charge, Reid is alight with sex and joy and utterly comfortable in his skin.

They never make it to twenty. At eighteen, Joaquim has had enough, flips Reid over and, holding his wrists to the bed, grinds against him hard. Impossibly wound up, they come in minutes and fall asleep in a tangle of limbs.

Twenty-one

JOAQUIM FIDDLES WITH THE MASK display far longer than necessary. They've been left a mess by a family that came through with unsupervised little ones. Organizing them gives Joaquim time to think about Reid. Reid loves board games. He loves his mother's cooking but has a strained relationship with her. His favorite color is blue. He loves live music but hasn't gone to a concert in months. His body is both a delight and a roadmap Joaquim doesn't know how to read, or even how to begin reading.

After Reid showed him his scars, it was painfully clear he wasn't willing to talk about or acknowledge them again. Joaquim carefully ignored them in the shower. Instead, he focused on Reid's lovely shoulders and how sensitive his neck is to touches and kisses. In the dark, Reid's skin read like Braille under Joaquim's exploring fingers. He touched Reid everywhere, though, and didn't let himself linger.

Yesterday, all of Joaquim's senses were trained to Reid. Being fucked senseless. Admitting he'd fallen in love: something he's never said to another man. Pushing and pushing down the worry and fear Reid's confession had inspired; Joaquim knows nothing about people who cut. He has no idea what he should be doing to help Reid.

He's got a million questions on the topic and a clearly shut door from Reid.

Worst of all, he can't talk to anyone about this. There's worry about the edgy and unreadable boy he shared with his sister, and then there are private secrets he's been trusted with.

Once he's back at the desk, Joaquim is buzzing with anxiety. *Is researching cutting a betrayal of confidence?*

He does it anyway. Well, he starts. With so much information available, he can't give reading the focus he needs while he's in the shop.

In his room that night, he reads until his eyes are tired and still has a list of questions only Reid could answer. He said it's like an addiction: Several websites have told him that self-harm can become this. *Does Reid only do it because he's addicted to it? What are his triggers? Why does he do it?* From what Joaquim reads, there are a variety of feelings or reasons ranging from expression of pain, numbness, and disconnectedness to a kind of self-soothing—and this seems so contradictory to Joaquim he can't begin to process it.

The most common advice he reads for people who have been told a friend self-harms is to ask if they can help, and to listen at the other's pace. That's pretty much what he would do anyway, and it doesn't help him feel less lost, especially because the advice he reads is for people who are currently cutting. He's not sure if what's going on with Reid counts as "current."

Joaquim shuts down his laptop with a frustrated snap and lies down. He stares up at the ceiling and misses his sister viscerally. Her voice alone would be a balm. However, her intuition and connection with him mean she would recognize instantly that something is wrong, and he'd have to fend off a lot of insistent inquiries into what's going on.

"J, it seems like all you have are boy problems," Bobby observes from across the room. Joaquim huffs and tries to ignore him. "Are you sure this is worth it?"

"What do you know?" Joaquim rarely gets angry enough to use this tone. "Seriously, Bobby, all you know or see are the hard parts. But the good ones outweigh those. He's amazing."

Bobby holds up his hands, "Sorry, man. Really. It's not my place to say anything."

Joaquim takes a breath and rolls over. "No, it is. You're my friend. But this is private stuff. And trust me, he's worth it."

"Okay."

"I'm sorry for snapping at you." Joaquim's anger is flash and burn.

"No worries, man. I don't know what's up, but what if you focus on something good right now. So what's good?"

Joaquim stares at the ceiling. Bobby has a point. Yes, Reid has exposed something private and painful. And Joaquim is lost as hell, but he can focus on loving Reid, on time they spend together, how Reid brings out a freer version of himself. He can connect with Reid from a different angle. When they've done that, Reid's opened up to him. Although the ceiling above him is unchanged, as always, Joaquim reads the flat surface as a plan forms.

✳   ✳   ✳

"So, where to, Captain?" Reid asks. The car is on, and the air conditioning has been running long enough that it's cool inside.

"Okay, bear with me. I'm going to ask you to do something weird." Joaquim slings the heavy bag he's carrying into the back seat.

"I didn't realize you were a kink guy," Reid says, playful and teasing.

"It's not a kink thing," Joaquim says and then pauses to think. "Although maybe that's a thing to revisit sometime."

Reid leans over the console and kisses him, dirty, biting and licking into his mouth, while his hand grips the inside of Joaquim's thigh.

"Why not now?" he whines against Joaquim's lips.

"Later, I promise."

Reid pulls back, pouting. He pulls out of Joaquim's dorm parking lot. "So what is the thing you need me to do?"

"Drop me off at the condo and then leave for a bit."

"Really?" Reid starts the car despite the skepticism in his voice. "Could I maybe go down to the water or something?"

174

"Only if you promise not to peek." Joaquim shoots a sideways glance at Reid and catches his slightly guilty look.

"All right, I promise." Reid opens the window to punch in the code for the gate. "So, what's in the bag?" He's trying for offhand, but clearly fishing.

"A surprise. Stop trying to figure it out. Let me surprise you."

Reid sighs. "I just like knowing what's going to happen."

"You totally read the end of books first, don't you?"

"Guilty," Reid says. He smiles. "I also watch the end of movies and look up spoilers for TV shows."

Joaquim shakes his head. He follows Reid into the condo when he opens the door, leaving the bag in the car for the time being. Before Reid can get too far from him, Joaquim snags his wrist, draws him back, and melts into a kiss.

"If you want me to leave," Reid says, husky, low and tempting, "you can't kiss me like that."

"Raincheck?"

"Of course."

Joaquim follows him onto the porch, pushing him lightly toward the door. "I'll call you when I'm done, okay?"

"Sure thing," Reid says, "I'll explore jellyfish town."

"Remember not to touch!"

"Yes sir!" Reid salutes, eyes saucy and bright.

"Reid!" Joaquim stands a few steps down, not wanting to have to go all the way to the beach only to climb back up.

"Coming!"

By the time Reid's all the way up, he's slightly out of breath but smiling. "I am ready for my surprise. You didn't install a sex swing in my grandma's condo, did you? I'd have a hard time explaining that away."

"No, you pervert." Joaquim takes Reid's hand. The sun is setting, leaving a lovely glow at their backs and a slightly dimmed living room. It lends the perfect ambiance. He covers Reid's eyes.

"Really?"

Joaquim glances behind himself as he walks backward while leading Reid in.

"Okay, we're going to die like this," he mutters. "Close your eyes." He comes around Reid, covers his eyes with his palms, and then leads him forward. "Sit," he whispers once they're in the middle of the living room.

"On a chair?" Reid waves a hand around blindly.

"No, on the floor."

Joaquim kneels and helps Reid onto the floor. Once they're down, he presses himself against Reid's back and whispers into his ear, "Now."

"J…" Reid says. All around them are small white candles in glass jars. Joaquim bought out the store with his measly savings. More than a hundred candles are on the table to their right, on the shelves by the TV, and surrounding the carefully laid, soft plaid blanket beneath them. Their light butters the hush of sunset through the glass doors at their backs. Strewn everywhere are rose petals and shells. Joaquim painstakingly removed the petals from the flowers, trying not to bruise or tear them; his fingers bear pinpricks from their thorns. At Shell World, he endured Delia's teasing after exacting a promise not to say anything to Reid about what he was planning. The stillness of Reid's body, though, speaks of the worth of the time spent.

"I've never…" Joaquim starts.

"No one has ever—" Reid breaks off, his voice is thick and unsteady. He turns his face to tuck it into Joaquim's neck. "How did you know?"

"That you're a hopeless romantic even though you try to hide it?"

"Yes."

"Because you're terrible at hiding it," Joaquim says. He holds Reid's hand in tender counterpoint to the light amusement in his voice.

"Fuck. I guess my cover is blown." His eyes, bright with tears, don't shy from Joaquim's.

"I hope," Joaquim says, and touches Reid's cheek, "that you know you don't need a cover with me."

Reid smiles, but looks away. *Too much?* Joaquim isn't pressuring. He's offering. He's laying something bare.

"I do." Reid kisses him.

Joaquim presses in, mindful of the candles around them; he breaks the kiss when he senses the changing tone. "I have food."

"It took you so long to set this up, surely you didn't have time to cook?" Reid glances around. Joaquim stands, steps over candles, and retrieves food from the fridge and the oven.

"Not here. I made the pão de queijo at the dorm. The fruit salad and dessert only required putting things together in the kitchen. It's not a full meal or anything, but..."

Reid examines the food Joaquim sets down. "What's pão de queijo?"

"It's a kind of cheese bread made with tapioca flour that we eat in Brazil. It's one of the things I crave the most."

"And you can bake!" Reid's eyes brighten adorably.

"Sure, some, I guess." Joaquim tucks Reid's excitement away for later.

"And fruit salad, too!"

Joaquim looks down as he hands Reid a small plate. "It reminded me of our first date."

"Joaquim," Reid says softly, "are you embarrassed?"

"Is this cheesy?"

"Other than the bread?" Reid jokes. Joaquim cracks a small smile. "No. This is perfect."

"Here." Joaquim holds out a piece of bread. "It's best warm. I had it in the oven."

Reid takes a cautious bite and then another. "Oh my god, this is so good! I was not expecting..."

"Right?"

"You said cheese bread, but this isn't quite. But it also kind of is."

"It's hard to describe."

"I can see why you miss it." Reid brushes his fingers off on a napkin Joaquim has handed him. Joaquim holds out a strawberry. Reid eats it from his fingers.

"One day, I want to take you somewhere where you can taste real Brazilian food."

"I would love that."

They eat in silence, feeding each other and feasting on small touches and matching glances. Once they are finished with their food, Reid lies down with his head pillowed on his folded arm, facing Joaquim. Joaquim puts the plates away. He moves some candles onto the table and lies across from Reid. Reid's picked up some shells and is toying with them, putting them on the blanket, scooping them up, and letting them plink onto one another. They make a beautiful tableau, their pinks and blues, their ivory complementing the dusky variegated pinks and reds of the rose petals.

"I've always wanted something like this," he says after a bit.

"But no one's ever—?"

"Felix wasn't one for romance. He thought it was…"

Joaquim waits it out.

"Dumb. He always said stuff like this was for girls and softies."

"Last I checked, you're definitely not a girl. Besides, who cares? Why does needing something have to be about stupid gender stereotypes?"

"Well, I don't know that I need it. It's a stupid thing I—"

"Reid. Do you know why I did this?"

"To get laid?" Reid jokes, a poor attempt to diffuse the seriousness of Joaquim's tone.

"Because you deserve the things that make you happy. That make you feel loved. To have someone want to meet your needs."

Reid closes his eyes. "How did I get here? This is so unreal."

Joaquim reaches for his hand. "I wasn't expecting it either."

Reid's laugh is hollow. "You know, when I chose to fight for myself, I didn't think I'd get this too. I chose to work recovery for the promise of happiness. And I've been happier. There's more happiness for me if I keep working and trusting. But I never imagined…"

"Reid," Joaquim whispers. He's sure Reid can hear the thudding of his heart. "Will you tell me more? You don't have to."

"I know I don't. And yeah. If you want. Should we move?" Reid shifts to get up, but Joaquim shakes his head.

"No," he moves closer to Reid. "Can we stay like this?" They're so close, face-to-face, hands together.

Reid takes a deep breath. "So, obviously, I have a history of, you know, um, cutting."

"Yes." Joaquim restrains himself from asking questions.

"And you've probably witnessed my mood changes. Or the effects of them."

"Oh," Joaquim isn't sure what to say. He has, but he doesn't want agreement to seem like judgment.

"Don't worry, I know it's there." Reid is playing with his fingers, as if to distract himself. "I'm cyclothymic. It's a mental illness."

"I've never heard of it," Joaquim admits.

"Most people haven't. A lot of people describe it as a 'milder' version of bipolar. Which…"

"Yeah?"

"I don't know. The thing is, I can see what's meant by that. It's a mood disorder, like bipolar. Only instead of experiencing some of the more visibly disruptive aspects of bipolar, such as mania, my moods are subtler; or, they were."

"So… no mania?"

"No," Reid says. "I get depressed or hypomanic. Which is like a stage below mania. Really energetic. Productive. Lots of people experience increased creativity. With me, I feel really outgoing. Like I can get so much done. My mind goes and goes and goes. But it's not… it's not bad. I don't mind that part. I actually like it."

"Really?" Joaquim says.

"Not the impulsive part, no. But I like feeling productive. The thing is, they say this is milder than being bipolar, right? Only with cyclothymia, your moods switch. It's different for different people. For me, my moods can cycle quickly, even as much as a few times in one day. I'll go from depressed to hypomanic. And the in-between…"

"You can feel it?" Joaquim guesses.

"Yeah. When I'm cycling, the feeling before or when it's happening is awful. Sometimes, too, I am both."

"Both what?"

"Depressed and hypomanic."

"Um." Joaquim squints; clearly his brain is trying to filter this information. "I don't understand."

"I don't know. They call it mixed states. Those are better with the meds I am on now."

Joaquim really wants to ask more about that, but bites his tongue.

"Anyway," Reid says. His smile is faint. "The mixed states and the cycling, that's where the cutting came in for me at first."

"You said..." Joaquim swallows the rest of his words.

"It's okay to ask questions," Reid says.

"You talked about the cutting like recovery. Does that mean it's, like, an addictive thing for you?"

"Yeah. For me at least. I guess. It's all tied together. The reasons why I used to do it, when it started. What it became. Why I couldn't stop. I mean, they've explained this to me a hundred times, and I've been working on this stuff in therapy. But honestly, sometimes I think it'll never be possible to explain it, to understand it. How it feels, not just the cutting, but everything else."

"It would be pretty presumptuous of me to ever think I could understand." Joaquim says. "I mean, not empathy or sympathy, but really get it, since I'll never experience it."

Reid's face is radiant. His kiss is tentative for one heartbeat, worshipful the next. He rolls Joaquim onto his back. "I know I said you could ask questions..."

"I can ask another time."

"If you want to still... I mean. If you still want this."

"By this do you mean you?" Joaquim runs a finger over Reid's ear, bumps the pad of his thumb over the piercings.

"Yeah."

"Of course. *Of course* I still want this, Reid." Fingers now on Reid's neck, Joaquim reads the rabbit-quick pounding of his pulse. "Kiss me, and maybe you'll know."

"That you want me?"

"And how much you can trust me."

Twenty-two

THE LAST TIME JOAQUIM SHARED a bed with him, Reid allowed him to touch every inch of his skin, including where his scars were—not that Joaquim asked, or that it was openly acknowledged. That touch had been transitional, a test of Joaquim's reactions and of Reid's willingness to share.

"Can we sleep in the bigger bed?" Reid asks, paused in the hall between the rooms.

"It's your condo; you get to choose," Joaquim says. The smile in his voice leaves Reid almost weak with gratitude. Despite the heaviness of the night and the weight of trusting Joaquim with parts of his story, Joaquim manages to make everything blessedly normal.

"Well, it's my grandma's bed, which has felt awkward. But the other one is too small."

"Lead, and I'll follow."

Reid supposes Joaquim intended for tonight to end with sex; he's pretty sure Joaquim would understand that Reid's not quite in the mood, though. Tonight, Reid craves closeness, reassurance. "Her bed it is, then."

In bed, in the dark, Reid takes off his shirt, strips to his boxers, and slips under the covers with Joaquim. "I wish I could open the window. Listen to the water and the night. But it's so hot here, even at night."

"I know what you mean."

Their silence is underscored by the whoosh of air through the vents and their breathing. Reid puts Joaquim's hand on his collarbone.

Joaquim's body is so warm under the covers; Reid doesn't know what he wants, just that under his skin he's trembling, loosening, and that maybe Joaquim's touch will ground him.

Joaquim traces his collarbone lightly, then down his chest. It's not sexual; it's comfort and learning. When he begins to trace the older scars on his ribcage, the ones that didn't heal well, Reid goes completely still. But Joaquim's fingers don't linger. They continue to touch Reid: his stomach and hipbones, his navel and where his tattoo is. In the dark it's not visible, but Joaquim seems to know exactly where it is.

"Is this about that?" Joaquim whispers. Reid needs a moment to work out what he's asking. He swallows hard.

"No. I got it after..."

Joaquim waits. They both press into that silence, but it's not a bad silence. It's a trusting one, patient.

"Last year I had a breakdown. My family had me, um, committed. Well. Not like... probably not like it sounds."

"Uh, I'm not sure what that means," Joaquim says at last.

"Well, most people have these loony bin images or ideas. Or like, a hospital."

"You weren't in the hospital?"

"Well, yes. At first. But that was maybe three days. Then my family sent me to this place called Sycamore Grove. It's a long-term psychiatric care place. They do long-term treatment programs for patients who haven't been able to function in 'real life.' I hated the way they used to say that. But it wasn't bad. They try to teach patients skills and how to manage their medications and treatments and stuff. Hold down jobs. Live independently."

"And you did—?"

"No, that's only one of the things they do. I was on a shorter treatment plan. I was there for three months."

"Reid, can I ask you questions?"

Reid rearranges himself on the bed, facing Joaquim and bunching the pillow under his head. His hands are shaky and sweaty, but overall he is much calmer than he anticipated.

"Yes. When I said that earlier, I meant it. I'd rather you ask than imagine things that are worse or wrong. I mean…"

"Yeah?"

"This is going to change how you see me anyway, right? I might as well do damage control. Let you ask questions and stuff."

"Reid," Joaquim says. His voice is faint and laced with sadness. "You don't have to do damage control. I'm *here*."

"True. You didn't run screaming for the woods when you found out I was crazy in the first place."

"*Reid.*"

"No, I know. Sorry. This is kind of a defense mechanism. So. Anyway. Ask away."

"Why were you there? What happened?"

"Okay. Well. So, for a long time, I knew something was different about me. We all did. But we didn't know what. I didn't know how to talk about it. I mean, I was a kid when this all started, and it's not like my parents had any experience with mental illness. Like I said, the cutting started when, as I now know, I was cycling rapidly and in mixed states. I had all of these awful weird feelings. I still do. I feel them in my body. Everything is overwhelmingly irritating. I have no control over my feelings; I am angry and everything is wrong. My skin feels all wrong. When I was younger, I was confused and had no idea how to describe these feelings or that wrongness, or explain why it was happening. Initially, the cutting came from that. The anger and the pain I was in. Then it became addictive."

"It was bad? Is that why—?"

"No. I mean, yeah, cutting isn't a good thing. I… controlled it differently. That's why the scars are different. It became less spontaneous. It was calming. I could control it. Or that's what I thought. But my parents found out."

"How?"

"My father. He saw the cuts one day when he accidentally walked in on me in the bathroom. And that's when everyone decided I needed help."

"Everyone including you?"

"I don't know," Reid says a little miserably. "It's all a little... I don't like to think about the whole thing that much, and with everything that happened after, some of it is hazy."

"What happened?"

"Well, I went to see a therapist. And she referred us to a psychiatrist. Cyclothymia is rare, or rarely diagnosed. It can fly under the radar, be mistaken for other mental illnesses. Anyway, initially, her diagnosis wasn't right." Reid's eyes are closed. Remembering and talking about this part—well, he's never done it. Nausea and aching pain bloom in his chest and stomach. "The thing about mood disorders is that everyone's chemistry is unique. And you have to be willing to adjust medications over time as things change."

"What things? Like moods?"

"More like... My therapist Nancy—a different one—says it's like trying to keep a balloon in the air. You have to keep tapping it to keep it afloat."

Reid lifts his hand to his mouth and bites the cuticle of his left thumb. The unsettled feeling in his body doesn't calm. It's dark enough that Joaquim can't see when he digs a fingernail, hard, into the same cuticle. It offers a sharper pain, a focus, and a tiny measure of calm.

"Anyway, the first meds she tried on me didn't work. Really. Things spiraled from there."

There's so much more to say: what it was like to have three days of feeling better, of calm and competence and feeling put together, and then the crash. Paranoia. Coming out of his skin with jitters. Persistent thoughts that his whole life was going to feel like that.

Reid has never been able to put into words why he did what he did next, not even in therapy.

"What kind of spiral, Reid?" Joaquim has a gift; he always sounds poised and level. The smallness of his voice now, the quiver in it, make Reid afraid too. He feels Joaquim's fear.

"It made me feel good at first. It was a fast-acting med, so I felt changes pretty quickly. But then one night I was so restless I couldn't settle down. Nothing was wrong exactly, just I didn't feel right. The next day was worse; even Felix wondered what was up. I figured that even with the meds, maybe I was going to start cycling. But the day after that it was unbearable."

"The restlessness?"

"It was *wrongness*. It was like coming out of my skin. I started to have intrusive thoughts."

"What are intrusive thoughts?"

"Persistent, bad thoughts you don't want to have but can't stop. That my life would always be like that. Awful. Always feeling the way I was right then, and that even if it got better for a little while, I'd end up back where I was. That there was no point anymore."

"Oh. Oh, *Reid*."

"J, don't cry," Reid says, his own voice thick with unbidden laughter. He kisses Joaquim's forehead. "I'm okay now. It's a thing that happened. It could have been worse."

"It's still pretty—" Joaquim cuts himself off. Reid twitches and tries to settle.

"Sending me to Sycamore Grove was a little reactionary anyway. I mean, I needed help. And other than three-day hospital stays, there weren't a lot of good options. Mental health care in our country is shit. Anything longer than that hospital stay is expensive and hard to find, where we were."

"Is it?"

"My parents paid for me to stay at Sycamore Grove. I didn't need a nine-month treatment plan to learn to reintegrate or anything. That's the shortest treatment plan they have. Good things came of it, but a lot of it was awful." Reid clears his throat and tries to modulate his voice. "There were a lot of really sick people there. Wonderful people, people who really needed the help. But I saw and heard a lot of disturbing things. It wasn't always a good environment, particularly for the people in my house, a lot of whom were classified as BPD. Borderline Personality Disorder."

"You have a personality disorder?" The *too* isn't said, but it's clear.

"No, not like you're thinking. It's a terrible name that doesn't at all match what it means."

Reid doesn't explain more. Suddenly deeply exhausted, he closes his eyes and moves closer to Joaquim's warmth.

"J?" he whispers

"Yeah?" Joaquim matches his voice.

"Can we be done now?" There's a pause, and then he feels Joaquim's hand on his hip.

"Of course."

"Don't be afraid, okay? Things are better now. They aren't perfect. But it's okay." Reid is still speaking words of comfort as he slips into sleep. Joaquim's fingers comb through his hair.

*   *   *

REID WAKES WITH THE SUN, as usual, despite how late they were up. Disoriented by the unfamiliar bed, he sits up with a startled heartbeat, clutching the sheets. Joaquim is next to him, and soon enough he recognizes the room. Then, with painful and visceral clarity, he remembers the night before.

Not wanting to wake Joaquim, Reid slips out of the bed and pads to the door. It shuts with a quiet snick. In his room, Reid pulls on thin pants and a pale yellow T-shirt he rarely wears because it's terrible with his coloring. He grabs water and his meds; as he does every day, he counts his pills and checks their colors and shapes. At Sycamore Grove, they had to do this when their meds were dispensed. It was a skill taught to help those who struggled to take or remember their meds: recognizing pills by color and shape, naming and counting them. Reid didn't generally struggle with taking meds, but the habit became reassuring.

Out on the porch, Reid surfaces from lethargy, rising into his body with the sun and the waking of the cicadas. His water is lukewarm by the time he finishes it. After half an hour, even being on the porch doesn't completely calm his nerves. He takes a towel down to the water and closes his eyes. He tries to give his body over to the sounds of a great big earth around him, understanding that he is very small, a tiny piece of something greater, a small glimmer of either light or darkness, depending on his choices and will. He might be small, but he matters, and Reid wants to be a light.

Every time he opens his eyes, the gray-blue water greets him with sameness, not awe. Reid rubs the palms of his hands against his knees, but the fiber of the fabric is too smooth. He puts his hands in the sand, but it's not right. The world is a gray sameness; it's all over his skin, and the longer he's awake the more he feels this. He bites his lip; that's different, yes, but it doesn't stave off the buzzing irritation in his chest.

"Morning."

Reid startles. Joaquim is climbing down the stairs with a mug of coffee balanced precariously in his hands. Reid bites his lip harder.

"Hi," he says. He reaches up to hold the coffee while Joaquim settles on the towel, squishing them together. Reid takes a deep breath and tells himself that his annoyance is tied to his own issues, not Joaquim.

Joaquim kisses him, whispers another good morning on his lips and, when he smiles, it's so fucking true. True and unbothered. A countenance of calm that's unabashedly genuine. He contemplates the water. Joaquim must be too sleepy to read Reid's body, because he settles his head on Reid's shoulder and sighs.

"You're up early," Reid manages. When he's not working, Joaquim is a late sleeper. He's also totally okay with taking a day to do nothing. Reid doing nothing feels guilt or has niggling thoughts that he should be doing *something* productive.

"Missed you in bed," Joaquim says. His murmured words do warm Reid a little. *What happens when Joaquim wakes up more, though? When he remembers everything I told him last night?* It's one thing to say it's okay in the moment, to promise not to judge, not to write Reid off as crazy. But the next day, and the day after, those are the days when the reality of promised words must be proven. Reid wanted something simple here on the Keys. He can no longer be not-Wisconsin Reid; he's unzipped that second skin and revealed this truth, this inescapable self.

Reid digs his fingernail into another nail bed and reminds himself firmly that this isn't true. The rest of his life isn't meant to be painful or awful. He is not obsolete. He's had real happiness here. Integrating the two versions of himself into this life doesn't have to be the writing on the wall for their relationship.

That reminder does nothing to settle the restless agitation in his body. He wants Joaquim gone; he can hardly stand to be with himself. At the same time, Reid doesn't want him to leave because he doesn't trust himself. Defenseless against any judgment Joaquim might have, Reid moves away slightly.

Occasionally his anxiety presents as the start of a mood change. Tracking his moods and anxiety carefully over the last year has helped Reid identify the difference between anxiety and a cycle most of the time. It's all a mess now, because Reid's pretty sure talking about his breakdown is a trigger. He's never had to talk about it outside of therapy, which is different because there's a communal understanding of need. His relationship with Joaquim, expectation-wise, was a blank slate; Reid's now scribbled all over it.

"I'm sorry I have to go upstairs there's something I need to do," Reid says, all in one jittery rush. "I'll be back, and we can plan today until you have to go back, right?"

Joaquim nods. Confusion slips over his face, but he lets Reid go without comment.

In the bathroom, Reid considers his options. If he takes a fast-acting mood stabilizer, he might settle down. But taking more makes him dizzy and forgetful. If he takes his anti-anxiety med, he'll be sleepy. Reid tries not to take either during the day unless he's home alone with no responsibilities. Everything is wrong. Wrong, wrong, wrong. Reid closes his eyes and grips the counter.

Calm down.

Reid leans over the sink and splashes water on his face.

I'm going to be okay.

No. *Nonono*, his body insists. Reid digs his fingernails into his forearm. He draws a line down the muscle, hard. Focuses on the sensation. Lets it ground him.

Stop. Breathe.

Reid breathes and tries to stop. He takes an anti-anxiety pill. He dries his face with precision, goes to the kitchen, and fishes in the ice dispenser. At the sink, he grips ice cubes and lets the water drip into the sink as he tries triangle breathing. Reid's rarely had patience for it, but right now, he's breaking out every suggestion from the Distress Tolerance unit they studied in DBT.

When his palms are numb, he dries them too. He should go back to the beach. It'll take a bit for the Klonopin to kick in, if it does help. No way he'll be able to hide from Joaquim that he's freaking out, though, and Reid is definitely not ready for him to see it. Talking about his problems was hard enough. Reid wants to keep these truths conceptual rather than factual for as long as he can.

He texts Rachel.

Reid: *J is here and I'm struggling. What do I do?*

Rachel: *Did he do something?*

Reid: *No, not that kind of struggling.*

Rachel: *Oh. OH. Do you need me to call?*

Reid: *No. I just need to tell someone I think.*

Rachel: *Did you try the ice?*

Reid: *Yeah.*

Reid makes a face. His fingers are still clumsy and cold.

Reid: *Why doesn't it work for me that well?*

Rachel: *It's a different pain honey.*

And that's another truth that's hard to explain to someone who hasn't experienced it. Different pains mean different things. Some pain is just pain, same as it would be for anyone else. Reid craves particular feelings. He's learned how to manage, mostly, with particular sensations. He thinks of the popcorn ceilings and has to wonder at himself because he's a little obsessed with them.

Rachel: *You don't want him to see? You haven't told him yet, have you?*

Oh, right. They haven't had a DBT session since he told Joaquim about the cutting.

Reid: *No I have. I'm not ready for him to see it.*

Rachel: *Go hide in the bathroom then. No one questions nature calling ;)*

In the bathroom, door safely locked, Reid sags against the wall opposite the mirror. Bright red lines stand out against the pale skin of his arm where he scratched himself. He didn't break the skin, but they're certainly visible. He is calmer now, feels as though he can control himself. That thing inside him, ugly and barbed, which presses on his chest and is too big to manage, it's smaller. His breathing is deeper and easier.

Five minutes later, he goes to the bedroom and finds the lightest-weight long-sleeved shirt he has. It's humid, but not unbearably so. He can claim he got cold inside the condo because of the air conditioning. In fact, he'll convince Joaquim to come up, and he won't question it.

He doesn't have to go to Joaquim. He finds him in the kitchen, eating leftover fruit salad.

"Sorry, I made myself at home," Joaquim says. Reid's smile is genuine; the fondness in his chest is very real.

"Please do." He wraps his arms around Joaquim from behind. "I like it." The kiss he presses between Joaquim's shoulder blades is vital somehow. Even through the fabric of his shirt, Reid's kiss connects him to this boy. Joaquim settles into his arms and sighs.

"Do you want some?"

"No, I'm good." Reid isn't a morning eater. Joaquim seems content to let Reid continue to hold him until he is finished eating. Reid feels sleepy now, weighed down with the lethargy that's part meds and part the crash that comes with anxiety. When Joaquim turns in his arms to smile at him, it abates somewhat.

"Are you all right?"

Bristling at being seen, and also at the question, Reid takes a step back. His life is nothing but a series of well-meaning people asking him if he's all right all the time. It's a sincere question, though; Reid's reaction is knee-jerk and may be unjustified.

"I'm tired all of sudden." Tired is an understatement. Reid closes his eyes and sways on his feet.

"Hey, babe," Joaquim says. He puts a hand on Reid's arm. "Let's go lie down."

"Okay." Reid acquiesces easily. He needs to sleep this off. Joaquim climbs into bed with him, lets Reid octopus-hold him, and doesn't speak a word as Reid drifts off.

Twenty-three

JOAQUIM ARRIVES AT THE CONDO at exactly six, as instructed. The door is locked, and Joaquim waits five minutes for Reid to answer.

"Hi, hi," Reid says, kissing both of Joaquim's cheeks in a rush.

"I've brought you over to the dark side, huh?" Joaquim smirks against Reid's lips when he pulls him in for a real kiss.

"Hmm?" Reid's curls his hands around Joaquim's hips.

"If you're going to start greeting people with cheek kisses, I should teach you the etiquette."

"Oh." Reid says. "I didn't realize I did that! No, I think I'll save them for you."

"So." Joaquim toes off his shoes. The condo smells delicious, like spun sugar. The kitchen is empty. Reid invited him over for a date night, his only instruction to bring comfortable clothes because they would be staying in. "What are we doing? I am here at your will."

Reid's cheeks flush, and his eyes flicker to the kitchen and back. "Well, there's been a change in plans. Do you have a bathing suit?"

"Reid," Joaquim says, leveling him with a look. Reid laughs and pushes him back out the door.

"I get it, I get it, you're always prepared. Just go get dressed."

Reid is bustling around the kitchen when Joaquim comes back in with his bathing suit. Joaquim knows the look of secrets and nerves, so he can tell something is going on. Reid seems happy enough, though, and as long as he's happy, Joaquim is content to play along. He lets himself be shooed off to get changed. Reid's left clothes on the floor in his room, and the bed is rumpled.

"Have you been taken by one of those—what are they called? Pod things?" Joaquim asks when he emerges.

"What?" Reid closes the lid on a cooler with a snap.

"Your clothes are on the floor." Reid rolls his eyes. "Well, if you're going to clean up, get on it," Joaquim says, and smacks Reid's ass lightly when he moves past him.

"Save that for later," Reid says, wagging a finger at him. *This*, this boy is the bright, beautiful person he's tried to describe to Nina and Bobby.

The cabinet door where the garbage is kept is open, and a roll of garbage bags unspools from the counter to the floor. Joaquim rolls them up. He's a little clumsy and sloppy; when he slides the garbage can out to put them behind it, he's surprised to find the source of the candied smell. What appear to be dozens of slaughtered cupcakes fill the can. Pastel frosting is smeared around the rim. There's even some frosting spattered on the inside of the cabinet door. Reid is making grumbling noises in the other room; fast on his feet, Joaquim unrolls the garbage bags once more, abandons his desire for a glass of water, and perches on a stool at the breakfast bar.

THEY HEAD TO THE POOL hand-in-hand. Reid carries a cloth Publix bag he won't let Joaquim look into. Joaquim lugs a surprisingly heavy cooler.

"We're going to break a few rules, so be prepared," Reid warns him.

"It's a little light out for public indecency," Joaquim says. Sunset is hours off.

"Keep it in your pants, buddy." Reid squeezes his fingers. The corners of his eyes crinkle with amusement. "Not that kind."

Joaquim doesn't respond. There's nothing he could say, no words to put around this happiness. He wants nothing other than to be in this moment, with this man. The pool deck is empty, with only pulled-out chairs at the shaded table to show that anyone was there. Half the chaise lounges are still folded.

"Oh, yay, no one is here." Reid sets his bag on the table with a loud clunk.

"You are so adorable," Joaquim says, snagging the front of Reid's swim trunks to pull him closer. They're new, a bright red that calls for attention. "If you wanted me alone, why bring me here? Talk about risky behavior."

Reid snorts and extricates himself with a look that's rich with a promise for later. "It's so warm; no one wants to get into a warm pool," Reid explains. "It's like taking a bath. No one has been here in the evening all week."

"All right. So what do you need from me?"

Reid fiddles with the straps of the bag. "Well, okay, I am realizing I didn't plan this well enough. I need you to close your eyes. Go over there or something." Reid waves to the far end of the pool.

"O—okay," Joaquim says.

"I had to recalibrate on the fly."

Joaquim runs his fingers through Reid's hair; it's an unstyled mess. Reid's face is naked, and he's utterly himself. Reid doesn't adjust to changes well, but he seems happy enough. "All right, lindo."

Joaquim busies himself cleaning the seldom-used lounge chairs in the far-right corner of the pool deck. The pool is rarely busy enough for anyone to want to sit here, under the trees. He tries not to decipher the sounds behind him, to suspend himself in the sweet moment before surprise.

"All right," Reid says. "Close your eyes."

"Oh, is it my turn now?"

"Yep. Please try not to fall; we're aiming for romantic." Reid guides him with one hand on his shoulder and the other at the small of his back, trusting Joaquim to keep his eyes closed. "Hand out," Reid says. He takes Joaquim's hand, puts it on the back of a chair, and lets Joaquim fumble into it. A whispered kiss to his lips, then two more to his eyelids and Reid's soft command to open his eyes make him viscerally aware of love, as if Reid's touch has become a living thing, something curled inside Joaquim, something he can cherish and hold and keep.

The table is set with candles Joaquim recognizes. There's also a beautiful charcuterie plate, chocolate-dipped strawberries dewing from the humidity, and tall drinks garnished with lime wheels.

"I'm breaking some rules with these. I did some research online and thought I'd try to make something that might remind you of home," Reid explains. He's twisting his hands nervously. "Also, we're eating on the pool deck, although no one really pays attention to that."

"Reid." Joaquim turns and presses his cheek against Reid's belly, closes his eyes into Reid's fingers ruffling through his hair.

"I had a plan for something else, but I fucked it up. Um, so the drinks don't match but, yeah. Caipirinhas?" Reid tests the word out slowly, fumbling over the pronunciation.

"Hey, hey," Joaquim says, catching Reid's fingers and kissing them. "This is wonderful." It also explains the cupcakes. "Thank you."

Reid's eyes are bright, and his smile is shy, sweet in a way Joaquim never could have expected when they first met. "You are so welcome." His next kiss is somehow even sweeter. It lingers, it promises, though it's not about the heat that so often sparks between them. It's love, is all. It is simple and full.

"Let's eat." Reid pulls up a chair. "Tell me what you like."

"I want to try it all."

"Well, then, here." Reid selects an olive, "These are my favorite." Joaquim allows him to slip it between his lips. He holds Reid's wrist carefully and nips at his fingers.

"Delicious." Joaquim doesn't let go. Reid cups his cheek briefly and smiles again.

They eat slowly, moving to the strawberries eventually. Night begins her sweet slide across the sky, slipping over the light.

"Wanna swim?" Reid asks after they're finished. His feet are in Joaquim's lap. He's been nursing his drink.

"Of course," Joaquim says. Everything is so easy. Joaquim doesn't want to look ahead, to think back, to wonder how fleeting these moments might be. "I'll race you."

Reid is off in a flash, faster than Joaquim anticipated. "You're predictable," he says with a chlorine-flavored kiss and an apology that is all mischief and no actual regret. "Hey, listen. I'm sorry tonight didn't go how I planned."

Joaquim squeezes Reid's waist. "Since I have almost no idea how it was meant to go, I must say with honesty, tonight has been perfect. What happened?"

"Almost?" Joaquim could read that deflection from twenty yards away.

"Reid." Joaquim adopts a singsong tone. "What happened?"

"Nothing. It's dumb." Reid won't look at him.

Joaquim pushes Reid away and splashes him. "Wanna play a game?"

"What kind of game?"

The water is rather warm. "Twenty questions?"

The light glints from Reid's eyebrow piercing when he raises his head. "Gosh, I really have changed your life if you can't get in the water with me without wanting to commit indecent acts."

Joaquim crowds Reid against the side of the pool. "Changed forever," he says, and when Reid kisses him it's with a heat that leaves him breathless.

Joaquim starts with easy questions; this time, when Reid asks him questions, he's better prepared to answer.

"Reid," Joaquim whispers. He pulls Reid as close as he can, arms tight around his waist, palms running up the back of his swim shirt. "What's the primary ingredient in a cupcake?"

"Oh, no," Reid groans, head thumping back against the side of the pool. Joaquim laughs.

"C'mon, I know you know it."

"Well, you definitely need flour," Reid says. "I'm sure everyone knows that."

"What if you were going to make special cupcakes?" Joaquim nips at Reid's earlobe.

"Unfair." Reid pouts and pulls away.

"Would you categorize any recent attempts at baking as your signature or showstopper product?"

"Oh my god," Reid says with a embarrassed gasp. "How did you know?"

"What's your deepest, darkest guilty pleasure, Reid?" Joaquim's lips are at Reid's throat in earnest now. Reid'll have marks tomorrow. He squirms away and ducks underwater.

"Too many questions in a row," Reid says from behind him when he surfaces. "I think that's cheating." He tries to swim out of reach, but Joaquim snags him before he can get away. "Ugh, this is so embarrassing."

"What? Why?"

"Seriously, how did you know?"

"Reid, your entire DVR is marathon episodes of *The Great British Baking Show*. If this is the way you keep secrets, I must advise you be more devious."

"Damn, I should never have left you alone with that TV." Reid still won't meet his eyes.

"So, final question," Joaquim asks, hand on Reid's cheek, coaxing him to meet his eyes. "Were you trying to bake for me?"

"Yes," Reid says. Joaquim has to bend to hear him.

"You know, that's about the sweetest thing anyone has ever done for me." Joaquim isn't lying. Reid can cook well enough, but Joaquim knows from passing comments that he can't bake worth a damn.

"Really?" Reid brightens. Joaquim wonders at the love Reid has in his heart, the sweetness and attention and affection. He wonders at Felix, who somehow missed this part of Reid, who didn't want it.

"Maybe..." Reid tucks himself close, with his face nuzzling Joaquim's neck and his hands laced behind his back. He swallows. "I was trying to make key lime cupcakes to go with the Caipirinhas. Maybe next time we can try together. God knows I could use a set of eyes to tell me what the hell I'm doing wrong."

"Yes." Joaquim kisses the crown of Reid's head and closes his eyes when Reid kisses him behind his ear. "I would love that."

Twenty-four

JOAQUIM IS A SELF-AWARE MAN. He's innately patient and has always been gifted with the ability to calm others, to make them comfortable. He enjoys adventure and travel and avoids sliding into lazy contentment in any place. He loves his family; they are his only true roots. He knew he was gay early on and never questioned it.

This kind of happiness is new knowledge: how it feels, how easily he accepts it, how it flows naturally through him. Reid makes him aware of his happiness, both in the joy being in love brings and in the stark difference in their emotional experiences. Reid is not always happy. It's clear that Reid wants desperately to be happy, that he savors and is grateful for the happiness he does get.

"Can I come over?" Joaquim asks over the phone for the third time. He's gentle with Reid's subdued voice and barely-there answers.

"You don't understand," Reid says. "You don't understand. Just. Can I call you tomorrow?"

The tightness in his throat makes it hard to reply. Reid's downswings make Joaquim feel helpless and frustrated; they're beyond his power to help or alleviate. And in the midst of them, Reid always shuts him out.

Reid told him that his mental illness isolates him. Even with family and friends, he was isolated. Without friends, and with only Felix for company, he was isolated. At Sycamore Grove. Here, before Joaquim.

Joaquim feels isolated himself, powerless and frustrated. Other than Reid, Joaquim is alone as well, with no one to help him understand what he and Reid are going through.

*   *   *

"Hey, babe." Joaquim kisses Reid's cheeks.

"Hi," Reid replies. He's a little pale; his smile is a tiny bit wan. But Reid's happiness at seeing Joaquim is genuine, if muted.

"You okay?" Joaquim asks.

Reid huffs and grips the steering wheel too tight. "Fine." Even his voice is tight.

"Um," Joaquim reaches to put a hand on Reid's thigh, then thinks better of it. "Did I do something wrong?"

Reid takes a breath. "No. No, I'm sorry, I'm sensitive right now."

Joaquim, at a loss, doesn't say anything. Despite Reid saying he's okay, tension fills the car.

"So," Reid says. Joaquim exhales, grateful that the silence has been broken. "We can eat inside or out overlooking the water. Do you have a preference?"

"Oh, I don't care. I guess it depends on how hot you are." Joaquim catches Reid smiling as well. "I mean, you're always hot. Just. Temperature."

"J, I got it." Reid pulls into the parking lot of the Buzzards' Roost, which Mike recommended to Joaquim.

"I want to be sure." Joaquim kisses him softly.

"Your inability to keep your hands and mouth off of me seems like a good indication," Reid says. His eyes are bright, framed by his eyeliner, and his smile is lopsided. Somehow, Reid is both sexy and adorable. Love and lust and affection swirl and ache in Joaquim's chest.

"You're finally wearing shorts regularly," Joaquim says. "Hopefully you've acclimated to the humidity, because late August and into September is truly a bitch, from what I hear. Let's try for outside." What he doesn't say is, he's learned that the sound and proximity of water calm Reid. Whatever tension was between them earlier has dissipated, but Joaquim is beginning to understand the truth Reid has been offering him: His moods are unpredictable, especially lately.

"Great!" Reid kisses him again, a fast, casual kiss, the kind that speaks of comfort and stability.

It's only four; the restaurant isn't too busy for them to grab a spot overlooking the water. And it's happy hour.

"Oh, that looks delicious," Reid says, eyeing Joaquim's margarita.

"I could probably sneak you a sip." Joaquim twists the drink by the stem of the glass.

"No, it's fine. If I want one badly enough I could make one at home, provided someone buys me liquor." Reid winks. "The other night was a splurge. I don't like the idea of mixing medicine and alcohol, though it's technically okay with my everydays. And I always regret what an ass I make of myself the next day."

Joaquim shrugs. "Can I ask about your meds?"

"Sure," Reid says. "What do you want to know?"

What Joaquim wants to know is, if Reid takes them, why does he still experience cycles the way he's described? Isn't the point to stop them?

"Um." Joaquim pauses and blows out a breath. Under the table, Reid's foot bumps his, and then both feet wrap around his ankles. "You said I can ask questions. But I can't lie; I don't want to ask something that seems offensive. I have no idea how to handle this."

His feet remain in contact with Joaquim's even when his eyes don't. "I'll keep that in mind," Reid promises.

"So—you take meds for?"

"Well, I take two for the mood disorder. They work in different ways. One keeps me level in the longer term. One is more short-term-acting; it helps with the agitation and the actual rapid cycling."

"It helps but doesn't…?"

"No, it doesn't get rid of them entirely. It helps a lot. And we've tried different things. The ones I'm on are great for a lot of reasons. The long-acting one I'm taking—Lamictal—is a great one for mood disorders, and I've had almost no side effects. Maybe in the future I'll have to change my meds again. It's always a balancing act. Right now my therapist, Nancy, thinks that part of what's making things rougher is the transition. I'm in a new place. And telling you about everything. She keeps telling me to set up a support network here."

"What kind?"

"Friends? Therapy? I'm not sure." Reid closes his eyes. "It's hard to trust people with this. I have my group back in Wisconsin. I Skype into the meetings remotely, but the distance changes things, I guess."

Reid's been alone with his truths here: Joaquim is unfamiliar with Reid's particular mental illness. Knowing it's there, though, couldn't that be a start?

"But now I have you," Reid says, echoing Joaquim's thoughts. "I mean, I want to be clear. You aren't responsible for my well-being. You don't have to take care of me. I don't want to be treated like I can't take care of myself."

"I know you can," Joaquim says, quietly but with conviction. "But I can be here for you, right?" What he wants is enough of Reid's trust to let him in when he's low, when he's struggling. He has no idea how to help, but being shut out the way he was this week was so hard.

"J. I love you. I do. But it'll be harder than you think," Reid says. Joaquim forces himself to linger on the love part, not the closed-off part.

"Is it crazy, falling in love so fast?" Joaquim winces as soon as the words are out. Reid only grins, though.

"You can say crazy with me. I do all the time, but it's a dark humor thing and I only do it with people I know. I'm not really a word-policing kind of guy, unless it's something racist or homophobic or misogynistic."

"Okay." Joaquim stops to thank their waiter when their food comes. He wraps his other foot around Reid's so that they are a tangle of semi-secret connection. It's a tether. And in the wind by the water, with greasy food on his fingertips, feeling the lovely weight of love shared, Joaquim promises himself he'll be more patient. He'll trust Reid with his questions and hold on when he's pushed away.

"So... love."

Reid's smile is brilliant. "Yeah. Wanna do this thing?"

"The being in love thing? Absolutely."

*   *   *

HOLDING ON WHEN BEING PUSHED away proves to be a bigger trial than Joaquim anticipated. Reid low and refusing to let Joaquim come to him is one thing. But his irritability, his quickness to assume Joaquim means something when he doesn't, is much more frustrating and tests Joaquim's patience. Joaquim noticed Reid's erratic moods before; now they seem to be constant. He can't tell if Reid's in a rough phase or if opening up to Joaquim triggered them somehow. *Was Reid working hard to hide them before?*

"Reid, I only asked if you were okay," Joaquim says, one night after dinner. Reid is at the sink in the condo washing dishes with jerky and angry movements. Joaquim noticed the spotlessness of the condo when he came in. Reid is regimented and organized; he's precise about cleaning, but by now Joaquim can spot differences when Reid is using cleaning as a coping mechanism. He knows better than to say anything about the cleaning as a sign of how Reid is doing. Asking if Reid is okay once felt innocuous; apparently, it was not.

Dinner was delicious, but Reid talked too fast and too much, then fell quiet. His leg bounced frantically all through their meal, but Reid seemed to be trying his best to act as if nothing was amiss.

Joaquim's question didn't only seem benign, it was born of genuine caring. He's absolutely clueless as to why it pushed Reid's button so hard: in response, Reid dropped his fork with a clatter, muttered something under his breath, and stalked off to the kitchen. They weren't yet finished with their meal, and Reid was already packing the food away and cleaning.

"Reid, come on," Joaquim tries. Reid's shoulders bunch under the faded black T-shirt he only wears at home. The seam is ripped where the inside tag was, and there's a hole in the front. It's soft as hell.

"Don't patronize me," Reid says, his voice barely audible above the rushing water from the faucet. The warning in his tone is clear.

"I'm not. I'm *not*." Joaquim insists. He doesn't dare touch Reid; he skirts the breakfast bar so he's in front of Reid and tries to catch his eye. "I don't understand what I've done. Why can't I ask if you're okay?"

"Because you need to trust me! *Fuck*," Reid turns the water off with a vicious twist of his wrist. His hands are still soapy. "No one trusts me to know myself, when I'm okay or not."

What the hell? Joaquim is reasonably sure that his question had nothing to do with trusting Reid with himself.

"Man, come on. It comes from a place of caring. You said you needed support systems." Joaquim gestures at himself. "I'm right here! How can I help if you won't let me ask if you're okay?"

"You're not supposed to! I come to *you*."

Okay. No. Joaquim bites his tongue in time. This is not how he understands support. When he's with his divers, it's his responsibility to read them, to offer encouragement or calm when he senses their anxieties mounting or when they panic. Joaquim's not about to tell Reid how backward and irrational he's being. In Joaquim's experience, arguing with someone when they're being irrational isn't productive.

Is judging Reid as irrational condescending? Joaquim closes his eyes and rests his palms on the counter top, trying to settle himself enough to think. Reid's anger comes from something. Strong emotions always have roots.

"Reid, is this really to do with me?" Joaquim asks, fully aware that the question might make Reid angrier. He promised Reid honesty and he promised himself that he'd ask questions.

Reid's hands are in fists and his eyes on the ground. Joaquim aches to touch him, to remind him of the connection between them and of the solid presence of his body, a tether to his *self*, a self in love with Reid's.

"I need a minute," Reid says. He doesn't meet Joaquim's eyes; he wipes his hands on his pants and walks past him through the condo and out the back porch. Stunned, Joaquim doesn't move. He has no means of transportation other than Reid, so he has nowhere to go. Following Reid is out of the question.

The silence is too loud and weighty, so, with nothing else to do, Joaquim settles onto the couch and flips through Reid's recordings. There's nothing new. Joaquim shakes his head and turns on the guide. He channel-surfs mindlessly. Obsessing over the fight leads him in circles, guessing what Reid might be thinking or doing, which leads back to annoyance and frustration, which is best solved or worked on with Reid, not when his imagination is spinning its wheels in *what ifs*.

"Hey." Reid says. Joaquim wakes from a light sleep when Reid shakes his shoulder gently.

"Oh god." Joaquim sits up and stretches. His neck is kinked from falling asleep at a weird angle. "What time is it?"

"Late." Reid won't look at him, but his voice is no longer brittle. Joaquim grabs his hand. "I'm sorry. I shouldn't have left you here so long; will you be in trouble?"

Joaquim checks his cell. It's well past when they lock the dorm doors, but he's not working in the morning.

"Don't worry about it."

Reid sits next to him and sighs. His eyes never lose their power when they meet Joaquim's directly. Joaquim wonders if being with Reid will always be like this: a punch to the gut of tangled feelings that make him helpless. Joaquim doesn't mind helplessness, so long as it's mostly the good kind, the heady helplessness of falling in love or the release of control that comes with being with someone trusted.

"I'm sorry," Reid says. "It's not about you; you were right."

Reid's apology is so direct, it takes the wind out of Joaquim's annoyance—and he's half awake and has had time to simmer down.

"Do you wanna talk or go to sleep?" Joaquim asks. Reid shrugs. "Can we talk tomorrow?"

"Yeah?"

"Promise me? I don't want to let this go without figuring it out." Joaquim can only be honest. "But we're both tired and things are okay. Right?"

"Yeah," Reid says. He takes a breath and repeats himself, sounding more confident.

In bed that night, they don't speak. They don't make love or fuck or even kiss, other than a chaste goodnight kiss. But Reid holds Joaquim on the edge of too tight, which is enough to communicate uncertainty. Nothing said can prove his constancy at this moment. Joaquim's had years of watching his parents practice constancy. He's never needed to do so himself, but with Reid, he will. They will. He doesn't want to imagine not being with Reid, so it's time to begin practicing.

Twenty-five

WELL PAST SUNRISE, REID WAKES up curled on the very edge of the bed. His grandmother's room overlooks the porch, so sunrises from bed are a distinct possibility. Somehow, the sound of the ocean isn't the same in here, probably due to the proximity.

Reid peeks over his shoulder. Joaquim curled up on his side, around a pillow, his back to Reid. He reaches out to touch a mole on Joaquim's shoulder blade, ready to trace a wake-up path to other ones on his back, when he remembers last night. He's going to have to face his own music.

Joaquim's body is beautifully settled into the rhythms of his deep, sleeping breaths. Reid is no longer angry. Well, he's a little angry at himself. *If I wake Joaquim with kisses, will that be enough? Will he remember the apology from last night and let it stand?*

Eyes closed, Reid scoots closer to Joaquim and puts a hand on his hip. He promised to talk to Joaquim. And even without that promise, they should talk. Joaquim is the potential for a healthy relationship, finally.

When Reid's body heat comes into contact with his, Joaquim stills and then stretches. Joaquim's body is a luxury: muscles tensing and loosening, all stunning bones and inviting skin. Reid *wants*. He wants to glut himself on this man, to soak up every moment with him while he can.

"Morning?" he whispers. His hand slides from Joaquim's hip to his stomach under his belly button.

"But will it be a *good* morning?" Joaquim arches a little, rolling his body, sinuous and promising, against Reid's. Reid puts his face between Joaquim's shoulder blades, as if he could breathe in the balm of that teasing, that ease. He kisses up to Joaquim's neck and then bites lightly.

Nothing more needs saying. Reid loves the hush, loves the ease and intimacy, loves the way Joaquim takes him so far out of his head and into his body he hasn't any words.

THEY LINGER AFTER SEX AND, when Joaquim's stomach rumbles, get out of bed. Joaquim showers first while Reid makes coffee.

"Mmm, warm," Reid says, taking Joaquim's casual kiss as they pass in the hall. Joaquim's face is still damp from the shower. "I made coffee."

"Thank you," Joaquim says.

A little later, out of the shower and with coffee mug in hand, Reid meets Joaquim at the table on the porch.

"You made breakfast?"

"It's just eggs," Joaquim says.

"Thank you," Reid says and means it.

"I never use to eat eggs like this," Joaquim says. "In Brazil it's not really something we eat for breakfast. Bobby is addicted to these egg sandwiches he makes, and he started making them for me too."

"And now you're addicted?"

"I wouldn't say addicted. Sometimes it's just nice to have someone make you something simple but good." Joaquim isn't laying traps; these aren't loaded eggs, a passive-aggressive power play like Felix would have made. Reid can eat these without nagging worry or prickling anger summoning his defenses. They're just eggs.

"With Felix, it wouldn't have been like this," Reid says.

"Hmm?" Joaquim's eyebrows are a question. He swallows. "Aren't all relationships different?"

"No. I mean, yes. They are. What I mean is that, when Felix and I fought, even after one of us gave in, it could go on for days. Some things never went away. These eggs would be a way to show me that he was a better boyfriend. A reminder that whatever I'd done, he was being... um, what's the word?"

Joaquim shrugs.

"Magnanimous. At some point, he'd remind me. Maybe when we were fighting again, or later that day. Like setting little traps. That he'd done this nice thing for me *despite* whatever."

"He sounds—"

"I did it too." Reid doesn't want to hear Joaquim's judgment; it would apply to him as well. "It's the way we were together. We weren't trying to be assholes. It's just how we were."

Joaquim takes a long sip of his coffee and inspects the gray morning. Blankets of clouds cover the bay, touching the horizon as far as he can see. Maybe it'll rain today. A rainy day indoors with Joaquim would be nice.

"I don't do that," Joaquim says at last. "The eggs are eggs."

"Yeah," Reid says. He bumps Joaquim's foot with his own. "I love that."

"So, if you make me eggs, will I have to ask?" Joaquim is matter of fact; there's no anger in his tone.

"I hope not." Reid tries to smile. "It's so different with you. I don't want to be like that. I haven't felt... pulled? I guess that's the word. Felix and I kept pulling each other into that. But it's a pattern, right? A habit? I don't want you to second-guess everything I do. But I promise I'm going to try not to do that passive-aggressive shit."

"A promise to try sounds good," Joaquim says.

Reid is swamped in gratitude. "Trying to explain feelings and actions and reactions and motivations is so complicated, man." He pushes his now empty plate away.

"I think you did pretty well," Joaquim says.

Reid shakes his head. "I meant, there's shit we have to talk about still. Have you ever tried to plan out what you want to say, only half of what you're feeling contradicts the other half? Like the rational and irrational parts of your brain both want to speak."

"I guess."

"I worry that I won't always be able to tell them apart. When I'm angry especially, but later too. Like, therapy is all, 'your feelings are valid.' Not because they're right, but because you're feeling them. They're happening. Don't tell yourself you shouldn't have them. Nancy always tells us that 'should' ought to be classified as a bad word. Even if your feelings or reactions make no rational sense, you need to look at what happened to figure out where they're coming from."

"Okay." Joaquim settles his elbows on the table and meets Reid's eyes.

Reid runs a shaking hand through his still-damp hair. "Like, if I said, when you did X, it made me angry. That doesn't mean you actually *made me* feel angry. It means my *reaction* was anger. With my family, with Felix, everyone was always saying, 'You make me feel.' But really, it's 'When you did this, I felt.'"

"And those are different?"

"Yeah, of course."

Joaquim mulls this over. Reid gives him some time.

"I'm not saying you should tell me what to say when we're fighting. Because if I'm already angry I don't think that'll go over well. But I'm working on it. Maybe later. Or I'll try to figure it out. That's why I left yesterday. I know that I'll keep going; I'll pick and pick and push when I'm mad or fighting. I can't be rational. The best I can do now is walk away."

"Okay," Joaquim says.

"You don't have to keep saying okay. I'm not... I don't want you to feel like you can't talk to me or, like, offer a differing opinion."

"So if I say okay again?" Joaquim's eyes crinkle with his smile. Reid grins back. "I'm not saying it just because, Reid. You're telling me about yourself. I'm learning."

"But is this too one-sided for you?"

"Uh, what?"

"I'm always an issue." Reid touches the tines of his fork, the edge of the plate, the bumpy plastic of the yellow and blue-striped tablecloth.

"You are not!" Joaquim protests. "It's not like people know how to balance a teeter-totter right away. You gotta learn that shit."

"A teeter-totter?" Reid cracks up.

Joaquim tosses a balled-up napkin at him. "What do you call them, then?"

"Seesaws."

"Whatever. You get my meaning, right?"

"Yeah."

They both rise to clear the table at the same time, as if planned. They do the dishes together, and then Reid goes into the bedroom. It's not too hot today, so he opens the sliding glass doors all the way to let in fresh air and the sounds of outside. When Joaquim comes to investigate, Reid pulls him into bed.

"Reid." Joaquim squirms when Reid pins him, then laughs when Reid tickles him.

"I know. I'm not changing the subject." Reid leans down to kiss him. Outside, the leaves catch the patter of the first raindrops. Reid exhales and kisses Joaquim again. He lies next to him and touches his lips and nose and, when Joaquim closes his eyes, his eyelids. The rain comes louder, and it feels as if, in the whole world, it's only them. Reid pulls up the sheet as a colder wind comes in.

"With my family, with Felix, 'Are you okay?' is code. It means someone else knows better than I do if I'm okay. It's not a question when they already have an answer."

"So when they ask, it really means they know you're not?"

"It means they *think* they know," Reid corrects him. The small changes make a big difference in meaning to Reid, who has learned that managing relationships involves precise words. Otherwise there's too much room for making meaning that isn't there. "It can be anything from placating to condescending. No one really cares what my answer is, because they don't trust me to recognize whether I'm okay or know what is good for me."

"That sounds frustrating," Joaquim says. His voice is as quiet as the moment calls for, under the cocoon of the sheet and in the privacy of the rain.

"And maybe sometimes I don't. For a long time, I didn't. I couldn't see patterns; I couldn't see the way my behavior looked to others. But what's the point of going through everything I have, all the therapy, and looking at my own patterns and behaviors if no one else is going to do the work too?"

"Your parents, you mean?" Joaquim says.

Reid cocks his head. "Oh yeah. Not you. It's not just being cyclothymic. We have bad patterns, all of us, with how we communicate. As a family, we could have done a lot of work together on recovery. But to them, *I'm* the sick one. I'm the one who needs help. They've suffered too."

"What the hell, no they—"

"Well, yeah, they have. Not like me. But watching someone you love go through what I did, they're living through it too… they did. But I'm the cause. I'm the root. I'm the one needing fixing. I'm patient zero."

"Don't you…"

Reid waits patiently while Joaquim works out what he wants to say.

"That sounds lonely."

Reid swallows hard, eyes burning. "It is."

"When I asked if you were okay. Is that, like, a trigger?"

"Have you been doing some Internet research?" Reid works to keep his tone teasing, so that Joaquim doesn't think he's taking offense.

"Yeah, of course."

Reid closes his eyes. *Of course. Of course this man would care enough to try to learn and support and be actively involved. God knows what wrong information he'll get from the Internet, but fuck. At least he's trying.*

"I'm so grateful for you," Reid says. He grips Joaquim's hand.

"And I you," Joaquim says. The words come easily, a quick response offered with no strings.

"I wouldn't call it a trigger," Reid says, after a while. "Trigger for me is a word that has to do with other things. The, um, anxiety and stuff."

"The self-harm?"

"Yeah. Or a panic attack. Maybe eventually a mood cycle. What happened last night was me being mad."

"I didn't mean it like that."

Reid bristles, but keeps his lips shut until he can think through his reaction to Joaquim's matter-of-fact tone.

"I know. I mean, before you came over, I didn't think my mood was changing. I couldn't see it. It kills me to say this, but I don't know that I was okay. And that's the worst of all of this."

"Not being okay?"

"No, people being right when I'm not okay."

Joaquim doesn't say anything.

"I don't know," Reid says and sighs. "I don't have the right answer. Because I need people to trust me. I am the single most invested person in my recovery. It doesn't matter what other people think about that. I mean, about me, yes. Maybe because I did… what I did," Reid swallows, "they won't ever trust me to be okay?"

"Because they're afraid?"

"Maybe." Reid plays with Joaquim's fingers and thinks his questions over. "That and more."

"I don't feel that way, though," Joaquim says. "I understand, in a sense, what you're talking about. But what happens if I'm worried, and you don't seem to see what's happening. Does that happen? Like, you haven't had a mood swing yet, or whatever, but there are signs?"

Reid closes his eyes. The intimacy of the rain and the pull of Joaquim's body burn through him now. He's too close; it's too rough on thin skin.

"Why can't I have just one thing?"

"What do you mean?"

"I want something that's not about this. I want to be a normal kid! I want to have regular issues and not have to figure this shit out, because I don't have the answers!"

Reid makes a frustrated noise into his pillow and lies with his face buried. Joaquim rubs his hand over Reid's back. Thank god he doesn't offer Reid any platitudes. He's on the cusp of sleep when Joaquim whispers *I love you*. Reid peeks over to find Joaquim's eyes steady on his, and shining.

THEY WAKE FROM A LONG nap tangled under a sheet. The rain has stopped, and everything is soupy; their bodies are slicked with sweat where they touch.

"I don't know the answer," Reid says before they're fully awake.

"All right," Joaquim mumbles into his neck.

"Do you need someone to talk to about this?" It occurred to Reid as he fell asleep that Joaquim's only person to talk to is the problem—not that Joaquim would call him a problem.

"Hmm?"

"Like a friend or something? To work through things?"

Joaquim pulls the sheet from his body to cool off. "Could I talk to my sister?"

Relief rolls through Reid. He'd offered with the fear that Joaquim would want to talk to a friend at the dive center. He isn't friends with them, but the fact that he might run into them or spend time with them wouldn't be great.

"Yeah." Reid rolls over and pulls the sheet off. "Yeah, that sounds okay."

Twenty-six

DESPITE HAVING REID'S PERMISSION, JOAQUIM doesn't speak to his sister at first. There's too much he doesn't understand himself. Joaquim values honesty above most things, but he's far from knowing how to navigate Reid's moods. Reid is right, though: knowing about Reid's issues, it's hard not to think everything could be related to a mood swing.

In the end, it's not a mood swing that tips the scales. It's not something he'd ever tell Sofia about in detail. It's something he doesn't understand.

"So," Reid says. It's dusk, and so hot and muggy Reid needed convincing to go outside. The bay water and pool water are tepid; everything has slowed until Joaquim is sure the sound of the cicadas and water is molasses melting, one long, ponderous, thrumming hum that won't end. "What to do now?" His eyes are bright, playful, and sure.

Joaquim's smile blooms; he needs no coaxing to unfurl. What Reid brings out in him is flash-bang response, as if an open, aching want has been there all along and Joaquim has forgotten to pay attention. He takes Reid by the waist and kisses him, a biting kiss that's both joyful and rough. They can't spend all day in bed, no matter how tempting it sounds. His muscles will get tight and achy; Joaquim isn't one for restlessness.

"We can go for a swim."

"The water's too warm even for me," Reid says. Reid's phone buzzes. "What's that?"

"Delia," Reid says. "She wants to go out."

"Ooooh, let's."

"I don't know." Reid's scrunches his nose and tosses his phone on the bed. "She's so intense; I don't want her scaring you off."

"Pleeease?" Joaquim kisses next to Reid's nose, one side and then the other, easing the frown. "I want to spend time with your friends."

"Friend," Reid says, holding up one finger. "I have one friend here."

"Two, actually," Joaquim says, capturing Reid's chin and looking into his eyes. Reid's eyes laugh back at him.

"Touché."

"So?"

"Okay, okay, I'll ask her."

DESPITE THE HEAT, THEY FIND themselves splashing around in tepid pool water half an hour later. Dinner at Salty John's with Delia isn't for a few hours, and Reid confessed to restlessness as well. The oppressive heat has kept Betty and crew inside today, so it's just the two of them.

"I wonder where the kids are," Reid says.

"Aren't you uncomfortable with your head like that?" Joaquim stands next to him. Reid is floating with his head propped on the side of the pool.

"Yes," Reid says. He rolls into the water and comes up with a kiss that tastes of salt and chlorine. He leans back against the wall. "There've been kids here this last week. Either visiting or renting for a week. Young. Lots of fun."

"You've been playing with them?" That's almost too cute to handle.

"Well, I've got to do something while my guy is busy." Reid's arms snake around his waist.

"Shell World?" Joaquim says, voice gone hoarse.

Reid laughs. "No. I don't want to do Shell World."

Joaquim retaliates, bites the side of Reid's neck, and notes how boneless he goes.

"Besides, I hardly work there enough hours to keep occupied. And kids are fun!"

"Yeah, they are," Joaquim says. Reid's playfulness flickers in and out, as do most of his personality traits. Joaquim has seen him be quite good with kids when he's in the mood. He always had fun with Erin during their class, and Joaquim could tell that his kindness and interest were never fake or forced.

"You still have those kids in your class?" Reid lets himself float away, then starfishes out. Joaquim stands next to him, touches Reid's now-pink cheek, and shakes his head. *Fuck. We forgot sunscreen.*

"No, they moved on last week."

"Wow, time flies." Reid closes his eyes and lets himself float for a bit longer. "I guess that means you're almost done."

"Yeah, less than two months." Joaquim puts a hand under Reid's head and draws him up, gives him a quick kiss before pushing him under the water, and shouts laughter when Reid wraps his arms around Joaquim's legs and pulls him under.

ROUGHHOUSING ISN'T JOAQUIM'S IDEA OF foreplay, but when he finds himself bending Reid over the side of the bed, both still struggling out of clinging suits, he has to concede that either it, or anything with Reid, is.

"*Ohmigod*, fuck, who cares," Reid grinds out when Joaquim insists on getting his swim shorts past his knees.

"I do." Joaquim bites the meaty globe of Reid's ass, then licks it and closes his eyes when Reid moans, utterly shameless.

"Do that again."

Joaquim struggles with the shorts and bites Reid again, high up on his leg, under the deep crescent where his thigh meets his ass. Reid vibrates and whimpers. Joaquim finally triumphs over his swim trunks. As desperate as Reid now, he pushes his legs apart roughly, puts a hand on Reid's back and presses him face-first into the bedding in one quick move. Normally here he'd laugh, or fuck, or swear; he'd make any noise if he weren't so on fire for Reid's taste. His knees protest when he drops to them. Reid churns his hips; jerky movements grind against the mattress. Rough and careless, Joaquim uses his strength to pull him back.

"Not yet." He punctuates this with another bite to Reid's inner thigh. He works Reid's body until it is live-wire tight, crackling with the nearness of orgasm. He pushes his face against Reid while he catches his breath.

"Bite me again," Reid says. His voice is hardly recognizable. "Please, J, bite me."

So he does. He bites Reid's ass and, when he demands it, his thigh, harder, then delivers a sucking, biting, bruising kiss to the other one. And when his fingers are as deep in Reid as they can go, when Joaquim's lost in dazed pleasure from the moisture of Reid's skin, Reid comes. He comes without noise, but with his body bowed gorgeously and Joaquim's fingers massaging it out of him, caught by the almost-violent clench and release of his orgasm pulsing.

"Fuck," Reid whispers, then rolls onto his back. When he reaches for Joaquim, his smile is full of filth, and mischief, and dazed pleasure.

"Wow." Joaquim pauses in dressing when Reid bends over to put his boxer briefs on. On the inside of his thigh is an impressive bruise bestowed by Joaquim's mouth. He's never done that to a lover.

"What?" Reid turns to him. Joaquim touches the mark.

"I'm sorry," he says. "I really got you. Does that hurt?" he presses a little, surprised when Reid shivers.

"A little, but that's okay. I like it." Joaquim takes Reid's kiss, and then the shirt Reid hands him. They're late for their meeting with Delia.

"God, I can smell the sex on you guys." Delia's at a table with one full and one empty beer bottle in front of her. Joaquim smiles, and Reid laughs. "You guys are way too cute. I don't know if I can be seen with you in public."

"Oh my god, I am famished," Reid says. Joaquim takes a sticky menu when Reid hands it to him, but doesn't bother to read it.

"Onion rings," Delia says, and Reid nods and puts the menu down. Joaquim observes the shorthand exchange and sits back. So often, he and Reid are alone; it's a treat to watch Reid out in the world with others. Now, his eyeliner is thick and smudged, and his hair is a riot of messy spikes. He's well and truly fucked, though he got ready *after* the fucking. It is a delicious look on him.

Joaquim orders a beer. Their waitress is impatient and on the verge of unfriendly, but the bar is filling up and Joaquim hasn't seen a single other server. Reid orders onion rings and potato skins, of all things.

"You want anything else or just to share those?" Reid asks.

"Those are good," he says. Greasy food sits in his stomach sometimes; he'd rather have the beer.

"Shel?"

"Oh god, inventory rampage." Delia says. She's finished her second beer quickly enough to impress Joaquim. "Took hours."

"Sorry," Reid says.

"No, you're not," Delia laughs. Joaquim's never heard her laugh. Either it's the beer or she just needs time to warm up. Joaquim is compelled to draw people out when they're like that. Delia exudes confidence, though. She doesn't need to be anyone but herself.

"Please don't tell me he's decided we need more personalized starfish lamps," Reid says.

"Excuse me, what?" Surely he heard that wrong.

"These lamps," Reid says. He gestures.

"They have starfish embedded in the bases." Delia says, and Joaquim nods. The lamps are the standard kitsch that's popular here. "Only these are personalized with names at the base. Like, you can do that cheesy shit, 'McMacken Family, 2007.'"

"Eh?"

"Family name, date they got married. Or kid's name, birthdate."

"Like, who the hell is giving their kid a lamp with their birthday on it?"

"Shel is *so* into this idea, I can't believe it."

"We've sold maybe two," Reid explains. "Shel is convinced it's a *thing*, though."

So the conversation takes off, starting with Shel facts and grievances that are more affectionate than anything else before leading Delia's most recent dating disaster, and then catching up on her friends. Reid doesn't hang out with them, but he definitely is up to speed on who they are and all about their lives. Joaquim is comfortably separate from the conversation, happy to rest his arm on the back of Reid's chair and nurse his beer. Every now and then he touches the back of Reid's neck. He's so beautiful, animated or upset or still. Reid's like the ocean: unfathomable, constantly changing, stunning, and dangerous. Joaquim doesn't think Reid will hurt him, but he could. Hell, he could hurt himself.

The thought is sobering. Joaquim remembers Reid begging him to bite harder. *Was that...?* Was Joaquim somehow a part of that? Obviously, he didn't think twice about it in the moment. He doesn't understand Reid's relationship to pain. Reid taps Joaquim's finger where it's wrapped around his beer bottle.

"You there?"

"Yeah," Joaquim says, smiling when Reid does. Reid turns back to his conversation. Joaquim likes that Reid checks in every now and then, but doesn't feel compelled to babysit or draw Joaquim in. From their conversations, he has the idea that this scene, played out with Felix, would end very differently. Joaquim breathes slowly and looks around the bar. He notices what people are wearing and the décor, the dim lighting and the scent of warm bodies in a room with closed windows. He pushes worries out of mind and marks them for later.

"So what's your deal?"

"Pardon?" Joaquim tunes back in at the sound of Delia's voice.

"Reid told me you're going for some, um, like. Diver master level? Something." She waves that off.

"An MSDT. Master Scuba Diver Trainer. Yeah, I'm almost done."

"Then what?"

"Not sure," Joaquim glances at Reid. "I guess I go where the wind takes me." Delia pauses, beer halfway to her mouth. She shrugs and takes a sip, but Joaquim doesn't miss the face she makes at Reid.

"Minha vida," Joaquim says when Sofia answers the phone.

"Fuck that," she says, sleep thick in her voice. He winces. "Don't butter me up because it's, fuck, midnight. Why are you awake? Why am I awake?"

"I don't know. I'm sorry." Joaquim sits heavily on the couch in the common room. He's whispering so as not to wake the others. It's way too late for the conversation he wants to have with her, and there's no privacy here.

"What's wrong?" Rustling noises come through; she's sat up. Joaquim takes in the dated colors and pattern of the carpet. He stands and walks down the hall to the heavy door to the outside and props the door open with a rock. Joaquim lets himself out into the muggy night.

"So, um. Reid told me some of his stuff."

"His stuff? Carinho, you need to give me more than that."

"You know what I mean." Joaquim kicks pebbles into the bushes.

"Listen, you called me this late for a reason. Do you want to tell me about it?"

"He's, he's got this thing. Called cyclothymia. It's a kind of mental illness?" He waits for her to speak. There's nothing but silence. "That sounds awful. Like he's crazy. He's not."

"I wasn't thinking like that. I was waiting. I've never heard of this."

"Yeah, right? I hadn't either. He said it's not commonly diagnosed. It's like being bipolar? Or not, but that's the closest comparison. He says it's a mood disorder, so not like being depressed. Although sometimes he is depressed."

"This is a thing I should look up, yes?"

"It might help, if you want to know more about the details so I don't fuck it up."

"Are you scared because he has this?"

"Well, no. I mean. I worry. But that's not—"

"Bebê, calm down. Take a breath. You told me you're in love, right? Keep that in sight first."

"SoSo, I miss you so much." Joaquim holds on to the door handle; the edges dig into his palm. He wants to ask her what to do about Reid hurting himself, or how he used to. *Could still?* He wants to talk about how, when they fucked, Reid seemed to like being hurt, and that only after had Joaquim stopped to think if he was perpetuating a harmful habit or desire. "I wanted to ask about some things, but I think maybe they're too personal."

Her laughter is warm; he wants to wind the sound around himself—the comfort and hominess. "Yeah, I don't need the sexy report."

He smiles. "We went out with his friend from work, Delia. Everything was great before, but then he was acting so weird on the way home. And I didn't want to ask if he's okay, because we had a fight about that already."

"About asking if he's okay?" Sofia makes a noise. *Frustration or disbelief?* Her face is so expressive, and without it he can't always translate her interpretation.

"Yeah, it was a thing. A real fight."

"You never fight," she says.

"Reid is different. In a good way. I feel... so much more." Joaquim blows out a breath. The stars are obscured by clouds. Rain is coming; he can smell it. "Anyway. He has a thing about people asking that, because of his family and how they treated him. Once we were calmer and he explained, it made sense. But how can I ask if everything is okay when it means something different to him? He thinks it's about people not trusting him to take care of himself or assuming he's having a mental breakdown."

"Quim, that's a thing to ask him. The language he needs must be different."

"I guess," he says. *She has a good point. But what if Reid can't separate the two?* "That doesn't help me figure out what happened tonight."

"And you think I can solve that in the middle of the night when you're depriving me of sleep over a boy I haven't met?" Joaquim laughs. Despite the sleep deprivation he's apparently forcing on her, her teasing is a leeway only she would give him.

"You make a good point."

"Okay. I love you. I must sleep, though. I'll look this thing up tomorrow. Text me what it's called?"

"Sure."

"Joaquim. Remember how much fun you've had with him? The things you've done that make this wonderful?"

"Yeah, of course."

"Well, do more of that too. This is heavy stuff. Bring yourselves back to the place where the good stuff started."

Joaquim tamps down a defensive answer. There's no criticism in her advice. Reconnection… not that they've disconnected. Joaquim remembers teaching Reid to trust him; easing him into the water, exploring the reef, the warmth on their salty skin, and the flirtation blooming between them. *Yes.*

"Te amo, Sofia. Boa noite."

"Pra você também."

Twenty-seven

REID LEFT THE DOOR UNLOCKED; Nina is dropping Joaquim off after they run errands. Reid woke up off. His body is alien-skin-covered. He made a big breakfast he couldn't eat. He washed the dishes carefully, took everything off the counters and cleaned behind them, wiped down all of the cabinets, cleaned the floor. He stopped every few minutes to shake his hands out, to breathe and try to remember the borders of his body.

When Reid went to make his bed, he ended up on it, obsessively staring at the ceiling. Rachel's been texting him all morning, wondering why he's been skipping therapy. *Joaquim.* Being with him, despite the complexity of their relationship, has trumped everything else.

I'll go where the wind takes me. Joaquim's words won't let Reid be.

Reid should text Rachel back. He should reach out, because he's on the cusp of trouble. He should tell Joaquim how much that both hurt and bothered him. He should, he should, he should.

Should. A bad word. Still, it runs through his mind in a loop. He stares at the ceiling. Nancy's never judged him for self-harm. But they've worked hard to find coping skills for him to manage it. Unlike other therapists, Nancy knows how hard it is to stop. *Small hurts*, he reminds himself. They are a transition away from cutting, a way to mitigate the worst of his impulses. He doesn't want to hurt himself. Self-harming stopped being about that long ago.

I don't want that. I don't.

Reid gets up and drags in a chair from the living room. He's reaching for the ceiling when Joaquim comes in, startling him enough that Reid almost falls off the chair.

"What are you doing?" Joaquim puts a hand on Reid's hip.

Reid bites his lip. Joaquim's shoulder under his palm is smooth and round. He's wearing a tank top and the heat of his bare skin is comforting. But even Joaquim's body and touch won't help right now. *Trust*, Reid reminds himself. He's let Joaquim in. Despite Joaquim admitting to an uncertain future, Reid's promised himself he'll try.

"I needed to touch the ceiling." As soon as he says it, hears it, Reid understands how insane he sounds.

"I don't know that you're tall enough, lindo," Joaquim says.

Reid stares at him; a pregnant pause lies heavy in the air.

"How are you taking this so easily?"

"Because this is something you need, right?"

"Yes," Reid says. He closes his eyes.

"I want to help you with the things you need. These things. And you trusted me enough to tell me what you need now. I want to be worthy of that trust."

"Fuck," Reid says. He leans down to kiss Joaquim lightly and blinks away tears.

"So. What if you stand on the dresser? I'll stand next to you."

"You are perfect."

"Reid, I am so far from that. Come on, let's get you up there."

Reid wishes that Joaquim's steadiness was enough. The burn of embarrassment hurts. But when he puts his palms on the ceiling, the texture digs into and imprints on his skin. The dual satisfaction of it rushes through him. Reid's been fixated on this ceiling for months; he never tried to explain it, and probably won't ever have the right words for the way compulsions get under his skin. Also, though, when he presses hard enough, the pain is centering. It's not hurting him. It's digging in, then spilling through him: small hurts, particular sensations that pull him back together. Nancy tried to explain sensory stuff to him once, but he's had a hard time getting past the *should* of it all. He *shouldn't* want pain, right? He *shouldn't* need it.

But now, he can breathe. He can absorb the steadiness of Joaquim's hands on him differently. His arms burn, which tells him he's been standing there for a while. When he pulls his hands away, they are sprinkled with indentations. Joaquim breathes out with him when Reid cups his face in his hands. He helps Reid down. Reid buries his face in Joaquim's neck. The fear of being judged broken or weird slips away when Joaquim's arms come around him.

They'll come back. All of those feelings. But Reid holds on to hope. *Because maybe.*

"Perhaps not the most convenient help, is it?" Joaquim says. Reid takes a moment to parse meaning from the strange phrasing.

"You think I'm totally crazy, don't you?" They're on the couch together for once. It's impossible to tangle up together comfortably on the chaise on the porch. Reid needs Joaquim's solid and steady body more than air and water.

"No. I promise. I meant, if you need to feel things… something like that. Um, it's probably not always convenient to have to climb furniture."

The hint of humor carries a lot of weight.

"No, you're right. Maybe I won't want to again, though."

"But…" Joaquim turns toward him. "This was a pain thing?"

"Well." Reid chews on his bottom lip, testing the words. "Yes and no. It's not because I want to hurt myself so much as a need for a sensation. And also, sometimes I fixate on things."

Joaquim frowns but doesn't speak, giving Reid room to stumble through explaining.

"I've been staring at that fucking ceiling for months. When I'm in a weird place, sometimes it's all I can think about. How it would feel."

"And now you know, so you think maybe you won't fixate on it?"

"Yeah."

"But the sensation thing?"

"Yeah. I don't know." Reid turns his gaze outside. The sun is so bright. He's through talking.

"Reid," Joaquim keeps his voice soft. "Do you wanna go somewhere?"

"Anywhere?" Reid asks. It's not as sarcastic or cutting as it could be, considering Joaquim's words he's been unable to shake.

"Well, I planned a date. A maybe-date."

"What's a maybe-date?" Reid kisses under Joaquim's chin, safe in the turn in conversation.

"Like, maybe you'll go with me. To Anna's Beach?"

Reid gazes up at Joaquim. "We recreating our first date?"

"Well, I don't have fruit salad, but we can take some drinks in a cooler." Joaquim winks at him.

"That sounds perfect."

"CAN I ASK YOU A question?" Joaquim pauses their trek in the shallow waters. They're still in the mucky parts near the beach, but Joaquim's promised him that it gets nicer a little farther out where the muck turns to sand.

"Sure," Reid says. The beach is empty, and the water and sun have made a huge impact on his mood.

"Um, so you've told me about the small hurts thing. And obviously, today. I was there."

"Yeah." Reid takes Joaquim's hand and pulls him forward a little. They can walk and talk.

"The other night, when you were asking me to bite you?"

Reid blushes. That night had been really fucking hot. "Are you worried that it was the same?"

"Well, I don't want to hurt you, is all. And I did. You liked that, right?"

"J, honey." Reid's the one who stops this time. "That's totally different. To me, there are different kinds of pain. I don't like *all* pain. Think about it more like sensations."

"But—"

"Babe, if I were any other guy you were fucking, someone you didn't know, and they asked for the same thing, would you worry?"

The water is a constant gurgle and shush, moving ceaselessly as he watches. "No. I guess not."

Reid squints at him. His face is unreadable. He chooses not to force the conversation; maybe Joaquim needs to figure this out for himself.

Hand in hand, they walk through the water; Reid tips his face toward the sun and enjoys its boosting effect on his mood.

"Mike told me they probably won't be able to hire me after the internship, at least not for now," Joaquim says.

Reid stops; the world, which had faded to the pleasant shush of the water and the cries of gulls, rushes back.

"What?"

Joaquim tosses him a small smile, totally oblivious to the tightness in Reid's voice and the panic swelling in his chest.

"Yeah, but we'll keep in touch. Maybe in the future. I'm not worried."

"You're not worried? But what happens next?"

"Oh, I don't know. But I was going home to visit when this was over anyway, right? I have between now and then, while I'm back home, to find something."

"To go where the wind takes you, right?" Reid snatches his hand away and begins to wade back toward the shore. The reminder that Joaquim is going home to visit his family is a cold slap of water. With Joaquim, everything else fades away. Their time together is a series of moments; bright, sharp, insular, strung together like pearls, each one separate. Joaquim makes him forget the outside world sometimes, helps Reid live in the present.

Apparently, too much in the present.

"Reid, what's wrong now?"

Wow. That *now* needles. Its implications and the exasperation elicit a response so strong, Reid bites his cheek until he tastes blood. Back on the beach, he begins to fold the towels.

"Reid, seriously." Joaquim stops his hands.

"Don't ask me to take this conversation seriously when *you're* the one who made promises you don't take seriously," Reid says.

"What on earth are you talking about?"

"*You*. You're so cavalier! It's like this," Reid gestures between them, "means nothing. Requires no planning. You don't give a shit about the future!"

"Reid, if I didn't care about the future, why would I have taken an unpaid internship where I had to work my ass off far from home?"

Reid squeezes his eyes shut. Joaquim's homesickness isn't a secret. Reid never let himself think he would lose him to it.

"Look, life is short. Sue me if I don't sit around stressing about my next move when I have time to figure it out. Something will come; if you're open to it, life can be a great adventure. I'm young. You're young."

"What do I have to do with it?"

Joaquim's face, a study in concern, shifts to puzzled. "What?"

"What do you mean *what*? I can't—" Reid is ready to pull his hair out. Dual frustrations—his inability to articulate and the redundant nature of this conversation—make him want to yell. Twining with his frustration is panic: white, numbing panic, so tight in his chest it's beginning to hurt.

"I guess I figured one of us would land somewhere and the other would come. We're not tied down."

"I'm not tied…?" *How on earth can someone be so obtuse?* Reid may not be tied to a job or to his grandmother's home, but he definitely has things holding him back. Reid works on drawing in air, on breathing normally rather than panting. His heart pounds too hard, a constant drumming in his ears, throbbing in his sinuses.

"Like I said," Joaquim takes Reid's hands, and Reid lets him. "Life is short."

"Oh, my god, *really*? Do you think I don't get that? I probably get it more than anyone, I'm the one who—"

"Do you get ownership?" Joaquim snaps, and Reid blinks.

"No, I—" Reid swallows. His mouth is so dry. "That's not, I'm just trying to…"

"I'm sorry. I need to take a break." Joaquim roots around for his flip-flops.

"What do you mean?" White spots sparkle at the edge of Reid's vision.

"I'm going for a walk to clear my head, okay? I'll be back." Despite his anger, Joaquim's face softens, and he kisses Reid's cheek.

Joaquim heads back to the boardwalk; Reid settles on the towel facing the water, determined not to watch for him. *Perhaps it's best that we clear our heads.* At the very least, Reid should use this time to bring himself out of his panic attack without depending on anyone else. When he closes his eyes, the sound of wind through the mangrove trees, the call of birds, the rolling of waves envelop him. Rather than run his fingers through it, he buries them in the rough sand. Sun-warmed skin provides a gentle boundary for his body. Reid imagines himself rooted to the earth, legs solid, crossed on the blanket, as if he is one of the mangroves with roots growing into the mud and water. Calm rises through him.

He opens his eyes and watches the water. He sorts his thoughts and the words he couldn't articulate in the heat of the moment. *Our future isn't here.* This tiny life in Key Largo was a stopping-off point for both of them, a transient moment they happened to land in at the same time. Reid's life needs order. He needs plans to help curb his compulsive tendencies.

He needs more than whims and wishes, though; Joaquim's casual confidence that something will work out *won't* work for Reid.

"Hey." Reid startles when Joaquim's hand touches his hair. His face is no longer drawn with anger. Reid pats the sand next to him in the hope that Joaquim will sit so he doesn't have to twist to talk to him. Joaquim does. Reid kisses his cheek, lingers next to his skin, makes apology in gentle touch. He's not yet found a way to explain himself to Joaquim, but he's no longer angry or panicking.

Joaquim leans into the touch; neither of them speak. Perhaps Joaquim hasn't found his words either.

"Ready to go?" Reid wants nothing less than to leave things as they are; his instinct is always to push for resolution. Waiting with anger and unsettled feelings is a skill he's been getting better at. Continuing to fight when either party isn't ready to talk isn't productive. Reid also tends to want a particular resolution. With Felix, he was always pushing for the *right* apology. Forcing it didn't help; forcing the "right" apology from someone isn't genuine. Creation of resentment is an inevitability when Reid does that.

"Yeah, I think so," Joaquim says. They fold the towels. Joaquim smooths Reid's wind-tossed hair and takes his hand. Reid kisses him lightly again. These are gestures of reassurance, offered despite silently acknowledged understanding that they must come back to this later.

The car ride is both too short and unbearably long. Silence hangs in the air and it's too much, straining against them.

"Call me?" Reid winces at the neediness in his voice.

"Of course." Joaquim touches his cheek, and Reid closes his eyes. He watches Joaquim until he's through the door, takes a breath, and drives home.

Twenty-eight

"I HAVE NO IDEA WHY he freaked out like he did." Joaquim stabs at a stubborn cherry tomato he's been chasing in his salad bowl. "I mean, I've told him I love him. *We're* in love. Why would I tell him these things if I was going to leave him?"

"Well, aren't you?" Nina asks. She's managing to eat *her* salad competently.

"No! God, I'm just going home for a little bit. I mean, obviously we'll work something out after that."

"Dude, is that obvious to him, though?" Bobby comes up behind them with his own lunch.

"How much of this conversation have you heard?" Joaquim struggles with his tone. "Because if you don't know what's going on—"

"Chill, man. I haven't heard it all, but I know you. You're all…" Bobby gestures indecipherably. "And he's not. I mean, isn't he like, a neat freak and stuff?"

"What does this have to do with—?"

"Maybe he needs more. Not everyone is as chill as you."

"Ugh," Joaquim moans and puts his head on the table. Nina takes his salad bowl and begins picking out the unfinished bits. "He accused me of being cavalier with our relationship! That's fucked up, though, right?"

"I don't know that I'd call it fucked up. That's harsh, sure. But he worries about shit, right? He's got issues," Nina says. Joaquim glares at her. She shrugs.

"Do not judge him; you don't know anything."

"Man, we've all gone on dives with him. You talk to your sister in the room sometimes," Bobby says, mouth full of a turkey and spinach sandwich. "We don't know details. I'm not judging him; I don't know his story. But we're not totally obtuse, man."

Joaquim struggles to hold back his words. He's not sharing Reid's story with anyone; it's never going to be his to tell without permission. And he wasn't expecting people who barely know Reid to take his side, though he knows it's immature to expect that they would take his. The frustration he felt when he and Reid fought hasn't left him; he's been stewing in it all night and into his morning shift.

Reid texts him sporadically throughout the day. They don't acknowledge their fight. Joaquim has a sense that Reid is working to maintain a connection. Whether for his own comfort or because it's the healthy thing to do, Joaquim doesn't know. He needs the connection too.

*   *   *

JOAQUIM HASN'T MINDED HAVING A roommate, for the most part. It's irritating on nights like tonight, when Bobby seems to be coming down with a cold and is snoring.

It's easier to blame sleeplessness on that and not on his argument with Reid replaying over and over. A defensive loop of arguments clutters his sleepless thoughts as he stares at the ceiling. He can barely make it out, smooth and white, in the absence of moonlight. Not everyone approaches life the way he does, with carefree willingness to uproot and land where circumstances lead him. Reid's resistance, his anger, seem to go beyond a difference in attitudes, as if he doesn't trust Joaquim. Perhaps Joaquim should have approached the situation differently. *It's a given that, no matter what happens, I'll find a way to be with Reid, right?*

While Joaquim understands that Reid has his own perspective on the fragile and tenuous nature of life, that doesn't entitle him to use it as a trump card. *Right?* Joaquim sighs, flips his pillow over, and rolls onto his side. The well-worn cotton is cool against his skin. The longer he thinks about the day, from finding Reid on the chair to their walk through the shallow waters and his own frustrated trek over the boardwalk through the mangroves, Joaquim senses both the folly and shortsightedness of his actions, as well as a thread of legitimacy to his frustration. He is allowed to have a different philosophy and outlook. It doesn't have to be like Reid's.

That said, Joaquim has a lot to learn about Reid—how he ticks, what things might trigger anxiety—just as Reid has a lot to learn about him. Neither of them is responsible for each other, but Joaquim wants a relationship where both are willing to *listen*—listen to understand, not listen to respond. Bobby was definitely on the nose about Reid's nature. *And* Joaquim's life as an adult has been a series of happenstance and luck leading him to new adventures. *Are we compatible enough to make a go of things?*

It's past one, but he slips his phone off his nightstand.

Joaquim: *I miss you*

Joaquim fires off the text before he can talk himself out of it. Reid responds before he can put the phone back down.

Reid: *I miss you too.*

Joaquim types *Are you okay?* and catches himself at the last second. He deletes the message and settles on wishing Reid a good night instead. They never got to the conversation about how they can communicate around particulars. An ache settles in Joaquim's chest: the pain of missing Reid, and regret and frustration that will linger until things can be hashed out. The missing is the biggest part of it, though. Reid in his arms right now would be perfect.

✼   ✼   ✼

IN THE MORNING, JOAQUIM SETTLES at his laptop and begins to research places he might be able to find work and contacts that could help get him a job. It's an imperfect plan, because it needs Reid's input. It must account for what Reid wants to do with the next period of his life. But it's a start, something he can take to Reid and begin a conversation that represents a compromise.

Joaquim: *Hey*

Reid: *Hi there :)*

Joaquim: *Did you want to hang out later? Can we, I mean?*

Reid: *Of course.*

Joaquim has an idea that's either brilliant or horrible, and he needs Nina's help. She's not through until one, though.

Joaquim: *I'm not free until afternoon, is that okay?*

Reid: *Yeah. I work until three, remember?*

Fuck, yeah, he'd totally forgotten. It buys him more time.

Joaquim: *How about I bring stuff to make dinner?*

Joaquim isn't a great cook, but he can cook.

Reid: *I'd like that*

Joaquim: *k. ILY*

Joaquim fires that off and then slips on shoes so he can walk to the shop to catch Nina.

Reid: *Grown-up version: I love you. But for you... ILY2, you dork.*

Joaquim smiles. *Things will be all right. Love makes them so, right?*

Joaquim arrives half an hour past when he'd planned. He grunts as he lifts all of the shopping bags out of the trunk of Nina's car at once. Sweat rolls down his spine; it's fucking hot today.

"Good luck," Nina calls through the window.

"Thanks," Joaquim calls back. Almost at the door, Joaquim tries to figure out how he's going to open it when Reid does it for him. His expression alone eases tension in Joaquim's chest. He drops the bags in the entry, pulls Reid toward him, and runs a hand over his hair. Reid smiles and leans into a kiss. Hot air rushes in through the open door, and when Joaquim steps closer he almost crushes a bag between them. Reid breaks away with a laugh.

"Let me help you," he says. Joaquim grabs the one paper bag that's not from Publix and puts it aside. "So, what are we making?"

Joaquim hands Reid vegetables from the bags they've hoisted onto the counter. "Stir fry."

"Have you ever made a stir fry?" Reid asks. He roots through a bag. "What the hell is this?"

"A ginger root." Joaquim takes it from him and puts it on the counter.

"I hope you know how to use that," Reid says, eyeing it.

"It's not going to bite. I promise. The Internet will tell us what to do with it. It was in the recipe."

"I leave the strange roots in your capable hands, then." Reid balls up the plastic bags and stores them under the sink in a holder. "What's in here?"

"Oh." Joaquim grabs the paper bag out of Reid's hands. "I, um. I got you a thing."

Reid's eyes light up, ice-blue and sweet; lines of exhaustion around them ease.

"But, I don't—"

"J?"

"I thought this might be a helpful thing. If it's not, or it's a bad thing, I'm sorry—hey!"

Reid grabs the bag out of his hand, "You need to calm down. You got something because you were thinking of me, right?"

"Yeah," Joaquim says.

"Well, thank you." Reid kisses his cheek. He pulls the paper-wrapped package out and opens it without tearing the paper, although he lets the paper fall to the floor. "This…" He pulls out a handprint impression toy, the kind with dulled metal pins.

"So, I definitely have a reason for this," Joaquim starts.

"My dad used to have one of these on his desk when I was a kid," Reid says, already playing with it. "This is cool. Um, but—"

"So, okay. Last night I was thinking about the way you like to feel things with your hands. The ceiling…" Reid winces, and Joaquim rushes to assure him. "...and the sand. And I thought maybe this could be helpful."

Reid pushes his fingers against the small pegs and then lets them down. He pushes his whole hand against them and flips it over to look at the shape of his hand pushing through.

"I don't know a lot about the sensory stuff you were telling me. Maybe you could tell me more? But this..." Joaquim takes it from him gently. "I thought maybe we could work on something to replicate the way the ceiling felt? Only, um, easier. So you're not climbing furniture."

Reid's eyes flash up to him, a little wary perhaps, but not upset. He turns and sits on the couch. "It's a cool feeling," he says. "But not really the same."

"What if you couldn't push the pegs through?" Joaquim pushes his palm against the pegs and then holds it out to Reid. "Put your hand against it now." He offers resistance against Reid's hand, and Reid's face clears.

"Oh!" Reid presses his index finger down and the pegs dig into Joaquim's fingertip as a result. "I understand."

"I don't know if this feels like the ceiling exactly, but it's maybe a start. I obviously didn't have time to shop around for anything else; this was hard to find. But we could look online. Or fiddle with this one."

"Joaquim," Reid says. He takes the toy from him and puts it on the coffee table. He turns away from Joaquim.

"God, I'm sorry; this was bad, wasn't it?" Joaquim puts a hand between Reid's shoulders and rubs them. Reid shakes his head, a tiny movement one could almost miss.

"It's good," Reid says. His voice is thick. Joaquim moves to kneel in front of him, a nearly impossible feat considering the lack of room between the sofa and the table. But he manages. Reid's cheeks are streaked with tears he wipes away with the back of his hand. "Don't— I'm a mess." He covers his eyes.

"Reid, come on." Joaquim, pulls at his wrists gently. "Why are you hiding?"

"I'm a mess," Reid repeats, crackle-voiced and shaky.

"No, no you're not." Joaquim speaks with conviction that's new to him. "You're *you*. And I love you. And I want to help you."

"Ugh." Reid puts his damp face into Joaquim's shoulder. "You could have anyone. You should."

"Stop." Joaquim kisses the top of his head. "Please."

Mercifully, Reid does. He pulls Joaquim onto the couch and curls into him. How unbalanced their relationship must seem to Reid, for him to say such things. Joaquim had never heard of half the things Reid is handling. But Reid acts as if Joaquim being here is an act of mercy, as if he has no idea what he brings to Joaquim's life, or the utter pricelessness of finding home in someone else.

"I'm sorry," Joaquim says slowly. "For the other day."

"What? No," Reid says. He's post-tears nasal and his eyes are slightly red. "That was me being hysterical."

"No. Don't dismiss yourself. Obviously there's something that needs working out. I think I can understand some of what happened, and why you got so upset. But I didn't really try to listen, did I?"

Reid moves away and curls his legs under himself. He props his head on his hand with his elbow on the back of the couch. He's wearing old jeans, tight and fraying past intentional distress into acute distress. *Acute Jean Distress.* Joaquim smiles at the thought. It would make a cool band name.

"I'll admit I was already stressed about what you said. And then I got flustered."

"That doesn't mean I shouldn't listen. And I was... I didn't even see that you were flustered. I should have—"

"Don't should," Reid says. His voice is soft. "Should is a banned word."

Joaquim tilts his head and studies Reid. "Regardless, I'm sorry I didn't see it. After I calmed down, and Bobby and Nina talked some sense into me, I think I understand. I came up with a semi-plan, thinking that you'd probably feel more comfortable with a plan, with something we can plan together?"

"You have wise friends." Reid shifts, and, when he curls up again, his legs press against Joaquim's.

Joaquim digs into his pants pocket for the list he made. "This isn't final or anything. It's more like ideas." He spreads it out, and Reid leans forward to see. "A list of places where I could find work. And also, see here? Maybe you can come visit me when I'm with my family. Assuming you have a passport."

"I don't," Reid says absently. His finger runs down the list. He sighs and closes his eyes.

Twenty-nine

"Reid?" Joaquim touches Reid's knee. "You with me? This is a tentative list, just ideas."

"I know," Reid says. He wonders how to word what's next, not only so that Joaquim will understand, but also because Reid himself isn't sure. "I... Joaquim, there are some hard truths. Things I don't know what to do about. I came here because I needed space from Felix and my family to try to heal and work on myself, to get stronger, healthier. And in a lot of ways I have."

"Yeah," Joaquim says. His face, with its light and lopsided smile, seems almost proud.

"But I had setbacks too. This tested a lot of things for me. I'm... I'm afraid."

"Afraid of what?"

"Of too much change, of more moving, of unsettling myself constantly or even just right now." Reid covers Joaquim's fingers with his. "Of being too far from home, even though I don't necessarily want to be there."

"It's too much change?"

"Maybe. Fear is... I know my fears are totally irrational—"

"Reid, of course they aren't," Joaquim says.

"I'm starting to feel like I have a grip on recovery. I don't know where I go from here. I don't know the answer. Half of this list is overseas or in a time zone that will make it hard to connect with my group."

Joaquim considers the list on his lap. He folds it and puts it on the table. "Okay." He draws Reid into his arms. "So we'll figure it out. I promise."

"Wanna make dinner?" Reid says. They've been on the couch, drowsing in silence. Reid's not used to comfortable silence with another person. Basking in it, despite the heaviness of their situation, has been lovely. Joaquim can't be the sole reason for his happiness or health, but he can be a part of it. Reid is coming to understand that partnership doesn't have to equal instability, that it can mean support—a different kind, too, from what he gets with his group or even his family, who try their best. This love is different and it could be so good for him.

"Yeah, definitely." Joaquim untangles himself from Reid and rubs his stomach. "I'm starving."

"All right. Let us stir and fry. Fire up the Internet." Reid pulls out vegetables and chops them, figuring he doesn't need the Internet to cut things up.

The kitchen fills with the smell of ginger, and Reid heats peanut oil in a pan, per Joaquim's instructions. They take turns stirring vegetables while chopping and mixing a sauce. They speak only to communicate about the food; they speak through gentle touches and glances, through small smiles and, when Reid is pouring the sauce into the pan, a light kiss on the back of his neck.

Silence follows them through dinner and out onto the porch, where they soak in the night soundscape together. In bed, Joaquim undresses Reid. When he runs his fingers down Reid's torso, he pauses. Reid lets him turn on the lamp. Joaquim has promised everything will be okay, that they are in this together. Trust, letting himself be laid bare, is vital. Reid's not sure how he knows it, but it's in his bones. It's still scary; his heart beats fast, and his breath is shallow and quick. Joaquim's fingers don't stray to his scars. Rather, they trace the tattoo.

"What does this mean? Why would you want to suffer?"

"It's my version of *life is short*," Reid quips. Joaquim's face is unreadable. "Sorry. I guess it's a reminder of surrender."

"Surrender to what?"

"This is my life. This is who I am. These things happened."

Joaquim's face doesn't clear.

"At Sycamore Grove, they had different 'jobs' and I got to work with the animals. One day, when I was walking down to the barn, I was so angry. I'd been angry. Resistant. I didn't belong there. That's what I was telling myself. Spring was coming. I was thinking about how the crocuses must be blooming at home, and something shifted."

"Crocuses?"

"They're purple and white flowers that bloom first in the spring. But the point is, they can bloom through snow. It's how you know spring is coming. I've always loved that. I couldn't care less about flowers, generally. But I like when winter is over."

"I can only imagine."

"I can't remember, have you ever seen snow?" Reid traces the ridge of Joaquim's nose.

"No. But maybe one day." They share a look.

"Anyway. I honestly cannot tell you what changed. But something clicked. I knew then that I had to surrender to the process. The only thing I could change in that moment was letting go of my resistance. And I knew, right then, that would mean letting myself feel all the bad shit. Looking at it. Not pushing it away or pretending it wasn't there. It's a scary thing, J."

"Yeah?"

Reid loves this about this man: He doesn't say he understands things when he doesn't.

"Something about that surrender... I knew that meant I'd suffer somehow. But it was the first time I ever felt hope. In my whole life, it was the first time I believed I could feel better, be better."

"And now?"

"And I've experienced radical acceptance. Shit fucking sucks sometimes. Hope is hard. I have to fight for that. But I trust it more now, because of that willingness. I'm not always willing. But I'm capable of it."

"I like that," Joaquim says. "That idea."

"I have to be honest. Things that go to shit and are hard, like... um. The cutting. Relapsing. Those are things I can examine, after a while. Other things, I'm not ready for. I haven't been able to bring myself to think about—" He begins to cry. Joaquim catches a tear with a fingertip. "I don't know why I tried to..." Reid forces a breath and the words. "... kill myself. And that is so fucking scary. I can't get close to acceptance, because I can't let myself think of it. I'm just not ready."

There's a long, painful silence. Joaquim closes his eyes. Eventually, he cups Reid's cheek. "But you have hope now?"

"Sometimes. Most of the time. Life is so much better. I have hope that I can hold on to that. I don't think that will ever happen again. There were mitigating factors when that happened; they think that new med I was trying added to it."

"Okay," Joaquim says.

"This is part of why I freaked out about what happens next. I can't pin my happiness on you, and I know that. You aren't responsible for it either. We can have happiness and make happiness and love each other, but I can't make you the reason I survive."

"True. That would be a lot of pressure, for both of us."

"I'm scared that you're already slipping away," Reid admits. "I'm scared that I'll slip away. Sometimes I can't believe that I'm here." Reid can't help it; he sees himself in his bathroom back home gathering handfuls of pills. He closes his eyes and tries to push the memory away. *How easily I could have missed this.* How easily he almost did something irreversible, and he still doesn't know what he was thinking. He covers his face.

"Oh, Reid," Joaquim whispers. Joaquim wraps his arms around Reid. He kisses his fingers, then kisses his Reid's scars gently and his tattoo more confidently. Then he rests his head against Reid's belly and waits for his exhalation. Reid listens to Joaquim's breathing.

"You're still here," Reid says on a wet and broken gasp. He must trust Joaquim's presence over his fears.

Joaquim's voice is thick, and he swallows his own tears. "*You're* still here."

Now Reid's hands are in his hair, and Joaquim lifts his head. Reid's kiss is wet, and he's shaking in Joaquim's arms, falling apart achingly but pressing into and against him. Instinct speaks when Joaquim wraps Reid in his arms. Reid tucks himself into them with his arms between them and his face pressed into Joaquim's skin.

"Tighter," he whispers. Joaquim holds him as firmly as he can.

"Don't be scared," Joaquim says. "I'm still here. You're still here."

"Gosh, are we the most emo couple of all time, or what?" Reid asks a while later. He's rewarded with Joaquim's laugh. "I think all I ever do with you is subject you to my problems or cry all over you."

"Naw," Joaquim says. He's running his fingers over Reid's shoulder absently; it's shivery pleasant. "We're finding our feet." He pulls away and settles his head on the pillow facing Reid. "And the sex is great."

"Ass." Reid laughs and pushes Joaquim's shoulders. Laughter should feel alien; perhaps this whiplash of pain and joy should overwhelm him. Reid's much stronger than people give him credit for, stronger than he gives himself credit for, sometimes. He can ride these waves. Joaquim's kiss takes him by surprise, but Reid doesn't stop it. He feeds that hunger, the need for connection. Joaquim is smiling into the kiss.

As Joaquim had before, Reid undresses him. They move in silence; soon all that's heard are their breaths, increasingly loud, and, as Reid slips into Joaquim slowly and carefully, Joaquim's stuttering moans. Reid coaxes them from him, draws him through pleasure until his muttering pleas break the spell.

"Reid, *fuck*, oh." The silence ripples and breaks apart as Reid does his very best to speak with his body to Joaquim's body, promising with every move everything he can give this man. Not just pleasure, but care and attention. Focus, and a promise to return Joaquim's steadiness, if in a different form.

Joaquim throbs around him, his body spasming as if Joaquim's orgasm comes in reverse, so that aftershocks pulse through him before he's come.

"Touch me, please," Joaquim's eyes are pure dark; his face is lax with stunned pleasure.

"No," Reid whispers. Joaquim writhes and moans. Reid shifts. He pulls back until he's on his knees, hauling Joaquim toward him by his hips. When he drives into him, hard and fast, just right, Joaquim comes with a surprised shout. His hands fly up above him, pushing against the wall so he can leverage himself harder onto Reid. He's the single most beautiful creature Reid's ever seen.

"Love you, love you, love you," Joaquim whispers later, into the dark, into the return of silence and their bodies, warm and sated, sticking and tangled under a sheet. Reid slips into sleep.

Epilogue

THE SUNLIGHT SCATTERS OVER THE chop of waves; the glittering light on the water is almost blinding. Joaquim's hand in his is sweaty. The rush of air as the boat rides the waves helps, cutting through the late-hanging summer humidity. From across the boat another diver glances at them; Reid's not sure if it's distrust, dislike, or curiosity.

"Are we a museum piece or a freak show?" Reid whispers to Joaquim. It's their first dive together with Joaquim as Reid's dive partner, not his instructor.

Joaquim kisses his cheek; the woman smiles at them. "We're a curiosity." Joaquim decides.

Reid can live with that. He'd rather not be stared at, but he'll take that grin over homophobia any day.

They're nearly at the reef. The cool water will be welcome. It's been weeks since his last dive. Joaquim lit up when Reid asked him if he wanted to go. They're still unsure of their future, for now they are living off Reid's meager salary in his grandmother's condo since Joaquim's internship is over. Next week Joaquim will be in Brazil.

The boat comes to a halt and floats with the current, and then the clanking of the anchor signals that they've reached their destination. They're back at Molasses Reef. Reid would love to visit others together, but this one holds precious memories of his first real dive and flirting, despite his nerves and anxieties, with Joaquim.

They get ready with the others, checking gear and laughing with their dive guide, Sam, as he cracks jokes. Joaquim steps into the water with ease and grace Reid admires. His entrance into the water is akin to a buffalo falling into the ocean, but they get to the same place.

When they pause on descent, Reid searches Joaquim's eyes and finds nothing but the steady peace he seeks so often. The water crackles with life around him; currents caress his skin. The sound of his breathing through the regulator fades to background noise.

Against the backdrop of the reef, vibrant with its bright splashes of life, Reid follows Joaquim's lead as he makes a beautiful tableau with the reef behind him and his gorgeous body sure in the water. Angelfish dart out around the lace of sea fans to Reid's left. Joaquim touches his arm. Reid is so entranced by the unpredictable swimming patterns of the fish into and out of the coral, he didn't realize Joaquim was next to him. He points: Right in front of them, moving to their right, a nurse shark glides past. Reid wishes he had a camera. He wishes he could capture the sense memory of this moment: Joaquim's hand on his arm, the teeming life in the deep water, and the huge happiness, almost too big, in his chest. This, this is his life now. They'll surface eventually. They'll go home, and soon they'll have to make decisions. But it's all beautiful. All around him is lovely, achingly present life, and he gets to be here for it. Because *yes*, he's still here.

Author's Note

For many years of my life, I struggled with mental illness in silence. I hid symptoms and intense suffering under an unbearable blanket of shame. I felt, in every corner of my life, the stigma associated with what I was going through. In this silence and fear and shame, I learned to repress and pretend; I tried so hard to be a different self that, by a certain point in my life, I had no idea how to express how I felt or what I was going through, even to myself.

The stigma and silence that cloak mental illness are devastating for those living with it and for family and friends who are trying to cope, support, and understand what a loved one is going through. Speaking into and against that silence is terrifying and painful but ultimately so, so necessary.

My own story is frightening and uplifting. Every time I speak to someone about my experiences, I have to take a deep breath and push headlong into my story: Yes, I had a mental breakdown that almost cost me my life and family. Yes, I struggled with self-harm. Yes, I live every day knowing that cyclothemia doesn't go away. I must learn to manage my anxiety and my compulsions regularly. I must face my traumas.

But I do all of these things willingly, because these are a part of my fight and because I love my life, I love my family and my friends, I love myself. And I tell this story because although I am just one voice, I hope that using it will help those who are afraid to speak feel less alone.

Like Reid, I want my life and voice to be a tiny piece of something greater.

I believe Reid's story absolutely must be told. Reid is a boy who is learning to thrive, who is beginning that fight for himself, with all of the ups and downs that come with recovery and wellness. But Reid, like all of us who live with mental illness, isn't his mental illness. This story isn't just about his wellness journey; it is about a boy on an adventure, a boy coming into his own and falling in love. For all of those living with mental illness, this story is for you.

Glossary

Tchau: goodbye
Mãe/Mamãe: Mom
Beijos pra todos: kisses for everyone
Tenho que ir: I have to go
Opa: oops or whoops
Te amo: I love you
Jesus, Maria, e José: Jesus, Mary, and Joseph
Caipirinhas: a cocktail made with cachaça, sugar, and lime
Lindo/Lindeza: Beautiful. Term of endearment
Carinho: Term of endearment indicating affection or fondness
Minha vida: my life
Pão de queijo: Brazilian cheese bread made from tapioca flour
Bebê: Baby
Boa noite: Good night
Pra você também: To you too
Obrigado: Thank you
Beijos: Kisses

Acknowledgments

First and foremost I must thank every person who was and is a part of my wellness and recovery journey: my therapists, my psychiatrist, the amazing team at Rose Hill, and every member of my DBT group. Each of you played a role in helping to save my life, and I can promise that I am not the only person who is utterly indebted and thankful to you.

This book benefited from the help of a team of sensitivity readers who mean the world to me: Taylor Brooke, Julian Winters, and Min, thank you for your honesty, support, and advice. Annie B., my lovely co-blogger, thank you for being the best first reader a girl could ask for. Avon Gale, S.J. Martin, and Pene Henson, thank you so much for letting me pester you with questions and for being willing to share your experiences with me.

To the amazing team at Interlude Press: you all make my books shine. Annie Harper, Candy Miller, and CB Messer, thank you for the continued faith and support you've given me over the past three years. I am endlessly grateful for Nicki Harper and Zoë Bird, whose editing challenges me to be and do better with every book.

I could not do any of this without the support of my friends and family. To all of you, and in particular my husband and children, so many thanks for your patience, your love, your belief in me.

About the Author

JUDE SIERRA IS A LATINX poet, author, academic and mother working toward her PhD in Writing and Rhetoric, looking at the intersections of Queer, Feminist and Pop Culture Studies. She also works as an LGBTQAI+ book reviewer for From Top to Bottom Reviews. Her novels include *Hush*, *What it Takes*, and *Idlewild*, a contemporary LGBT romance set in Detroit's renaissance, which was named a Best Book of 2016 by *Kirkus Reviews*.

interludepress™

🌐 interludepress.com
🐦 @InterludePress
📘 interludepress
🛒 store.interludepress.com

interlude press

also by Jude Sierra...

Idlewild

Named one of Kirkus Reviews' Best Books of 2016

In a last ditch effort to revive the downtown Detroit gastropub he opened with his late husband, Asher Schenck hires a new staff. Among them is Tyler Heyward, a recent college graduate working his way toward med school. When they fall for each other, it's not race or class that challenges their love, but the ghosts and expectations of their pasts.

ISBN (print) 978-1-945053-07-8 | (eBook) 978-1-945053-08-5

What It Takes

Publishers Weekly Star Recipient

Milo met Andrew moments after moving to Cape Cod— launching a lifelong friendship of deep bonds, secret forts and plans for the future. When Milo goes home for his father's funeral, he and Andrew finally act on their attraction—but doubtful of his worth, Milo severs ties. They meet again years later, and their long-held feelings will not be denied. Will they have what it takes to find lasting love?

ISBN (print) 978-1-941530-59-7 | (eBook) 978-1-941530-60-3

Hush

Published by Consent, an imprint of Interlude Press

Wren is one of "the gifted"—a college sophomore with the power to compel others' feelings and desires. When Cameron, a naïve freshman, enters his life, Wren grows to discover new and unexpected things about himself. Will Cameron's building confidence break through Wren's emotional walls, or will Wren walk away from his chance at love?

ISBN (print) 978-1-941530-27-6 | (eBook) 978-1-941530-31-3